Praise for *New York Times* and *USA TODAY* bestselling author RaeAnne Thayne

'I've been following RaeAnne Thayne for some time now, and have watched her readership grow with each title. She's a rising star in the romance world. Her books are wonderfully romantic, feel-good reads that end with me sighing over the last pages.'

#1 *New York Times* bestselling author Debbie Macomber

'In Thayne's latest, her beautiful, honest storytelling goes straight to the heart. Her characters are authentically vulnerable and the light, amusing banter between them adds to the sweet warmth of this story... [A] moving yet powerful romance.'

RT Book Reviews on *Wild Iris Ridge*

'A sometimes heartbreaking tale of love and relationships in a small Colorado town.... Poignant and sweet, this tale of second chances will appeal to fans of military-flavoured sweet romance.'

Publishers Weekly on *Christmas in Snowflake Canyon*

'Once again, Thayne proves she has a knack for capturing those emotions that come from the heart.... Crisp storytelling and many amusing moments make for a delightful read.'

RT Book Reviews on *Willowleaf Lane*

'Thayne pens another winner by combining her huge, boisterous cast of familiar, lovable characters with a beautiful setting and a wonderful story. Her main characters are strong and three-dimensional, with enough heat between them to burn the pages.'

RT Book Reviews on *Currant Creek Valley*

'Thayne, once again, delivers a heartfelt story of a caring community and a caring romance between adults who have triumphed over tragedies.'

Booklist on *Woodrose Mountain*

'Thayne's series starter introduces the Colorado town of Hope's Crossing in what can be described as a cozy romance... [A] gentle, easy read.'

Publishers Weekly on *Blackberry Summer*

Snow Angel Cove

RaeAnne Thayne

MILLS & BOON

HQ
An imprint of HarperCollins*Publishers* Ltd
1 London Bridge Street
London SE1 9GF

This paperback edition 2018

1
First published in Great Britain by
HQ, an imprint of HarperCollins*Publishers* Ltd 2018

Copyright © RaeAnne Thayne 2014

RaeAnne Thayne asserts the moral right to be
identified as the author of this work.
A catalogue record for this book is
available from the British Library.

ISBN: 978-1-84845-751-5

MIX
Paper from
responsible sources
FSC **FSC™ C007454**
www.fsc.org

This book is produced from independently certified FSC™ paper
to ensure responsible forest management.

For more information visit: www.harpercollins.co.uk/green

Printed and bound in Great Britain by
CPI Group (UK) Ltd, Croydon, CR0 4YY

Dedication

So many people have a part in bringing a book to life. In the craziness of life and kids and deadlines, I am sometimes remiss in expressing how very grateful I am to everyone who has played a part in helping me along this writing journey, from idea to completion. First, I need to thank my brilliant brainstorming partners, Nicole Jordan and Victoria Dahl, for all the hilarious breakfasts. Someday, they're going to get tired of us and kick us out of Village Inn! To my agent, Karen Solem, for her thoughtful guidance, thank you for keeping me on track! To my amazing editor for over forty books now, Gail Chasan, for having faith in me from the very beginning. Mere words are not enough!

My heartfelt gratitude goes to everyone at Mills & Boon—from Susan Swinwood and everyone else on the editorial team to the art department and the spectacular covers they give my books to the sales and marketing teams who work so hard to get my stories into the hands of readers. You are all wonderful! I offer my deepest thanks to my family for their patience, their encouragement and their unending love. And finally, to my readers. I am so very grateful to you for your letters, your emails, your Facebook messages—and especially, for the amazing gift you've given me of being able to watch with awe and wonder as my dreams come true.

CHAPTER ONE

OH, THIS WASN'T GOOD. At all.

Eliza Hayward stood with sleet pelting her like hard little pebbles, gazing at the blackened, charred bones of her future. Cold dread wormed its way beneath her coat like the wintry wind blowing off Lake Haven, just a few hundred yards away.

"I don't like this place," Maddie muttered, gripping her hand tighter. "It's ugly and scary."

"Yes. Yes, it is."

This couldn't be real. She had driven the two hours from Boise with such eager anticipation, singing Christmas carols all the way, loud and silly enough to make a five-year-old giggle. She had been so excited about this new chapter of their lives in this lovely Idaho town nestled in the raw and stunning Redemption Mountains.

It had been an amazing opportunity all the way around—a big jump, career-wise, to her first hotel manager position, but also a nice salary increase, a really attractive benefits package and, best of all, an included apartment on the property for her and for Maddie so she could keep her daughter close.

Now that cute apartment, the salary bump, the

insurance, *everything,* had disappeared in a puff of smoke. Literally. Though she couldn't see any flames, tendrils of smoke still curled from the rubble of the building.

The air smelled harsh and acrid, far different from the sweet, citrusy scent of pine she remembered permeating the town when she had visited the month before during the interview process.

The fire had to have flared within the past few hours. Fire crews still worked busily all around the burned hotel coiling hoses, stretching yellow crime tape around the perimeter, putting out a hot spot here or there.

No wonder she hadn't heard from Megan Hamilton. The woman was probably still in shock.

Oh, Eliza hoped no one had been hurt.

That dread sidled up to her again, menacing and dark. What was she going to do now? She had tied off every single loose end in Boise. Her job, her apartment. All gone. Their things had been packed and put into storage until she had a chance to figure out what she might need here in their new life, this new start.

She had even used a big chunk of her savings as a down payment on a newer SUV to get around the mountain roads.

Now what?

She gripped Maddie's hand more tightly. She would figure something out. Isn't that what she had been doing for three years?

"That's not where you're going to work, is it?"

"Well, it was supposed to be." She forced a smile for Maddie, doing her best to ignore the flutters of panic taking wing inside her. "I guess they had a fire today."

She drew in a calming breath, trying to make her brain cells snap into gear so she could come up with a plan. The sleet seemed to sting harder with each passing second and the wind had picked up in the past few moments. Apparently the big storm the forecasters had been predicting—the reason she had come to town early instead of waiting until the next day or Sunday—had blown into Haven Point.

Maddie shivered a little and Eliza was just about to take her back up the small hill toward the parking lot where she had parked when she spotted a familiar woman about her age in jeans and a sooty jacket, talking to a firefighter in turnout gear with the word *Chief* written on his helmet.

When she saw Eliza and Maddie, the other woman's eyes widened, looking huge in her lovely features that looked taut with stress and exhaustion.

She cut off her conversation with the fire chief and headed in their direction. Though they had only met twice—once for Eliza's initial interview and then the follow-up where she had been offered the job—the woman held out her arms and folded Eliza in a hug that smelled strongly of smoke.

"You're here. Oh, Eliza." Her voice wobbled and her slim frame trembled, too, like a slender branch shivering in the wind. "I should have called you. I'm so sorry. It didn't occur to me. I only... It's been such a terrible afternoon. I thought you weren't coming to Haven Point until tomorrow or Sunday."

She imagined receiving this sort of news over the phone and was almost grateful she had driven in early and had witnessed the damage for herself. "I wanted to beat the storm. Was anyone hurt?"

"Not seriously. Thank heavens. One of the house-keeping staff suffered some smoke inhalation while trying to help us evacuate the guests. Other than that, everyone is fine. We were only about half-occupied and we were able to get everyone out quickly. It's been a nightmare few hours trying to find other places for them all to stay."

What if this had happened a week from now, when she was in charge as the hotel manager? She hated even imagining it.

"What happened? Do you know?"

Megan rubbed at her red-rimmed eyes. "I was just speaking with Chief Gallegos about it. The investigators aren't sure yet but all indications point to some kind of electrical event. They think it started near the guest laundry. It's a miracle it happened when it did, on a slow week, first of all, and then late morning before the weekend guests checked in, when we were fully staffed with the maintenance crew and the housekeepers to help evacuate. If the fire had started in the middle of the night, things might have gone very differently. The situation could have been much, much worse."

Eliza could certainly appreciate that from Megan's point of view. As far as she was concerned, though, the fact remained that her exciting new opportunity was now a pile of ash and debris.

Megan suddenly spied Maddie, pressing her face now into Eliza's wool coat to keep out of the wind. "But you. And Maddie. I'm so, so sorry."

She wore the same sorrowful expression that Eliza had seen on her friends and neighbors after Trent's funeral.

"I can't believe this happened right before you were supposed to start. I've been so excited to have you on board, too. I just feel like we really clicked during the interview process. Your ideas were innovative and exciting, exactly what this old inn needed to shake things up."

Eliza heard the "but" and knew what was coming.

"Obviously everything has changed. Oh, Eliza." Megan's eyes welled up and spilled over, trickling down her soot-grimed face. She pulled a bedraggled tissue out of her pocket.

"I understand."

"I don't know what we're going to do. We have to close indefinitely. I guess that's obvious. I need to speak with the insurance company to find out if we should rebuild what is left or raze the whole thing and start over. And to have this happen right before Christmas! I feel so terrible for my staff. Some of them have been at the inn since before I was born, when my grandparents owned it."

Though that leashed panic inside her wanted to break free and ravage everything, Eliza forced a smile, cuddling Maddie closer for comfort and warmth. "You obviously don't need a new manager when you've got nothing for me to manage. Don't worry. I understand."

Megan gave a little whimper and more tears dripped out. "I'm so sorry I dragged you out here. You quit your job and everything. Can you go back to it?"

She wouldn't, even in the unlikely event that they might hire her back. With the owners' son firmly entrenched in the top managerial position and mismanaging everything from the linen orders to the payroll, she suspected it wouldn't be long before the Diamond Street Inn would go under.

"Don't worry about me. I'll be fine." She had no idea how, but she would figure something out.

"Don't cry. It will be okay." Maddie spoke softly to Megan, looking bewildered at the situation but distressed, too. She was such a sweet little soul, always concerned about the pain someone else might be experiencing, whether at the hospital or on the playground.

Megan gave her a watery smile, then reached down and hugged her. "It will be. You're absolutely right. Not immediately, but things will eventually be okay."

"Is there something I can help you do now?" Eliza asked. "I can find somewhere to stay and help you cancel bookings or something?"

"I appreciate that, but I've already got the front desk staff taking care of that. Thank heavens our computer system was backed up off-site and we can still access all those reservations."

"That is good news."

She squeezed Eliza's hands. "Again, I'm so, so sorry."

"Stop apologizing. This wasn't your fault."

"At least I can give you a small severance package. Something to tide you over while you look for another position."

Megan had already been so generous, offering to pay her moving expenses and including the apartment as part of her compensation package. Eliza didn't want to burden her with one more obligation.

"Don't worry about it," she said, even though that panic fluttered harder. She wasn't destitute. She had some savings left, as well as monthly survivor benefits. She also had several solid years of experience as the assistant manager at the Diamond Street Inn.

She wondered if she could possibly return the SUV and get her down payment back—but what would she drive to interviews if she did? Her sedan had been on its last bald tire.

Job-hunting less than two weeks before Christmas wasn't ideal timing, nor did she want to move her fragile child into some grimy pay-by-the-week hotel until she found a position and could lease a nearby apartment. Right now she couldn't see any other choice.

All in all, this might be another in a string of miserable holidays.

Emotion welled up in her throat and she was very much afraid she would burst into tears like Megan.

"I have your cell number. I'll be in touch as soon as things settle down," the other woman said.

"Okay. Thanks."

"Hey, Megan," the fire chief called. "Do you want us to put up temporary fencing to keep out the looters?"

"Looters. I didn't even think about that. I'm sorry. I need to…"

"Don't worry about us," Eliza said firmly. "I'm going to go get Maddie out of the cold. Good luck with everything."

She gave Megan a hug, very sorry suddenly that she wouldn't have the chance to get to know the other woman better. She had been certain they would have been friends—and she could always use a few more of those.

The wind and sleet had died down a little while she had been speaking with Megan. The calm before the storm, maybe? She should climb into the SUV she could no longer afford and drive back through the mountain passes toward Boise before the snow began in earnest, but she didn't trust herself to drive right now, with her emotions in turmoil.

With the vague intention of grabbing a bite to eat at one of several restaurants she had spied in the town's small commercial district, she headed away from the scorched remains of the Lake Haven Inn.

"Was that lady sad because her hotel burned down?" Maddie asked after a moment.

"She was. It's been in her family for many years."

Eliza had learned during the interview process that Megan Hamilton had had no inclination or aptitude to run the hotel after she'd unexpectedly inherited it. Her interests lay elsewhere, Megan had told her, which was why she had hired Eliza in the first place.

"We can't live there now, can we?"

"I'm afraid not."

"Where will we put all our boxes?"

"Why don't we grab a bite to eat at that diner across the street from where we parked and we'll try to figure out our options?"

"Do they have macaroni and cheese?"

"I wouldn't be at all surprised."

They headed for the crosswalk and waited for the light to change. Eliza took a moment to look around, cognizant of her surroundings for the first time since she had seen that pile of rubble.

She could see the downtown business owners had done their best to decorate their charming little clapboard-and-brick storefronts. Lights hung on nearly every facade and most had Christmas trees in the windows. A few had ornaments with nautical themes, in keeping with the vivid blue of the lake that dominated the view in every direction.

"Mama, the light is green. Green means go," Maddie declared.

"So it does."

Maddie slipped her hand free of Eliza's and scampered ahead of her into the crosswalk. Eliza followed close behind her, keeping an eye on a black SUV headed down the hill toward them.

The SUV was slowing down, she saw, the driver hitting the brakes in what should have been plenty of braking distance but her insides suddenly froze.

The vehicle's tires spun wildly, ineffectually, unable to find purchase on the road. He tried to turn into the skid but she could tell in an instant he wasn't going to be able to completely stop in time—and he was sliding straight for her child.

No. This couldn't be happening!

"Maddie!" she screamed. Acting on a mother's frantic desperation, she leaped forward to push her daughter out of the path of the vehicle.

She had only an instant to feel deep gratitude and overwhelming relief that her daughter was safe before the vehicle struck her. Though the driver had almost stopped completely by that time, the impact still stole her thoughts, her breath, and she crumpled like that ragged tissue of Megan Hamilton's. Her head struck concrete and she knew a moment's screeching agony before everything went black.

AIDAN CAINE FUMBLED for the door handle in the unfamiliar SUV he had rented from the paunchy dude at the Lake Haven airstrip. It took him a moment but he finally worked the handle and shoved the door open, panic and nausea roiling in his gut.

He had just hit a person! Maybe two. A woman and a little girl crossing the road had been the last thing he had seen as he frantically tried to pump the brakes during the slide and turn into the skid.

This couldn't be real. He wanted to rewind the past twenty seconds of his life to that horrible moment the SUV hit that patch of ice and started sliding down the hill, wheels spinning.

When the light changed and the pedestrians had started across, he had tried frantically to turn into a streetlamp or something but the vehicle had been completely out of his control by that point.

He thought he would be able to stop in time, until he heard that horrible crunch.

A child's cries reached him, strident and fearful. Crying. Crying had to be a good sign, right? At least it meant the girl was alert enough to be upset.

He raced around the vehicle to assess the situation and found the source of the crying was a little girl with wavy dark hair beneath a pink-and-purple stocking cap. She knelt in the snow and slush of the road next to a crumpled, motionless figure.

"Mama! Mama!" she cried out, trying to shake the unresponsive woman.

He knelt down beside the girl and put his arm around her, mostly to keep her from jostling the figure unnecessarily. "Okay. Okay."

The girl trembled in his hold. "She won't wake up! Mama!"

"Ma'am?" he called. "Hello?"

She wasn't dead, at least. He could see the steady rise and fall of her chest. Beyond that, he had no idea the scope of her injuries. He thought he had barely tapped her but that crack as she went down still seemed to reverberate through him like a gunshot.

He reached in his pocket for his phone and with fingers that felt heavy and thick he started to dial 911. He couldn't seem to make his brain function, which sent icy fingers of fear crawling down his spine.

Only natural, he told himself. Normal and expected. The accident had severely rattled him, just as it would anyone else. This had nothing to do with his health situation—nor did the accident. He *hadn't* blacked out or had a seizure or something similar. He knew that unequivocally as he could remember each second of those terrible few moments.

His head ached like somebody was drilling him over and over with a nail gun, but that was nothing new.

"I already called for paramedics," someone said. "They're on the way."

He looked up and found a young woman dressed

only in jeans and a sweater coming out of one of the nearby businesses.

"Thanks." He shoved his phone back in his pocket as she came closer to them and knelt beside the woman and the little girl.

"I saw the whole thing. You hit the bad patch of black ice at the top of the hill, didn't you? I'm so sorry!"

"You are?" It was hardly her fault he hadn't checked the condition of the vehicle before he endangered other people by taking it on the road.

"Three times I've told the road crew supervisor we need to have the crews come by and put deicer on that patch. Every time we have a little melt, water just collects there and then freezes, causing all sorts of issues. When I take over as mayor after the New Year, I can promise you, fixing the drainage in that spot is going to be Priority One."

He didn't give a damn about the road problems in Haven Point. Right now, his Priority One was the woman who still hadn't moved.

"Oh," the shopkeeper suddenly exclaimed as she looked at him for the first time. Her mouth sagged open. "You're—"

Aidan supposed he shouldn't be surprised she recognized him. He wasn't exactly a celebrity on par with Bezos or Zuckerberg, but he had some renown in certain circles. Closer to home, he was quite sure word had trickled out that he had taken over Ben's property in town, including Snow Angel Cove.

That he was Aidan Caine, founder and CEO of Caine Tech, was the least important issue right now, even less important than the poor precipitation drainage. He cut her off before she could say anything more about it by turning back to the injured woman. "Ma'am," he said again, gently nudging her. "Ma'am, can you hear me?"

When she didn't answer, he turned to the little girl. "What's your mother's name?"

"Eliza Jane Hayward," she answered promptly, though her voice wobbled on the words. "My name is Madeline Elizabeth Hayward."

He tried to give her a reassuring smile, though it was completely fake since *he* wasn't reassured by anything that had happened in the past few minutes. He did his best to push away the headache that had become his constant companion the last few months. "Hi, Madeline. My name is Aidan."

"Why won't she wake up?" the little girl asked with a worried frown. "Is it her heart?"

He blinked at what seemed an odd question. "Her heart? Oh, I don't think so. Sometimes when people have an accident and hurt their heads, they can go to sleep for a minute. That's probably what happened. Ma'am? Eliza?"

Her eyes fluttered a little but she didn't awaken so he tried a little harder. "Eliza? Come on, ma'am. You have to wake up. Your daughter is here and she needs you."

At that, long eyelashes brushed her skin again,

once, then twice and finally she opened her eyes with what looked like supreme effort.

They were the same rich green as dewy new leaves on an aspen tree, he noted—a completely inconsequential observation but one that couldn't be helped. Just now they looked dazed, unfocused. She mumbled something incomprehensible and then in the next instant, she blinked rapidly and he watched as full consciousness returned in a mad, frantic rush.

Her gaze shifted wildly. "Maddie? Maddie!"

The little girl moved closer. "Right here, Mama. I'm right here."

Eliza gave a sob of relief and pulled the girl to her chest, holding her tight. "I thought you were... Oh, honey."

"You didn't wake up and I was so *scared*."

"I'm here. I'm sorry. I'm sorry." Tears leaked out of those stunning eyes and dripped into her hair and her daughter's. After a moment, the girl sat up and her mother tried to follow her but Aidan rested a hand on her arm.

"Easy. Don't get up. The ambulance is on the way."

"Don't be silly," she croaked. "I don't need an... ambulance."

"You were hit by a car. My car. You need an ambulance," he said firmly.

"Where are you hurt? Can you tell us?" the storekeeper asked in a kind voice.

"Everywhere," Eliza Hayward muttered. "But…I don't think anything's…broken."

She again tried to scramble up but Aidan set a hand on her shoulder, careful not to apply pressure anywhere until they had a better idea of the extent of her injuries.

"Please. Just stay still. By the sound of it, help is almost here."

She didn't look thrilled at the reminder as the siren's wail approached them but she subsided on the cold ground again. Heedless of the weather conditions, he took his coat off and folded it under her head so she didn't have to lie on asphalt, just as the ambulance pulled up behind his rental vehicle.

A couple of frazzled-looking emergency medical technicians—probably volunteer firefighters, if Haven Point was anything like his hometown of Hope's Crossing—raced over carrying boxes he assumed contained medical supplies.

The EMTs greeted the woman who had come out of her store to help.

"It's that stupid patch of ice we've had such trouble with this year," she said. "Mr. Caine couldn't stop in time and he slid right into her."

After quick, furtive looks in his direction that made him squirm, the EMTs turned their attention to Eliza. Aidan quickly stepped out of the way to give them more room.

He noticed Madeline—Maddie, her mother had called her—standing to one side, watching the activity with eyes that looked very large suddenly in her pale face.

He stepped closer and leaned down to her. "Don't worry, Maddie. The paramedics are taking very good care of your mom. Everything's going to be okay."

She looked skeptical. "How do you know?"

He could appreciate someone who demanded verification. "Your mom was talking to us. That's a great sign. She said she was okay. I think we're going to have to believe her until we find out otherwise. What about you? Are you okay?"

The little girl's chin wobbled a little, as if she had been trying all this time to be brave and had finally lost the battle. "My knee hurts," she said with a sniffle. "My mom pushed me and I fell and now I think it's bleeding.

"See?" She pulled up her purple jeans and he could see she had a scrape about the size of a quarter just below her little kneecap.

"Look at that. You *are* bleeding. I bet we can find a Band-Aid to put on that for you."

"Will it have a princess on it?"

She reminded him forcefully of his niece Faith, which seemed odd as Faith was a few years older, slender and blonde. This little curly-haired imp with the big personality and the dimples probably had more in common with Carter, Faith's younger brother. They seemed about the same age.

But there was something about her, a kind of fragile sweetness, that made him want to blindly promise her everything would work out—and then tuck her against him to protect her from further harm and do everything in his power to keep his word.

"I'll see what I can do," he said.

He spent a few more moments talking to the girl while the paramedics were working on her mother and learned, much to his surprise, that she and her mother weren't from Haven Point.

"We were just moving here. All our things are in boxes," she revealed. "I was going to sleep in my new bed *tonight,* but then my mama's new job burned down. See?"

She pointed down the hill toward the lake, where he could see the charred remains of the comfortable inn where he had stayed on his first visit to the area.

"Your mother was going to work at the Lake Haven Inn?"

Maddie nodded, curls bouncing. "Yes. Only now she can't and the lady was really sad. She cried and my mama told her not to worry, that we would fig-ure something out. That's what she always says."

He was still mulling that and the atrocious luck that had hit Eliza Hayward in the past hour when the woman who had first come out of the store to help after the accident approached him.

She was young, he could see now, no more than twenty-seven or -eight. *This* was the new mayor of Haven Point?

"You're Aidan Caine, aren't you?"

She said it bluntly and without any of the kind

of embarrassing awe he sometimes encountered. In fact, her voice and expression were completely devoid of any kind of warmth.

"I am, yes. I'm afraid I didn't catch your name."

She wasn't overtly hostile but there was definitely a coolness in her tone and expression. "I don't think I told you. I'm McKenzie Shaw. That's my store over there. Point Made Flowers and Gifts."

Was she trying to drum up business? This really wasn't the time.

"I like your Christmas tree," Maddie said.

The woman smiled at her with considerably more warmth than she had shown Aidan. "Thanks, honey. If you come in with your mom, I'll give you an ornament made out of a pinecone. I make them myself."

"Wow! Thanks," Maddie said.

"You're welcome."

Ms. Shaw turned back to Aidan. "I'm also the newly elected mayor of Haven Point and will take office in January."

"So you said."

"I apologize again on behalf of the town for the poor road conditions," she said stiffly. "You can be assured, it won't happen again."

Was she afraid he would pursue legal action against the town? The fault was entirely his own. If he had been driving a vehicle with better tires, this wouldn't have happened. He was already planning on purchasing an additional vehicle besides the ranch Suburban and pickup truck—one with excellent tires—that he could leave at the Lake Haven airport and use for ground transportation on future visits.

Before he had the chance to tell her that, a police officer approached them. "I'm Officer Bailey with the Haven Point police department. I understand you were the driver of the vehicle that struck Mrs. Hayward while the light was red and she was in the crosswalk," she said sternly.

"Yes," he answered. By her unfriendly tone and set jaw, he had to wonder if he was going to end up behind bars over this whole thing. He wasn't sure the town even *had* a jail but he had a feeling he was about to find out.

"I saw the whole thing from my shop window, Wyn," McKenzie Shaw said. "He wasn't speeding and definitely tried to stop in time."

He blinked, shocked by the would-be mayor's unexpected defense.

"It's that stupid patch of black ice," she went on. "How many times have I tried to get the road department to lay down extra salt solution there?"

"Plenty," Officer Bailey said. "Regardless, it's still considered a failure to yield situation. I'm going to need to see your license and registration."

"You know who this is, don't you, Wyn?" McKenzie said, giving him a significant look.

The police officer—who looked only a few years older than the new mayor—gave a shrug. "Sure I do. No matter what Mr. Caine might think, owning half the town doesn't give him any special privileges, as far as the law is concerned."

Why the hell were all the women in this town pissed at him? This was only the second time he had even stepped foot in Haven Point. What had he done?

"I don't expect special privileges," he insisted.

"Good." She smirked. "Then you'll understand that I have to give you a citation with a hefty fine."

"Absolutely," he said, with a coolness to match hers.

"Mr. Aidan! Where are they taking my mama?" Maddie spoke in a frantic voice, adding several progressively more insistent tugs on his shirt for emphasis.

While he was talking to the new mayor and the police officer, the EMTs had started to load the stretcher into the back of the ambulance, he realized.

"Where is the closest medical facility?" he demanded of the two women.

"Lake Haven Hospital," Officer Bailey answered. "It's the closest and *only* medical facility around here. You'll find it at the halfway point between Haven Point and Shelter Springs."

Maddie tore away from him and raced over to the ambulance. "No! Don't go, Mama. Don't go!"

Eliza looked equally distressed. "Please. My daughter. I can't leave without her!"

One of the EMTs, a man with a completely bald head and a bit of a paunch, gave her an apologetic look. "It's against our department policy, ma'am, to take uninjured minors in the ambulance. But Officer Bailey over there can transport her to the hospital in her patrol vehicle. She might even beat us to the hospital."

"I want to go with my mama!" Maddie exclaimed. "I'm hurt, too! I scraped my knee!"

"It's true," Aidan offered solemnly. "She definitely needs medical attention."

"I'm sorry, but—"

"She's a little girl who's been through a terrible ordeal, seeing her mother hurt like that. It's cold out here and she's frightened. What's the harm in letting them stay together?"

"The rules—"

"Just let her ride the bus, Ed," the police officer said, her voice weary. "I'll clear it with Chief Gallegos. He's too busy dealing with the fire at the inn to mind a little breach in protocol this once."

After a moment and another whispered conversation between the EMTs, the bald dude shrugged. "Fine. Come on up here, little lady. You have to promise not to touch anything, though."

"I won't," she promised.

Aidan lifted her up into the ambulance and she paused in the door opening to give him a little wave before the EMTs climbed in after her and closed the door. A moment later, the ambulance pulled away, lights flashing, and drove away from the scene.

He shivered a little and realized his coat had disappeared somewhere. Maybe they had used it to cover the woman in the ambulance. He hoped so.

"Mr. Caine. I need your license and registration, please." The police officer's expression had once more returned to a stern, uncompromising line.

He found the necessary information inside the rental vehicle—not an easy task since the glove compartment was packed with all kinds of paperwork, from the last time the tires were rotated to a receipt for pizza from a place called Pie Guys Pizza.

By the time they finished, he was freezing. The mayor had long since returned to the warmth of her store, with its cheery Christmas tree in the window.

"That should be all," Officer Bailey said, still without smiling once. "You can find all the necessary instructions for paying your citation or where and when to appear before the judge if you want to contest it. If you have any questions, there's also a number there you can call."

"Thanks. Am I free to go, then? You're not going to arrest me?"

"Not today, anyway."

Was that a joke? It was tough to tell, since she seemed completely humorless.

"Can you tell me again how I get to the hospital?"

"Take a left and go a block until you hit Lakefront Drive, then head north about a mile. You can't miss it. Big redbrick building. The storm is picking up. Drive slowly and leave plenty of room to stop, especially with those tires."

He nodded and climbed back into the rental SUV. His headache had ratcheted up about a dozen notches. He wasn't in any hurry to drive anywhere except his lodge at Snow Angel Cove after the trauma of actually hitting a person, but Dermot and Margaret Caine had raised him to do the right thing, even when it hurt.

CHAPTER TWO

AIDAN'S PHONE RANG with the signature ringtone for his father just as he pulled into a parking space near the sign for the emergency department at the modern-looking redbrick hospital along the lake.

He briefly entertained the temptation to ignore the call. He loved his father dearly but at the moment his primary focus centered on finding out Eliza's condition and checking to make sure Madeline had someone looking after her.

On the other hand, after such a traumatic afternoon, he was drawn to the safe, warm, familiar connection with his father.

"Pop. Hi."

He pictured Dermot Caine—hearty, strong, still handsome even as he headed toward seventy. Wherever his father might be when they spoke on the phone, Aidan always imagined him in his favorite environment, the Center of Hope Café, where he ruled as master and commander—pouring coffee and serving up pie and conversation to tourists and locals alike.

"Are you in the country?" Pop said. "I wondered if you might be abroad."

Aidan winced a little as he watched the snow pummel the windshield with increasing intensity. Calling his father had been on his to-do list for a week.

"I'm here. I got your messages. Sorry we never connected. I've been in the middle of some pretty intense negotiations this week."

"You work too hard, son."

He couldn't argue. He had been working twenty-hour days for the past week trying to iron out some contract disputes with one of their vendors in China and for several weeks before that, he had been neck-deep in product development projects.

Everything seemed harder since September. He wanted to think he was almost back to full throttle but he still had times when he had to collapse and sleep for almost twenty-four hours straight.

He didn't tell his father any of that, of course.

"How is Katherine?" he asked, choosing a topic certain to distract his father.

"Lovely. Just lovely." The delight and satisfaction in his father's voice made him smile, despite the bleakness of his errand. "I had forgotten so many little things about sharing a home and a life with a woman. How she straightens up the towels in the bathroom and fills the house with fresh flowers and scented candles and little fancy soaps. She's had such fun decorating for Christmas. The house is beautiful."

His father, who had been a widower for most of

Aidan's adult life, had married just a few months earlier to a woman he had secretly cared about for years.

Aidan was deeply happy for his father, who deserved to find love and joy again after all these years on his own.

"And how are things coming there?"

"Good, I guess. I haven't been up to the house yet."

"Katherine is anxious to see it. We all are."

"Everyone is still coming, then? I was afraid you might be calling to tell me you've decided to stay in Hope's Crossing, after all."

"No. We're all excited to be together for once. No one else has any place big enough for all of us, now that we've absorbed all these new people into our midst."

In the past year, two of Aidan's siblings had also married and another had become engaged. When his family was already unbelievably large, every new person added a little more chaos into the mix.

"You're sure about having us all, then?" Dermot asked.

"Absolutely. I'm looking forward to it."

He was, even if he was beginning to have a few misgivings as the holidays approached. The whole plan to host everyone for Christmas had been his idea, actually, during that dark time in September while he waited for test results and feared the worst.

He had only recently come into possession of the property here at Lake Haven and his initial visit had convinced him the rambling ten-bedroom lakeshore lodge would be the perfect place for his overlarge family to gather.

Now that the reality of it all was sinking in, he was beginning to wonder if this was yet another decision he had made when he wasn't precisely in his right mind. He loved his family best in small doses. Having everyone at Snow Angel Cove was certain to be noisy, chaotic and intense.

"I wanted to talk to you about the travel arrangements." His father's voice turned disapproving. "That's the reason for my call."

He braced himself for the lecture he knew was coming. "What don't you like about the arrangements?"

"A private jet, son? Really? You're sending a private jet for us?"

"Yes. And?"

"And it's a ridiculous expense, that's what it is. Why, we can drive there in no more than thirteen, fourteen hours, on a few tanks of gas."

"Do you have a school bus I don't know about, big enough for twenty people plus luggage?"

"Smarty. We could take separate cars. We could each drive our own and it would still cost less than a chartered flight."

He sighed. His humble, hardworking father couldn't quite grasp the fact that Aidan was loaded, even after all these years.

"I don't want everybody to have to spend their

whole holiday in the car. I can get everyone here from Hope's Crossing in less than two hours."

"It's a big waste of money. That's what it is."

"It's my money. If I want to waste it giving my family a happy Christmas, that's my prerogative, isn't it? I'm excited for everyone to be here. We haven't spent a Christmas together in years. It's too bad Jamie can't make it."

"Yes." He could tell his father was still fretting about the expense.

"Just relax and let me worry about the details, okay? The flight is already arranged. It's too late to back out now so you might as well just sit back and enjoy it."

"I don't see that you've given us a choice, if you've already paid for it."

He would have smiled at Pop's reluctance if he wasn't parked outside a hospital, about to go in and check on the woman he had injured.

"I've got to go, Pop. I'm sorry."

"I know. You're a busy man."

"I'll see you in a few weeks, though, and we'll have plenty of time to catch up."

"You know I love you, son."

"I love you, too, Pop."

He had said those words whenever he spoke with his father since September. Each time, they seemed to carry a new weight, to ring with resonant depth.

He loved his family, each crazy one of them. His father had set a fine example of the way a man should live, with dignity, compassion and Dermot's inherent goodness. As a result, his brothers were all men of honor and strength and he admired each one of them for different reasons—and the women they had chosen.

He only had one sister, the sweet and kind Charlotte, who impressed the hell out of him for the determination and courage she had directed toward turning her life around the past few years.

Aidan had neglected them all. For years, he had been immersed with single-minded focus on building Caine Tech into the powerhouse it was today. Something else had to slide along the way and his personal life had, by default, dwindled to nothing. As a result, he had missed countless birthdays, holidays and special occasions over the years.

This year, he wanted everything to be different. Life had taken an unexpected, disconcerting turn for him in the fall but he had emerged from it with a new determination to tighten and strengthen those ties binding him to his family.

He wanted this Christmas at Snow Angel Cove to be perfect for all of them, his way of making up for all those years of neglect.

First, he had to make sure the woman he had injured would be able to enjoy a merry Christmas of her own.

OH, HOW SHE hated this.

From the drafty hospital gown, to the smell of

sickness and disinfectant, to the frustrating and unsettling sense of being completely out of control of her circumstances, Eliza heartily disliked hospitals.

She had a great respect for medical professionals and understood that certain instances required their services but she would rather be standing out in the middle of that storm out there in bare feet than be tucked here under warmed blankets in the emergency department of the Haven Point medical center.

Okay, she seriously loved the warmed blankets. They made her feel sleepy and cozy and safe. She probably should be ashamed at her fierce desire to just curl up on the uncomfortable exam bed and sleep for a few days.

All the more reason she had to get out of here. She didn't have the luxury of dawdling under blankets, warmed or otherwise, when she and her daughter were now basically homeless.

"I'm fine, I promise," Eliza insisted for at least the twentieth time. "Can't I just go?"

The lovely red-haired young woman frowning at her appeared far too young to have earned that stethoscope and the name tag on her lab coat that read Dr. Devin Shaw.

"You were hit by a car, Ms. Hayward. The head CT showed a concussion."

"And you said yourself, you saw no evidence of bleeding or swelling."

The doctor made a dismissive gesture. "Yet. Sometimes those things can develop hours or even days after the initial injury. With all that's been in the news lately about professional athletes and concussions, you surely understand that any head injury is potentially serious."

"I know. I will be very careful, I promise."

The doctor jotted a note on her chart. "I would still like to X-ray that wrist and possibly your shoulder where the vehicle struck you."

All of which would take time and money, both of which she had in very short supply right now. "That's hardly necessary. The SUV barely tapped me. Nothing is broken."

"You sound very certain of that."

"I'm sure I would know if I had any broken bones. Besides the concussion, I've got some scrapes and bruises and possibly a sprained wrist. That's all. I don't need to waste any more of your time."

"You're not wasting anything. It's my responsibility to make sure we don't let you leave the hospital until we're absolutely certain it's safe for you to do so."

She shifted in the flimsy gown, wanting rather desperately to be done here. It was growing dark and a storm was poised to deliver a hard uppercut to this little corner of western Idaho. She didn't have *time* to lie here being coddled and fretted over, not when she needed to find somewhere safe and warm for her daughter to stay.

"Look, I appreciate what you've done so far but, really, I'm fine. Please."

She couldn't stay here. The hospital was nice enough. Over the past five years with Maddie, she had seen the inside of more than her share of medical facilities and as far as she could tell, the Lake Haven Hospital was small but modern and seemed to have all the necessary diagnostic equipment.

The doctor might seem young but she also projected a calm, comforting bedside manner that Eliza appreciated.

That didn't make her any more eager to stay a moment longer than necessary.

She craned her neck to see Maddie curled up in the visitor's chair, watching one of her favorite Disney movies on Eliza's tablet while she colored a picture with crayons and paper provided by the hospital staff.

Maddie had plenty of experience with hospital rooms and didn't seem at all distressed to be in a new one. In fact, she had spent the past hour chatting up all the doctors and nurses in her usual friendly fashion.

Every time Maddie touched a surface, Eliza wanted to cringe and grab the spray disinfectant. Having a child with a serious health condition had given Eliza a severe case of germaphobia, at least when it came to hospitals.

No matter how good the hospital's housekeeping department might be, most emergency departments were a breeding ground for viruses and bacteria by the very nature of the cases they treated.

She had to get out of here.

"Look, I appreciate your concern and I understand you're just doing your job, but what do I have to do to convince you I'm fine so you'll let me go? As I said, the SUV barely touched me. I don't need X-rays or stitches and I don't want any pain medication."

"You might be singing a different tune in the morning. You're probably going to hurt everywhere."

She *already* hurt everywhere but she wasn't about to tell this earnest, concerned young doctor that. "I promise, I'll pick up a bottle of ibuprofen and take them faithfully."

The doctor still didn't look convinced so Eliza decided to appeal to her sympathy, if nothing else. "I appreciate your concern. Everyone here has been really great. I can highly recommend the hospital and will be happy to post good reviews on Angie's List or wherever you hospitals need reviews, but I have had a really miserable day. The worst."

The doctor gave her a sympathetic look. "The paramedics told me you were supposed to start work at the Lake Haven Inn. I'm so sorry. What rotten timing."

"Almost as bad as being in the crosswalk at the exact moment a driver coming down the hill hit a patch of ice, right? Haven Point hasn't been really great to me. Right now I just want to take my daughter and go."

The doctor frowned again, looking torn. She studied the computer screen again and studied Eliza carefully.

"If I were to release you, where will you go?"

"I was going to drive back to Boise. I have friends I can stay with for a few days, until I figure things out."

That was a blatant lie. Yes, she had plenty of friends but she wouldn't feel comfortable calling any of them a few weeks before Christmas and inviting her and her daughter over for an open-ended visit.

She didn't like the bleak option of an extended-stay hotel somewhere, but she would figure out a way to make it work for a while.

Dr. Shaw chewed her bottom lip, looking more like a middle-school student prepping for an algebra test than the attending physician at an emergency room.

"I'll be honest, I don't feel good about you driving two hours back to Boise when we haven't properly assessed your injuries, especially with that storm. It's already snowing pretty hard out there and I can imagine the mountain passes between here and Boise are restricted to chains or four-wheel drive only."

"I have four-wheel drive on my vehicle and chains in my trunk."

She also had a pounding headache that would make even driving to the mountain pass an interesting exercise, but that was another thing she decided not to mention to the physician.

"How about this. I'm all right with releasing you

from here but I don't feel good about sending you out into the storm. Do you know anyone in town you could stay with tonight?"

She shook her head then fought a wince as her pain cells reacted quite negatively to the gesture. "Megan Hamilton is the only person I know— besides the nice EMTs and your staff here, of course. I imagine Megan has her hands full right now, dealing with the fire at the inn. I can't add another burden onto her plate."

"We're at a stalemate, then."

"What if I were to find a hotel room for the night and drive back tomorrow?"

"I'm afraid that might be easier said than done. A lot of our hotels are only open seasonally, during the summer. With the fire at the inn, we lost half the available hotel rooms in town. All their guests had to scramble to find lodging here or in Shelter Springs, from what I understand."

She sighed. Finding a way through this quandary was more effort than her aching head wanted to handle right now. "I suppose that's our answer, then. I can't stay overnight in the hospital simply because of a lack of hotel rooms. Not with Maddie to think about, too. I'll drive back to Boise to stay with friends. I'm sure I'll be fine."

The doctor was quiet. "I'm still not crazy about that option. You've got a sprained wrist and a concussion. We both know you're in no shape for driving under perfect conditions, forget about driving at

night during a winter storm. Give me a few moments
to see if I can arrange something."

"I may have the solution."

The sudden masculine voice in the room startled
both of them. Only Maddie, happily watching her
show with her headphones on, didn't jump.

Eliza and the doctor both turned to find Aidan
Caine standing in the doorway, looking lean and
sexy in a blue sweater, jeans and worn leather boots.

She knew who he was now. She had figured it
out during the ambulance ride, when she heard the
EMTs mention his name. She should have recognized
him immediately but she had been too dazed after
the accident to place why the face of the man whose
vehicle had hit her seemed so familiar.

Aidan Caine. The Geek God. That's what the
magazines called him. He was a tech genius whose
company had recently been named one of the five
most influential in Silicon Valley. Though only in
his midthirties, he was reported to be worth well into
nine—possibly ten—figures.

She had never met the man in person but they
were connected by a tangled web that went back
far further than the events of this afternoon. What
an odd coincidence, that he had been driving in the
little town of Haven Point at the exact moment she
was crossing the road.

If she didn't know better, she might think Aidan
Caine had some kind of vendetta against her and was

determined to ruin her life—all while looking like a cover model for Sexy Geek Monthly.

"Hi!" Maddie exclaimed suddenly, distracted from the Disney princess movie she was watching. She pulled off her headphones and beamed at Aidan.

"Hey, Mama, look! That's my friend! The nice man who helped me when you were hurt."

Nice man? Aidan *Caine?* She really needed to have a talk with her daughter about developing more discriminating taste. From all reports, the man was ruthless and cold, used to taking what he wanted, to hell with the consequences.

He had just mowed *her* down with his car, for heaven's sake.

Eliza had plenty of reason to know Mr. Caine and the people who worked for him only cared about the Caine Tech bottom line, not about all the people they stepped on to protect it.

Oblivious to just how much this man had indirectly altered the course of her young life, Maddie slid off her chair and trotted over to him holding out her paper. "Look, Mr. Aidan. I'm coloring a picture. It's a Christmas tree. You can have it, if you want."

Eliza braced to swoop in and protect her baby, fully expecting him to be impatient and brusque with a little girl's childish drawing. Instead, he surprised her by taking the paper with apparent delight. "Thank you. It's very nice. I especially like the angel on the top."

"We always have an angel on the top of our tree,"

Maddie informed him. "Except this year. This year we don't even have a Christmas tree. Isn't that sad? We were going to have one at our new apartment but it burned down. Now I don't know *what* we're going to do. All our ornaments are in boxes. So are most of my toys, even my Barbie Malibu Mansion."

Dr. Shaw stepped forward before he could answer. "This is a secure area, Mr. Caine," she said, her voice cold. "How did you get back here?"

The young doctor didn't seem very impressed or intimidated by Aidan's reputation, either. She faced him down, chin up and arms crossed over her chest like she was a one-hundred-pound offensive lineman protecting Eliza, who had the ball.

"I asked where I could find Eliza Hayward and the receptionist gave me the room number. Is that a problem?"

"Yes! We have strict security protocol. This area is restricted to family and friends of patients. As far as I know, you're neither."

"He's *my* friend," Maddie said firmly. "I want him here. He's nice."

Eliza flushed. Maddie had become very good at pushing her weight around in hospitals.

"There. You see?" Aidan said, after flashing a rather devastating smile to her daughter. "I'm Maddie's friend. And I do believe I have an answer that might help everyone."

She sincerely doubted that. Eliza pulled the warmed blanket—quickly losing its comforting capabilities, anyway—up to her chin, wishing she were wearing something other than this atrocious hospital gown.

A little battle armor would be nice when confronting a man like Aidan Caine.

"You need a place close by to stay for the night so you can leave the hospital, is that correct?"

Eliza didn't want to answer but she could see no point in dissembling. "I want to drive back to Boise to stay with friends but Dr. Shaw is concerned about the storm."

"With good reason. It's really coming down out there."

He was not helping her position with the doctor. Maybe he *was* trying to sabotage her life.

"Here's the thing," he said. "I recently took ownership of some property in town."

Dr. Shaw gave an inelegant snort. "More like half of Haven Point," she muttered.

To Eliza's surprise, a hint of dusky color rose on the man's cheekbones. "Not quite. But one of the properties is a large lodge on the southeastern shore of the lake about two miles from Haven Point."

"Snow Angel Cove," Dr. Shaw offered.

He looked surprised. "You know it?"

"I grew up on the lake, Mr. Caine. Everyone knows Snow Angel Cove."

"Then you can confirm that there's plenty of room for Ms. Hayward and her daughter to stay while she recovers from her injuries."

He really thought she would just merrily pack her daughter up and go move to a stranger's home? Either he was unbelievably arrogant or ridiculously clueless. She would bet on the former.

"That's not necessary. I'll figure something else out," she said, her tone stiff. Her head throbbed as if someone had wedged it in a car door and was slamming the door against it again and again for fun. The rest of her wasn't faring much better.

After the miserable day she had endured, she just wanted to be alone somewhere where she could whimper and sniffle and lick her wounds by herself.

"There aren't any hotel rooms left in town. You heard the doctor. I don't feel good about you leaving town, either, in the middle of that storm. I promise, I'm not a homicidal maniac."

No. Only a fiercely ruthless competitor who had built his business from nothing in only a few years—and the man who had indirectly contributed to her husband's death.

She didn't want anything to do with him.

"That's impossible," she said. "Completely out of the question. I'm not staying with you."

Surprise flitted in his blue eyes, as if he had never expected her to refuse. "If it makes you feel any better, a very nice couple has been overseeing the renovations on the property for me the last few months. They're staying on the property, as well."

That made the whole thing sound more like a genuine offer to help her out of a tough situation and help her get released from the hospital and less like he planned to drag her to his evil lair for his own nefarious purposes. But still.

"This is stupid. I'm fine to drive back to Boise. I'm used to driving in snow. I've got a four-wheel-drive SUV *and* I have good tires on my car. Unlike someone else I could mention," she said pointedly.

Where was all this snarkiness coming from? She was never caustic or sharp. She considered herself a nice person, darn it. Apparently, leaving one job and apartment, losing another of each in a terrible fire and then being mowed down on the street, all in the same day, tended to bring out the worst in her.

Unfortunately, reminding him of his contribution to her situation only seemed to strengthen his resolve.

"That is exactly the reason you should stay at Snow Angel Cove for the night. I feel responsible that you were hurt."

"You *are* responsible," Devin Shaw murmured.

He nodded. "There. What the good doctor said. I *am* responsible for you being hurt. I would offer to put you up in a hotel for the night but as Dr. Shaw pointed out, I doubt there's one room to be found in town. This is the next best thing. Please, Ms. Hayward. Better than some cramped couch at a friend's house."

"Do you have a Christmas tree?" Maddie asked eagerly.

He looked down, apparently disconcerted by the question. "Um, I don't think so. Not yet, anyway."

"That's okay," Maddie said.

She seemed to accept this failing—and the whole situation—with far more equanimity than Eliza. She also seemed to have developed an immediate liking for Aidan.

Eliza wanted to pull her daughter close and whisper to her a bit of maternal advice about being careful about the men you decide to trust, but this probably wasn't quite the time.

"It's not a bad solution," Dr. Shaw said with a pensive nod. "As a last resort, I was going to offer my own house for you to stay. It's not far from here and I have an extra bedroom. The only problem is, I'm on shift all night tonight and you and your daughter would be alone there. I'll tell you quite frankly, I feel much better about you staying somewhere with people around than I would even if we could find you a hotel room here or up in Shelter Springs."

Eliza studied all three of the people in the room, looking at her with varying degrees of expectation. She was too tired and battered to make this kind of decision right now! This whole thing was so ridiculous.

If she only had herself to consider, she would jump up from this bed, grab her coat, tell them all to go to hell and drive to Boise, against medical advice or not.

But she would be a poor mother not to be concerned about her daughter's well-being. Maddie had already had a long, hard day. She was a trouper but she had to be exhausted. Subjecting her to at least a two-hour car ride in poor conditions—and with a driver who, like it or not, probably wasn't in any shape to drive—would be foolhardy.

He had an abundance of bedrooms and a caretaker couple in residence. She likely wouldn't even see the man before she and Maddie left in the morning.

The thought of having a safe, comfortable bed suddenly held enormous appeal. One night. What would be the harm in that?

And anyway, what choice did she really have in the matter? She had a feeling it was either stay with him or be stuck here in the hospital overnight.

"I suppose we could stay for one night, if you're certain you have the room."

Relief blazed across his features and she realized with some surprise that his concern was genuine.

"Absolutely," he answered. "We have more than enough room."

"The place is huge," Dr. Shaw said.

"Yay. Now we can help you get a Christmas tree!" Maddie exclaimed.

"Great," he answered another quick flash of that devastating smile.

"I do have one caveat," Dr. Shaw said. "Someone will have to check on Eliza during the night. I would prefer every two hours but at least once or twice will suffice."

"That can be arranged," he said.

"Great. Then I'll start work on your discharge papers."

She hurried out of the room, leaving Eliza alone with the man who had put her in the hospital bed in the first place.

CHAPTER THREE

BY THE TIME the nurse brought the final paperwork to release Eliza from the emergency department an hour later, Maddie's patience with hospitals had trickled away, leaving her tired, hungry and cranky.

"I want to go home," she said several times. Each time, panic trickled through Eliza at the reminder that she didn't *have* a home for her daughter.

"We're going to stay overnight at Mr. Caine's house," she finally explained just as she was shrugging back into her coat.

At least she assumed that was still the plan. She hadn't seen the man in an hour, not since he left with her car keys to call his employee to retrieve her vehicle from downtown Haven Point and take it out to his property so she would have all her things waiting for her when they arrived.

"Are we having a slumber party?" Maddie asked with excitement. She had been hounding her mother to let her stay overnight at a friend's house but Eliza had always been too nervous, given all the medication her daughter required. Apparently this was the next best thing.

"Something like that," Eliza murmured.

The more thought she gave to it, the more ridicu-lous the whole concept seemed. What in the world was she thinking? She didn't even want to *speak* with the man, forget about staying in his home.

She was a smart, capable woman. She never should have let herself be railroaded into this whole thing, storm or not.

When they walked out to the reception area, they found Aidan leafing through a magazine in one of the uncomfortable-looking chairs.

He rose when she and Maddie came through the door. "Are you free to go?"

"So they tell me," she said glumly.

She had no choice, she reminded herself. She had her daughter's welfare to worry about first and fore-most. A safe, warm place for the night, even with Aidan Caine, was the best option for Maddie.

"Excellent. I've already brought the car around."

He gripped her elbow as they passed through the outside door and she caught a whiff of some kind of expensive peppery aftershave before the wild swirl of icy wind and blowing snow snatched away her breath.

"It's so cold!" Maddie exclaimed.

"Come on. We'll get you warmed up."

Still gripping her arm, he headed for a very fa-miliar vehicle and opened the door to the backseat.

"Hey! This is my SUV," she exclaimed.

He nodded. "It seemed the safest choice, since you had a car seat and everything. I drove the rental with the lousy tires into town while they were discharging you and swapped with the key you gave me. I hope you don't mind."

"I don't mind. What about your rental?"

"I called them to pick it up," he said grimly, "with a few choice words about renting out an unsafe vehicle."

She would *not* like to be on this man's bad side.

After he made sure she and Maddie were both settled securely, he pulled out into the snow.

Within the first few minutes of observing while he drove along at a crawl, the wipers valiantly trying to beat back the snow, she realized driving back to Boise would have been a nightmare. She wouldn't have made it, not with the headache still throbbing through her to the same rhythmic beat of the wipers.

"Are you doing okay?" he asked after a few moments.

She shrugged then realized he couldn't see her in the dark interior of her SUV. "Yes. Fine."

"Thank you for giving me this chance to try to make things up to you," he said, his voice low. "I can't tell you how sorry I am about what happened today. I've been having flashbacks ever since that terrible moment when I thought I had hit both of you. I'm not sure I'll ever be able to forget it."

She relived that moment of helpless terror when she had seen Maddie racing directly into the path of the oncoming vehicle and realized he wouldn't be able to stop in time. A fine-edged shiver rippled down her spine. "I doubt I will, either."

If she had any doubts about his competency behind the wheel, they were quickly allayed as he drove through the snowy night around the lake. Though they encountered few other vehicles on the road, he was cautious, alert, leaving plenty of time for braking at the few stop signs they passed through on the way out of town and then progressing at a sedate pace.

She had a feeling this was more a reaction to the events of the afternoon than his usually driving patterns. That didn't make her appreciate his vigilance less, given the dangerous conditions.

"Tell me again about what you were doing in Haven Point, the job you were supposed to be starting," he said after a few moments without taking his gaze off the road. "I only caught bits and pieces of the story at the accident scene and then a little more at the hospital."

She released a long breath and shifted in the seat. Just that slight movement hurt and she sincerely wished she had taken the doctor up on her offer to write a prescription for pain medication.

"I have a degree in hotel management and was hired to take charge of the Lake Haven Inn."

"What were you doing before today?"

"Until yesterday I've been working as the assistant manager at a small hotel in Boise. I've been there for three years, since my husband died."

"I'm sorry. About your husband, I mean."

"Thank you." Manners compelled her to acknowledge the condolences, though it felt strange, *wrong* somehow, when they were coming from Aidan Caine.

She stared straight ahead at the snow blowing against the windshield. When she was a little girl, she used to think the snow reflecting in the headlights looked like stars and she would pretend her dad was piloting a rocket ship through hyperspace.

That time of imagination and fun seemed a long time ago. Now driving through snow was at best an inconvenience, at worst, an experience fraught with tension and peril.

"It seems an odd time to start a new job, right before Christmas," he observed.

"I suppose. I was actually hired in early November but it took a little time to tender my resignation and end the lease on my apartment."

"You really did pack up everything, didn't you?" He jerked his head to the back, piled high with boxes.

"Most of our things are in storage. These were only the essentials. Moving to Lake Haven was supposed to be a new start for us. I guess that didn't work out so well."

That panic hovering just beneath the surface since the moment she'd seen that blackened building seemed to bubble up all over again. For a moment, she wanted to just close her eyes and wallow in self-pity. She had pinned such high hopes on this move. Running a hotel in a small town had been her dream since she was just a girl working the front desk at the Seaswept Inn on the Oregon Coast.

She loved the idea of raising Maddie in this small town, finally putting down roots after Trent had moved them from job to job, opportunity to opportunity, always in search of pay dirt.

The charming town of Haven Point and the whole Lake Haven area had seemed the perfect location— quiet part of the year, bustling during the summer months, and close enough to Maddie's specialists in Boise that they could still go to appointments with relative ease.

She had loved Haven Point on previous visits and had felt welcomed from the first moment she stepped into town.

She was so tired of disappointments, of constantly being forced to rechart her life's direction.

"I'm sorry about your job situation," Aidan said quietly. "I can only imagine how upsetting that must be for you and for Maddie."

What did he know about upsetting job situations? He came from a completely different world and probably had no idea what it was like to struggle, to wonder which bills she could afford to pay off that month and which she would have to make token payments on until a better time.

"Upsetting. Yes. It certainly is."

"If you don't mind me asking, what are your plans beyond the next few days?"

She didn't have a fallback position. Why would she ever have imagined she needed one?

"I don't know yet," she admitted. "I haven't exactly had a great deal of time to go over my options, considering I've been at the hospital since five minutes after I found out the inn burned down."

"True enough. Being hit by a car can be such a distraction."

"Who knew?" she said dryly, earning a short, surprised-sounding laugh.

"I will probably try to find a short-term lease on an apartment back in Boise somewhere while I send out resumes," she finally answered.

"You don't have family you could stay with?"

"No," she said. To her dismay, her throat started to close at that single harsh word. For a moment, she missed her mother fiercely. It had been sixteen years since her mother went to work and never came home and it still sometimes seemed like yesterday.

She could drive to Portland and stay with her father and stepmother but she knew just how that would go. They would be squeezed into a sofa bed in the corner of the family room. Her teenage stepbrothers would resent her presence in what they considered *their* home and would complain about having to share a bathroom and about Maddie's chattering. After a week or so, her father—prodded by Paula—would take her aside and quietly tell her he was afraid things weren't working out.

She didn't want to put any of them through that.

"My father lives out of state," she said. "He doesn't really have room for us."

In his house or in his life. Though she didn't add the words, she acknowledged them with a familiar little pang, then forced herself to focus on the positive.

"I have many friends in Boise and could call several of them in a moment and they would gladly open their homes until I can find a place."

Her best friend, Joan, had an extra bedroom and had ushered her off tearfully just that morning—Lord, it seemed like a month ago—after extracting promise after promise that Eliza would come back for frequent visits.

He didn't have a chance to answer, as they had approached a massive carved wooden gate. The gate opened smoothly before they reached it—she had no idea how—and he proceeded up a long driveway.

"It's like a tunnel," Maddie exclaimed. Pine trees rose up on either side of the driveway, blocking the view of the house—not that they could have seen much, anyway, through the darkness and the snow that was blowing almost horizontally.

She could see a glow in the distance that gradually took shape as a rambling log home ablaze with lights. The lodge was set on a hill, angled in such a way that Eliza imagined it would have magnificent lake and mountain views during better weather conditions.

"Welcome to Snow Angel Cove," Aidan said as he pulled into a porte cochere in front of the house.

The moment he opened the driver's side door, two people hurried out of the house toward the passenger side to open the doors for Eliza and Maddie.

The woman was lean to the point of being scrawny, with lined, leathery features and black and iron-gray hair pulled into a ponytail. She beamed at Maddie as she took her arm to help her from the car.

"Hello, my dears. Oh, you've had a time of it. Come inside where it's warm."

Maddie, who must have fallen asleep a little in the car without Eliza realizing, gave her a bleary-eyed smile. "I'm Madeline Elizabeth Hayward. I'm almost six years old."

"Hi, Madeline. I'm Sue Stockton and this is my husband, Jim."

Maddie waved at him and the man solemnly shook her hand. Jim was just as leathery, just as gray, but with a sweet smile and a bit of a paunch.

She liked them both instantly, though it was one of those snap judgments that had no real basis in reality.

"You must be Eliza," Sue said. To her surprise, the other woman wrapped her in a warm hug, as if they were old friends reconnecting after a few years.

When Eliza confirmed her identity, Sue said, "Don't dawdle. Come inside. It's freezing out here."

She opened the door wide and ushered them into a massive great room, with a ceiling that had to top thirty feet, dominated by a huge open river rock fireplace and raw timber mantel. The space was big enough to contain at least four couches she could see, in separate seating areas, along with a giant Christmas tree that was currently unadorned.

Aidan came in behind them with her purse and Maddie's backpack in one hand and a suitcase in the other. He was followed by Jim, who carried a few more suitcases.

She wanted to tell them not to bother bringing everything in since they were only staying one night, but she didn't have the chance before Aidan set her things down on a chair and swept the woman into an affectionate embrace.

He bent down and kissed her cheek. "Sue, darling, you are more gorgeous every time I see you."

The woman blushed and shook her head. "And you're still a rascal, aren't you?"

"Sue and Jim have been with me for many years," he said to Eliza and Maddie.

"Almost since the beginning of Caine Tech. What has it been? Twelve? Thirteen years? You bought that little ranch outside San Jose and hired us to look after you and we've been doing it ever since."

"Something like that. She and Jim retired a few years ago but I managed to talk them out of retirement for a while to help me get things organized here at Snow Angel Cove."

Sue gave her another hug. "When he called to tell me he was bringing you here, Aidan told me everything that's happened to you today. I'm so sorry, honey."

She ached in every muscle and under normal circumstances she would have tried to extricate herself from the woman's hug but she found something so comforting and warm and *genuine* about it.

Tears welled up, much to her dismay. "Thank you," she murmured with a watery smile, trying to wipe them away on the cuff of her sweater before anybody noticed.

"You probably haven't had time to eat a thing all afternoon, have you, what with going to the emergency room and all. Well, I hope you're hungry. I've got vegetable beef soup on the stove and fresh rolls just set to come out of the oven."

Maddie perked up. "I *love* fresh rolls!"

"You and me both, young lady," Jim said with another of those slow, sweetly charming smiles.

"We'll work on bringing in your things while you grab a bite to eat," Aidan said.

"I don't need everything," she said. "We've got boxes and boxes in my car. Just the suitcases you've already brought in should be sufficient for one night."

"Are you certain? We don't mind bringing in whatever you think you might need."

"Positive. I should be fine."

"In that case, I'll have dinner ready for you quick as a wink," Sue said.

Eliza wanted to protest that she wasn't hungry. What she needed most was a horizontal surface to stretch out on. Maddie needed to eat, though.

"If you care to wash up, there's a powder room just down that hallway. First door on the left."

"Come on, Maddie."

She almost didn't want to look in the big carved wooden mirror in the lovely little half bath. The damage was as bad as she feared. She had a darkening bruise above her temple and an abrasion on her cheek. Her hair wasn't as bad as she feared but running a brush through it was an exercise in pain for both her head and her sprained wrist.

By the time she set Maddie's hair to rights, she had to stop and lean against the sink for a moment to catch her breath.

When they returned to the great room, they found Sue, Jim and Aidan seated at a massive dining table on the other side of the pass-through fireplace.

Maddie quickly climbed into the chair next to her new friend.

"I like your house," she told him. "It's pretty."

He smiled. "Why, thank you. This is the first time I've seen it since I bought it last August. I'm amazed at all the work that has been done in just a few months."

"Only a little paint and some varnish," Sue said, ladling soup into bowls. "I've had the cleaning crew working their fannies off, I can tell you."

Maddie giggled. "You said fanny!"

"Why, so I did."

"That's a funny word. Fanny, fanny, fanny."

"Maddie," Eliza said in a warning.

Sue chuckled. "I'll have to be more careful. I'm afraid Jim and I might both need reminders that we're not on the ranch with roughneck cowboys. Now, eat up while it's warm."

"We have to pray first!" Maddie exclaimed.

Aidan cleared his throat. "Why don't you go ahead."

Maddie offered a sweet prayer, asking a blessing on the nice lady who cried because her hotel burned down and for the nurses at the hospital and for Dr. Mendoza, her own cardiac specialist. She even remembered to bless the food before saying amen and taking a bite of her roll with the next breath.

Conversation flowed between Aidan and his caretakers—who were obviously more to him than just employees. Eliza listened with half an ear. She was so tired. She judged it couldn't be later than 7:00 p.m. but she couldn't see a clock anywhere to confirm her guess.

Though it was grand and spacious, with those huge log supports in the great room and the wide wall of windows, it seemed...cold, somehow. The lodge reminded her of a new hotel in Boise she had toured about a month prior to opening, before all the finishing touches had been added to give it a welcoming air.

"How are you holding up?" Aidan asked.

"Okay, for now."

"Would you prefer a tray in your room? I should have thought to ask."

Yes. Quite desperately. She wanted a long, hot shower and then a bed. But she could manage to keep it together for a few more moments. "No. This is fine. It's delicious, Sue." The rolls were perfect, crusty on the outside and fluffy on the inside while the soup was probably the best she had ever tasted, even though she could only manage a spoonful or two.

"Thank you, darlin'. It seemed just the thing for a stormy night."

She would have expected Aidan Caine to dine on gourmet meals every night but he seemed more than content with the rather humble fare.

"Oh. I almost forgot the pasta salad," Sue said.

She headed out of the dining room just as a phone rang. Aidan pulled a cell phone out of his pocket. He glanced at the number.

"I'm sorry. I've been waiting for this call. I've got to take it. I'll be right back."

He excused himself and answered the phone on his way out of the dining room as Sue came in from the kitchen Eliza could see through a doorway.

"Where is he going?"

"Phone call," Jim answered, taking another roll out of the basket.

"Oh. That man! I swear, he hasn't had a warm meal in a decade. One of these days, I'm going to drop his blasted phone right in the soup bowl."

Maddie giggled at the image and Sue and Jim both smiled at her. Her daughter had a way of charming everyone, even crusty old ranchers.

"He'll put his phone away quick enough when

he has the chance to get out again with the horses," Jim said.

Maddie inhaled sharply. "You have *horses* here?"

Oh, dear. Here we go, Eliza thought.

"Why, we certainly do!" Jim said proudly. "Six of the prettiest horses you could ever meet, including a little pony that's just the right size for a girl such as yourself."

"Oh. Mama, did you hear?"

"I did."

Maddie was a little obsessed with all things equine. Okay, a *lot* obsessed. Her daughter loved horses with a deep and abiding passion.

Eliza didn't quite comprehend the depth of the obsession since her daughter had never actually ridden a horse and had only seen a few closer than out the car window. Yet Maddie drew horse pictures, she had horse toys, her favorite pajamas featured horses and every time they went to the library, she wanted to check out books about horses. She even pretended she was a horse sometimes and made clippy-cloppy noises when she walked and her imaginary friend— who seemed to appear and disappear in their lives with rather alarming and random frequency—was a black horse named Bob, for reasons Eliza had yet to determine.

"Do you think I could *see* the horses?" Maddie asked, as if the prospect was far more exciting than even meeting Santa Claus on Christmas morning.

"Don't see why not," Jim answered. "Maybe you could even help me feed them in the morning."

"Oh, could I?" she asked Eliza with eager entreaty.

"We'll have to see."

It was her traditional maternal nonanswer but Maddie barely heard her, too enthralled by the idea that Snow Angel Cove had six horses, including a girl-sized pony.

"I have a horse," Maddie declared. "His name is Bob."

"Is it?" Jim looked interested.

"Yes. He's black with a white nose and he can gallop as fast as the wind. He says hello."

The couple exchanged surprised looks. "He...says hello?" Sue asked.

"Yes. Didn't you hear him? He's right next to you."

They both looked baffled, until Eliza mouthed *imaginary friend.*

She had been concerned enough about Bob to speak with the unit mental health counselor during Maddie's last hospital stay, who assured her imaginary friends were both normal and healthy for children, whether or not they had chronic conditions.

"I guess I must have missed him," Jim said. "Black with a white spot, you say. That must be why. He blends right into the dark window there."

"He likes it here. So do I."

"Maybe he'll like making new friends with the other horses tomorrow," Jim suggested.

"He will. He loves new friends. I do, too." She beamed at the grizzled man, who seemed to visibly melt. People tended to do that around Maddie.

An alarm suddenly went off on her phone. She and Maddie both knew what it was without looking and her daughter gave a little groan.

"Do I have to?"

"You know you do, honey."

Eliza reached into her purse to find the four medications Maddie took twice a day, morning and evening. She shook them out and set them on her daughter's plate. Maddie sighed but obediently picked up her water glass and swallowed them, one after the other, with the ease of long practice.

"My goodness," Sue exclaimed. "What's all this?"

"I have to take pills for my heart," Maddie said. "It doesn't work the way it's supposed to and the pills help it, plus I have a little machine in there to make sure it beats the right way. When I get bigger, I might get a new heart like my friend Paige."

"Oh. Oh, my."

Jim and Sue both looked astonished. It wasn't an uncommon reaction. Maddie seemed healthy most of the time. She *was* healthy, just like other children—to look at her, it would be impossible to know she had a rare, idiopathic form of juvenile cardiomyopathy, a thickening of the lining of her heart.

For the past few years, her condition was wonderfully stable. While the disease was incurable, the pacemaker helped steady her irregular heartbeats and the medications she took slowed the progression of her condition but she would probably need to be put on the heart transplant list before she hit puberty.

The harsh reality constantly prowled through Eliza's thoughts like a huge, voracious beast that never slept. With the help of her specialists in Boise, Maddie was a happy, well-adjusted girl who was hardly bothered by the fact that she lived with such a serious condition.

Eliza intended to keep it that way.

"She has a heart condition," she explained. "It required the implantation of a pacemaker when she was two. But she's doing very well now."

"I'm a trouper. That's what my mom calls me."

"Sounds like that's exactly what you are."

She looked up at the voice to find Aidan had returned to the dining area while her attention was focused on Maddie. He watched them with an inscrutable expression.

"You're a trouper with a horse named Bob," Jim said.

"Bob comes to the hospital with me when I have to stay there. He likes the nurses a lot, especially when they feed him candy."

"Well, sure. Who wouldn't?" Aidan said as he sat back down.

Eliza shifted, uncomfortable that he had overheard the discussion for reasons she couldn't have explained. She was, no doubt, already an object of pity to him, the widow who had just lost her job and had been hit by a car within five minutes. Throw in a daughter with a serious heart condition and it was a wonder she didn't have her own personal violin trio following her around playing mournful tunes.

This man had everything he could ever want or need. He was insanely wealthy, powerful, successful. She, on the other hand, probably presented a pathetic picture to him and she hated it.

Aidan Caine, of all people. Why did her path have to cross with him?

She had nurtured a completely unreasonable resentment toward him and Caine Tech since Trent's death. Logically, she knew he wasn't to blame directly. He hadn't even been at the fateful meeting that afternoon.

Her emotions weren't very rational, however. It was easier to blame him than to accept that her husband had been on a self-destructive path since Maddie's diagnosis.

She took another spoonful of soup as she listened to Aidan speak with Jim about one of the horses. She had to get over this. The man had been kind enough to give her and Maddie a comfortable— even luxurious—place to stay for the night. She could manage one night in his home and then she would move on without having to speak with him ever again.

Maddie yawned suddenly and set her spoon down with an impolite clatter that made Eliza wince a little. "I'm tired, Mama," she announced. "Where are we going to sleep tonight?"

Aidan set down his own spoon and slid his chair back from the table. "You both look like you're ready to drop. I'm sorry to keep you so long out here. Let's go get you settled."

She wanted to protest that he could at least finish his dinner but in truth she *was* exhausted and was more than ready for this miserable day to be over.

The sooner she went to sleep, the sooner she could wake up and begin to figure out how she was going to put life back on an even keel for her and for Maddie.

CHAPTER FOUR

AIDAN LED THE way through the house toward the bedroom suite Sue had suggested might be best for Eliza and her daughter. He really hoped he was going in the right direction. How embarrassing would it be if he got lost in his own home?

He couldn't believe all the work that had been finished since he'd last seen the house. Though Sue and Jim had kept him apprised of the progress with pictures and even a few videos, the change was remarkable.

When he first saw the house, the logs had been dark and dreary. Since then, an army of workers had sanded and varnished them until they glowed a warm honey.

The changes he had wanted to make to the bones of the house had been completed in record time and Snow Angel Cove now boasted new paint, new carpet and updated electrical and plumbing systems.

A decorating tcam had come in with new furniture over the long Thanksgiving weekend. He was happy with the result as he studied the furnishings, though he couldn't help thinking something still seemed missing.

He wasn't very good at that sort of thing, which was why he tried to hire people who were.

"Is this our room?" Maddie asked when he paused outside the guest suite Sue had suggested.

"Yes. Do you like it?"

She walked into the room, with its gas fireplace, four-poster bed and floor-to-ceiling windows facing the lake. "I like rooms that are pink, usually, but this one is nice," she said. She looked tired, he thought, more concerned about her than ever now that he knew she suffered from a heart condition.

"It's a lovely room," Eliza said. "Thank you."

Like her daughter, she showed clear signs of exhaustion. Her mouth drooped a little at the corners and she gripped the back of the armchair in the room to steady herself.

The bruise above her temple looked dark and ugly against the pale loveliness of her features. He couldn't look at it without guilt drenching him like somebody had tossed a bucket of ice water in his face.

He could have killed her and Maddie both.

Yeah, the tires had been terrible on the rental vehicle and black ice had contributed to the accident, but some part of him would always wonder if his own reflexes had somehow been slower than they should have been.

Could he have stopped a few seconds earlier than he had and avoided hitting her altogether if he were a hundred percent back to normal?

He couldn't know the answer to that, for all the metrics and algorithms in the world.

"I thought you might like a bedroom on the main floor so you don't have to tackle the stairs, but if you would prefer one with a better view of the lake, those are on the second floor. I'm having an elevator installed but it won't be done for a few months."

"This should be fine. It's very nice. We can share the bed."

"Not necessary."

He reached down and pulled a wheeled trundle mattress out from underneath the bigger four-poster.

"I wanted these rooms designed with flexible bedding for when my family comes to visit."

"Oh, I love it! Look! My very own little bed."

"Nice." She smiled at her daughter, though she hadn't moved from her spot where he suspected she would fall over if she moved away from the chair propping her up.

She belonged in the hospital. He frowned, wishing he could pack her up and drag her right back there. At least she was here, where he could watch out for her, and not trying to drive back to Boise. It was small comfort.

"Your home is lovely," she said.

"It's a work in progress," he said.

"All the best homes are. That's part of the fun, isn't it?"

"I suppose."

Purchasing a home on a mountain lake in Idaho

had never been on his radar. He enjoyed the home he had built in San Jose and had leased another property on the coast near Big Sur for his recovery.

For some time, he had been thinking about buying a ranch, maybe something closer to Hope's Crossing and his family, until a friend and business partner mentioned his family property here on Lake Haven.

One quick visit later and a look at the stunning, restful view of the lake and mountains, and Aidan had purchased it on the spot, along with the other property that came with it.

He might not have been a hundred percent in his right mind but he refused to regret it. He needed a retreat, a place away from the constant pressure and stress of his regular world—especially now. He was on strict orders to rest and be patient with himself as he healed and slowly returned to his regular activities.

Where better to do that than this sleepy little Idaho town where he could ride horses and cross-country ski on untrammeled snow during the winter and stand hip-deep in the Hell's Fury River with a fly rod in his hand during the summer?

His scar itched like crazy and he wanted to reach back and scratch it but he curled his hand into a fist at his side instead.

"It lacks many of the finishing touches I want," he said after a moment, looking around the room. "I have family coming for the holidays the Tuesday before Christmas. I'm hoping we can whip it into shape before they arrive."

"The other guy, Jim, said you have six horses," Maddie said, bouncing her bottom a little on the trundle bed.

She was really an adorable little girl, with those dark curls, dimples and the big green eyes she had inherited from her mother.

Cardiomyopathy. Poor thing. Sometimes life really sucked.

"I do indeed have six horses."

He loved to ride and had since he was a kid spending a few weeks each summer with his maternal grandparents, who had a ranch in southwest Colorado. All his brothers would stay with their grandparents but he was the best rider of the six of them. He didn't need a psychoanalyst to explain his enduring affinity for horses. It was rare for him to excel at anything physical that one of his brothers hadn't already conquered.

Even at his house in San Jose, he had a few horses and would take them up into the mountains along the coastline whenever he had the chance.

"I love horses," Maddie informed him. "I have a horse named Bob. Mom calls him my imaginary friend but he's real. He is!"

"I'm sure."

"Jim said Bob and me could visit your horses tomorrow."

"I don't see why that would be a problem. I'm sure they would love a visitor."

"He said I could maybe even ride one!"

He didn't miss the way Eliza's mouth tightened at that idea. Did it have something to do with her heart issues? Not wanting to stir the pot, he simply shrugged. "I don't know about that. We'll have to see. Sometimes they're not in the mood to have people ride them."

"Can I still visit them, though?"

"I don't mind, if your mother doesn't," he answered.

"That really depends on how early we leave tomorrow," Eliza said.

"Okay," Maddie said with an equanimity he found surprising in such a young girl. Perhaps she was used to disappointments, a notion that left him sad for her. His nephew Carter, about the same age as Maddie, would never be so sanguine.

Or maybe she was simply too tired to argue. She yawned and drooped a little more.

"The bathroom is through there," he said, pointing to the en suite. "You should find everything you need, as far as linens and toiletries."

"Thank you."

He was strangely reluctant to leave them. How was it possible he had only met Eliza Hayward and her daughter a handful of hours before? He felt an odd connection to her, as if the events of the day had forged a bond between them.

"If I haven't said it in the last hour or so, I'm sorry again for what happened today."

"It wasn't your fault, Mr. Caine."

"Please. Call me Aidan."

Her lips tightened. "Aidan. It was an accident. I completely understand that and don't blame you at all. If Maddie hadn't raced into the road at just that moment, we would have been safely on the sidewalk when you hit that patch of ice and I would be back in Boise right now trying to find a new apartment."

"Is there anything else we can get you before you settle in for the night?"

She shook her head and then winced a little as if the slight motion pained her. He wished she had taken the painkiller Dr. Shaw tried to foist off on her in the emergency room but he was the last one to encourage the use of opiates, since he hated them, too, and only used them as a last resort after his surgery and with his lingering headaches, much to his own doctor's frustration.

"The master bedroom is upstairs but tonight I'm going to sleep in one of the guest rooms in this wing. If you need anything, I'll just be across the hall."

"I won't need anything," she said firmly, even as she swayed slightly then gripped the chair a little more tightly.

"I promised Dr. Shaw I would check on you during the night. What's the best way to do that so I don't wake up Maddie?"

"Totally unnecessary. I'm fine."

He wanted to tell her not to bother arguing with him. He was far more stubborn than she could ever be. "Sorry to disagree but it's *absolutely* necessary," he said. "Also nonnegotiable. I promised the doctor."

"And if I lock the door?" she challenged.

He simply raised an eyebrow. "Then I'm afraid I would most certainly wake up Maddie when I have to kick it down."

She glared at him, two bright spots of color on her pale, lovely features. After a moment, she sighed and all the fight seemed to seep out of her. "Fine. I'll set an alarm on my phone. Should we say about 2:00 a.m.?"

"Works for me."

"Maddie is a heavy sleeper. I'm not. Just knock softly on the door and I should hear you."

He didn't want to have to wake her when she so obviously needed rest, but he had promised the doctor. "You'll leave the door unlocked?"

"I would hate to be responsible for you ruining such a lovely door," she said dryly.

Good. At least she understood when he was serious.

Maddie had pulled out a couple of improbably colored horses with rainbow tails and manes from her backpack and was galloping them across the quilt of her little trundle bed.

He smiled, though he wasn't quite sure why. He enjoyed his nieces and nephews, though usually from a distance. Something about Maddie Hayward touched his heart—especially after learning of the trials she had already endured in her young life.

"Good night, young lady. Be good for your mother, okay?"

"I will, Mr. Aidan. Night."

"Try to get some rest," he said to Eliza.

"Until you wake me up, you mean?"

"Something like that. Good night."

After he closed the door behind him, he headed back through the house toward the kitchen, where he could hear Sue singing "Let it Snow" in her Western twang.

Her sharp ears heard him come in. "Did those two sweet things get settled?"

"They did," he answered. "I'm taking the guest room across the hall so I can hear if they need anything."

"You want me to do it for you? I can take the room across the hall and check on her. You're not exactly in tip-top shape yourself to be staying up all night."

"I'm fine," he said shortly, fully aware of the irony that he sounded exactly like Eliza.

Out of habit, he grabbed the dish towel off her shoulder and started drying. After all these years of working for him, Sue knew better than to argue with him or shrug off his help. He grew up working at the Center of Hope Café, the restaurant in Hope's Crossing his father owned. He had been washing and drying dishes since he was old enough to pull a stool up to the sink.

"I'm sorry to throw a couple of last-minute guests in your direction. I know you've got plenty to do, with the family coming in a little over a week."

"Oh, never mind that. How is the poor thing?"

"Peaked. That's how my father would have described her."

Dermot would have swept into the situation and wrapped Eliza and Maddie under his considerable wing. That's just the way his pop was, a natural nurturer. Aidan hadn't inherited those tendencies. His own natural inclinations—and a few bitter experiences—had left him reserved and slow to trust. He kept most people except a reliable few at arm's length.

The door to the mudroom off the kitchen opened and a moment later, Jim came in looking like the abominable snowman in a Stetson.

"You wanted snow, darlin', you're getting snow. I was outside for five minutes and look at me. It's really coming down. I think we've had four inches in the last hour. Maybe six, altogether, since it started."

"The weather lady said we were in for a doozy," Sue said. "I love a good storm. Good thing all your Christmas decorations finally got here this afternoon before the snow hit or I might have had to put you to work making paper chains to put on that monster tree in the great room."

"They only just arrived? They were supposed to be here by Thanksgiving! I wondered why the tree wasn't decorated yet."

"Better late than never. I guess I know what I'll be doing tomorrow."

Too bad his brother Dylan and sister-in-law Genevieve couldn't come out to Lake Haven early. He had it on good authority from Charlotte that the two of them were whizzes at Christmas decorating at A Warrior's Hope, the recreational therapy program his brother-in-law had started to help wounded veterans.

The idea of his rough army ranger brother—a wounded veteran himself—decorating anything boggled his mind, but then a guy did crazy things when he was in love.

Aidan had seen plenty of evidence supporting that hypothesis since four of his brothers suffered from that particular malady—Brendan twice, now that he had found happiness with Lucy again after the tragic death of his wife a few years ago.

"Can you handle everything that needs to be done before the great horde descends?" he asked Sue now as she handed him the big soup stockpot to dry.

She shrugged. "I'll do my best. Might need to look for somebody from town who might be in need of a little extra Christmas cash. There are plenty of folks struggling in Haven Point who might appreciate the help. From what I can tell, jobs here are few and far between."

A germ of an idea found purchase and began to sprout as he dried the stockpot and set it on a counter. He thought of Eliza, out of a job and a place to live just a few weeks before Christmas.

He had to help her somehow. Fate couldn't have thrown her into his path and then just expected him to stand by and ignore her plight.

While it would be easy to give her a comfortable cash settlement—he wouldn't call it guilt money but he *did* owe her something—he sensed she would reject him flat if he tried.

He might not be as good as Dermot at intuitively tending to people's needs, but he had learned a few tricks from his pop. People were more inclined to accept help if you could convince them they were doing you a favor, instead of the other way around.

He sensed Eliza wouldn't be easy to persuade but he owed it to that sweet little girl to try.

CHAPTER FIVE

HER PHONE BEEPING softly in her ear woke her from a dream about giant monster trucks with ferocious-looking grills barreling toward her from every direction, intent on mowing her down.

She fumbled under her pillow for the phone then rolled over to turn off the alarm. Ow. She swallowed a groan as various and sundry muscles complained quite loudly at just that small movement.

Beside her, Maddie stirred and made a huffing little noise but quickly subsided back to sleep. She hadn't even made it to the trundle. After her bath, she had climbed into the big four-poster—the princess bed, she had called it—for their regular story time. They were reading a Junie B. Jones holiday book but had both fallen asleep about five minutes into the story about the mischievous kindergartener.

In fact...Eliza patted around the comforter until she found the book where it had slipped out of her hands as she drifted off. She moved it safely to the bedside table so the pages didn't get crinkled, then enjoyed the luxuriously soft sheets for a few moments as she listened to her daughter's deep, even breathing.

She did this sometimes, just slipped into Maddie's room to listen to her breathing and to offer up earnest prayers for that weak, courageous heart to stay strong as long as possible.

Right now, she wanted to hug her daughter close and remain snuggled under these cozy blankets, safe and warm from the howl and moan of the storm she could hear outside.

Though she had no recollection of doing it, she must have turned the reading light off sometime in the night. The only light in the room came from the flickering glow of the gas fireplace.

Wouldn't it be lovely to stay here in this nice, protective bubble and pretend the figurative storms in her life weren't swirling around with equal menace to the actual blizzard outside, where she didn't have to worry about any pesky little details like finding a place to live and a job that would provide decent health insurance that Maddie's cardiac specialists would accept?

This time she couldn't hold back her groan. Only a little of it was from the aches and pains of the accident.

What was she going to do? The natural optimism that had kept her from completely falling apart during the past three years of dealing with everything on her own seemed in short supply right now, as the reality of her situation seemed to seep beneath the blankets and grab hold of her skin with icy fingers.

She had options, she reminded herself. She wasn't

completely destitute. She had already taken care of Maddie's Christmas presents, so that wasn't a worry. Beyond that, she had a little left in savings, enough to tide them over for a month or two and to make a first and last month's rent, and she received monthly social security benefits that would help.

She had been trying to save all of Maddie's survivor benefits for her college education but the hard truth was that survival today had to take priority over tomorrow's tuition payments.

The snooze on her phone alarm chimed softly again and she turned it all the way off, wide-awake now. Something told her Aidan Caine was a man who kept his word. He said he would be knocking on her door at 2:00 a.m. and she had a feeling he would be there precisely at that moment.

She gingerly eased out of bed, feeling about a hundred and ten years old. Her robe was packed in one of the boxes still in the back of her SUV so she grabbed a decadently soft throw from one of the plush chairs by the fire and wrapped it around her nightgown for warmth.

With one last check on Maddie, she padded out into the hall, hoping to intercept him before he knocked on her door. She could see a light on underneath the door across from hers but she didn't quite have the nerve to knock on it. Instead, after a moment's indecision she headed toward a padded window seat at the end of the hall upholstered in rich, deep colors that fit well with the lodge look of the rest of the residence.

The window was a little frosted but through the darkness she could see snow falling steadily, whipped in all directions by the wind.

She shivered, grateful for the comforts of the house. It really was a lovely place, with those massive beams and logs the color of sun-warmed honey.

What had led Aidan Caine to purchase the house? He didn't strike her as the outdoorsy cowboy sort, more like a sexy computer geek. Maybe there was more to him than she would have suspected from what little she knew about his public persona.

The Geek God.

He seemed a very complex man. Yes, he was a powerful and successful man with this grand, expansive house, his own company. To achieve so much at his relatively young age he was no doubt a workaholic, just like Trent had been, a man whose entire focus revolved around making money.

On the other hand, he was obviously very fond of Jim and Sue and he had been extraordinarily kind to Maddie. He had been visibly upset about the accident and had gone out of his way to make sure she was all right, even coming to the hospital and eventually bringing her here for the night.

All that hardly seemed the actions of a heartless, cold businessman, which was the image she'd had of him before today. How did she reconcile the man she had met that day with all the anger she had nurtured toward him and Caine Tech over the last three years?

His company had stolen the heart right out of her husband. Plain and simple. The people he had met with at Caine Tech had taken Trent's dreams of fame and fortune, his ideas for a new productivity app he was certain would revolutionize the business world, and had shut him down fast and hard.

He had called her from California in despair to tell her about it and she had never heard him sound so defeated. She had tried to be encouraging but by that point she was exhausted and out of patience from trying to be a supportive wife in his endless chase for financial security for her and for Maddie.

She couldn't blame Aidan for the mess. Not really. Knowing the nature of big companies as she did, he probably didn't even have any direct knowledge of that final meeting between his associates and her husband.

Shifting her mind-set would be a difficult task where she had demonized him for so long. She could manage it for the few hours she might see him in the morning, before she left Snow Angel Cove.

At exactly one minute to two, she heard the door just across from theirs open. Aidan walked out into the hallway in jeans and a T-shirt. Had he forced himself to stay awake into the early hours so he could check on her or was he habitually a night owl?

He was wearing dark-framed glasses that only magnified the impact of those stunning blue eyes and his hair was a little messy, rumpled a bit on the right side of his head behind his ear. Perhaps he had been leaning his head against one side of a wing-back chair or maybe propping his head on his hand while he read or watched TV. Or maybe he just had a cowlick on that side that resisted his hairstylist's attempts to tame it.

It hardly seemed fair that the man could have a zillion dollars and be gorgeous, too. She swallowed, suddenly aware of a completely unexpected quiver in her stomach. Oh, for heaven's sake. Where did *that* come from? She hadn't experienced the tiniest flutter of attraction to a man in so long, she thought maybe that part of her had withered and blown away like dry leaves in an October wind.

She quickly shoved it down deep, where she put every other ridiculous urge she knew she could never act upon. While she was tempted to hide away under the throw, she didn't want him knocking on her bed-room door, then barging in and waking Maddie when she didn't answer.

"I'm over here," she murmured.

At her soft words, he shifted in her direction. Her eyes had become accustomed to the darkness during those few moments she had been sitting in the win-dow seat and she clearly saw his frown of surprise before he headed over to her.

"What are you doing out here?" he asked in the same low tone.

She shrugged. "I told you Maddie is usually a heavy sleeper but I thought she might be thrown off

her routine by finding herself in a strange place, especially with everything that's happened. I didn't
want to wake her up."

"Ah."

As he moved closer, a shaft of moonlight pierced
the gloomy clouds and she saw that while he might
be a little on the lean side, his unadorned blue T-shirt
clung to surprising muscles.

He was a tech genius, responsible for dozens of
apps and devices dominating the market. She would
have expected him have the pudgy, soft frame of
someone who spent most of his waking hours staring at a gadget or screen. Instead, he apparently spent
some of those hours at a gym.

To her dismay, he perched on the other end of
the window seat. Theoretically, there was plenty of
room for both of them but she couldn't help feeling
crowded, edgy, especially in light of this extremely
inconvenient physical awareness she didn't want.

"How are you feeling?" he asked.

"Oh, you know. Like I've been hit by a truck. I
have a feeling I'm going to be saying that a lot from
now on."

He made a sound that wasn't quite a laugh. "I
guess that was a stupid question. Let me be more
specific. Does anything new hurt?"

"No. I'm fine. Don't get me wrong, I have aches
and pains but they seem fairly generalized right now.
Nothing is broken."

"And your head?"

"Not bad, actually. My wrist hurts more than my head right now."

"I suppose I should ask you how many fingers I'm holding up, just to make sure you're not delirious."

"Four. I promise, I'm not delirious. I know what year it is, who the President of the United States is and my birthday, social security number and email password."

"That should cover it, then." He sounded amused. "Definitely not delirious."

"You didn't need to check on me but now you can report to Dr. Shaw that I'm fine."

"Except for feeling like you've been hit by a truck."

"Right." Because she was already growing a little tired of people asking her how she felt, she quickly changed the subject by gesturing out the window behind her. "That snow is crazy. Have you seen it?"

He shifted around and peered out. His eyes widened behind his lenses. "Wow. I've been catching up on some year-end reports and not paying attention. I knew we were supposed to have a storm, but that looks intense. Jim said he thought we would have eighteen inches by morning. When he said it, I thought he was exaggerating. Looking out there, now I wonder if he underestimated things."

"Makes me glad I'm in here and not out there." She couldn't quite bring herself to admit she was grateful he and Dr. Shaw had encouraged her to stay in Haven Point for the night, though she was. She hadn't been in any shape to drive back to Boise.

"I hope this isn't the start of an intense weather pattern. I would hate for my family to be trapped here over the holidays in the middle of a storm like this."

"Your family is coming to Snow Angel Cove for Christmas?"

He stretched out long legs, apparently settling in for a while. So much for demonstrating her mental acuity and then returning to her warm bed. She tucked the blanket more tightly around her shoulders, not minding a little conversation as much as she ought.

"Just about everybody will be here—barring my brother Jamie, who's in the military and stationed overseas."

"That will be lovely for you. Do you come from a big family?"

He gave a rough laugh. "You could say that. Five brothers and one sister."

She blinked. "Seven children. Oh, my. Your mother must have been a saint."

"She was. The closest thing to it I ever knew, anyway. She died when I was in college. Cancer."

Though he spoke in an even tone, she sensed an undercurrent of lingering grief that shouldn't have touched her but somehow did, anyway.

"I'm sorry. My mother died the summer before my junior year of high school."

Unlike Aidan, she didn't offer an explanation. Not only did she dislike discussing it but he already considered her an object of pity, the poor widow with the ill child who had lost her job and been hit by a car within minutes. She didn't need to add to that extremely unappealing picture.

She didn't consider herself a victim of anything. She preferred to see herself as a survivor, someone who had been through some tough things—and who hadn't, really?—but who endured with dignity and strength and tried to move through the hard times to the other side.

Yes, it was a little Pollyannaish, maybe, but she liked that narrative better than the pathetic alternative.

"Do you still have your father?" she asked.

He smiled, his teeth flashing white in the dim light. "I do. And a new stepmother, as of a few months ago. She's quite wonderful."

Eliza was aware of a twinge of envy. She also had a stepmother but theirs was an awkward, tense relationship—mostly because of her.

"Does your family live close by?" she asked, wondering if that explained why he had purchased Snow Angel Cove.

He shook his head. "My dad and most of my siblings live in a little town in Colorado. Hope's Crossing."

So much for that theory. "And yet you chose to

buy a house several hundred miles away from them on a remote Idaho mountain lake."

He was silent for so long, she wondered if her question had been unforgivably rude. After a long moment, he sighed. "I love my family. Don't get me wrong. We're all very close and I enjoy being with them. I consider my brothers my best friends. I'm flying the whole crew here for Christmas, aren't I?"

"But?"

He sighed again. "But when a guy is the middle of seven children, he can sometimes have an overwhelming need to find his own way. Whenever I go to Hope's Crossing, I'm always Dermot's boy, the one who invariably had his nose pressed to a computer. There's something very appealing about the fact that nobody in Haven Point knew me when I had braces on my teeth and bad acne and a crush on the head cheerleader, who was only interested in my younger brother, Jamie the stud—which, by the way, is fairly traumatic to the ego when you're fifteen and would like to think *you're* the stud, despite all evidence to the contrary."

She couldn't help a startled laugh, shocked that he would reveal something so personal to her.

"Did I just say that out loud?" he asked ruefully. "I must be more tired than I realized. I don't believe I've ever shared that with another human being on the planet. Or articulated it so clearly, even to myself."

She knew perfectly well she shouldn't find the man appealing here in the quiet hush of the night when the rest of the world slept, but this evidence of past vulnerability made him seem less like a mythical, larger-than-life personage and more like someone who had weaknesses and insecurities.

"Don't worry, Mr. Caine. I'm good at keeping secrets."

He made a face. "I told you to call me Aidan. When I divulge embarrassing secrets to somebody, I usually insist they call me by my first name."

It felt strange but she did her best. "Aidan, then."

"Eliza," he mused. "It's not a very common name anymore."

"My mother's name was Elizabeth and everyone called her Betsy. She wanted to be called Eliza but nobody ever did so she decided to give the name to me. I always thought it was old-fashioned. My friends in school called me Ellie but it seemed a little young-sounding as I grew up."

"I like it. Eliza. It fits you, somehow."

They lapsed into a not uncomfortable silence. She knew she should probably muster the energy to go back to her bedroom but she couldn't quite manage it. She found something strangely appealing about sitting in this darkened hallway with him, talking softly about nothing in particular while the storm raged outside.

"I hope the snow stops soon or it will be an interesting drive back to Boise in the morning."

He rubbed at the side of his head. "I'm glad you brought that up, actually. I intended to wait until the

morning to talk to you about this but the time somehow seems right."

"Oh?"

He gave her a long look. "How would you feel
about staying here longer than just one night?"

"That's very kind of you," she said, choosing
her words carefully, "but I'm afraid I don't have the
luxury of an extended vacation. I need to return to
Boise and start putting my life back together. I need
to find a job."

"I actually had a great idea earlier tonight."

"What sort of idea?" she asked, with no small
amount of wariness.

"You could work for me."

Her mind seemed to spin in a hundred different directions. She wasn't exactly a Luddite but her
technological skills were limited to remembering
that email password she had mentioned earlier and
knowing how to reboot her laptop.

"Doing what?"

"I told you my entire family is coming for Christmas. This is the first time we've all been together for
the holidays in years, for various reasons."

"That will be lovely for you."

"I hope so. It's important to me that everything
is perfect for them."

"You don't ask for much, do you?"

"My family has suffered some tough things in
recent years. My brother nearly died fighting in
Afghanistan. In the middle of all that, my other

brother's wife *did* die of pregnancy-related compli-
cations. We're finally finding our way back from
all the heartache. I'll admit, I haven't been there for
my family during everything. Not really. I was always too busy and figured they didn't need one more
Caine brother getting in the way."

He rubbed the side of his head again, just behind
his ear. That must be why his hair was a little rumpled there, she thought. It was actually a rather endearing habit, one she wasn't sure he even realized
he was doing.

"These last few months, I've...come to realize
how necessary that connection is to me. I've missed
it. I have this new house this year that's finally big
enough to fit us all. We've had several new marriages
and a lot to celebrate and I want to do my best to
make the holidays amazing, you know? Memorable."

She found that endearing, too, though she knew
she shouldn't. "And how would I fit in to help you
with that?"

"Sue has been doing her best to get everything
ready. She's wonderful in the kitchen, don't get me
wrong, but with twenty houseguests, she's going to
have her hands full with all the meal planning and
cooking. She just can't do everything herself. She
and I were talking earlier about hiring someone to
help her. As I see it, with your hotel management
experience, you're the ideal candidate."

"Me?"

"I have a confession here. I called the owner of the Lake Haven Inn after you and Maddie went to sleep."

"You called Megan?"

"Right. Megan. Hamilton. She seemed nice enough. By the way, she was horrified to find out you were hurt today after you spoke with her. She wanted to rush straight here to fuss over you but I assured her you seemed to be doing all right and we are keeping a careful eye on you. She confirmed my suspicions, that you are just the woman I need."

His words sent a completely inappropriate little shiver rippling through her. For the job. He was talking about a *job*. She forced herself to get a grip as she struggled to take in the completely unexpected twist.

"You want me to come work for you here? I was the assistant manager of a small three-star hotel. What do I know about providing luxury hospitality services in a private home?"

"If you knew my family, you would understand the Caines don't need luxury. You won't find more down-to-earth people anywhere. I think you'll like them and I know they'll like you and Maddie."

How was she supposed to respond to a job offer extended in the middle of the night when she was wrapped in a *blanket,* for crying out loud?

"It can't be that much different from what you would have been doing as the manager at the Lake Haven Inn, just on a smaller scale. As I see it, the goals are the same—making everybody feel welcome and keeping them happy. All you have to do

is make sure Pop stays out of the kitchen, find entertainment for the little ones and make sure the teenagers have enough to keep them busy and out of
trouble."

"That's all?" she said faintly.

"I just want everyone to enjoy the holidays together, whatever it takes."

"You basically need somebody to play hostess to
your family."

"Wow. In a manner of speaking, I suppose that's
exactly what I need."

What he needed was a wife. But of course, she
could never say that.

"Look, I'm the first to admit, I have many bad
habits," he said. "One of them is a single-minded
focus on whatever project I'm working on. I can get
a phone call and forget everything else but solving
whatever problem is on the other end. If that happens, I would love to know somebody else is here
besides Sue to make sure my family doesn't feel ignored."

She wanted to suggest he just turn his phone off
but, again, it wasn't her business.

"The job would include room and board for you
and Maddie as well as a salary I think you'll find
more than fair," he said, naming a gulp-worthy sum
that made actually made her palms begin to sweat.

"That's entirely too much."

"I promise, you will earn every penny of it. My
family is great but they're crazy and wild, too."

She didn't know how to answer him. On the one hand, this would be an answer to her prayers. Working and staying at Snow Angel Cove through the holidays would give her a little breathing room, time to send out some feelers about who might be hiring and to really plan out her next step instead of jumping out of desperation into a job that might not be a good fit.

In addition, the compensation he was offering for only a few weeks would provide a much-needed financial cushion to tide them over for several months.

She wasn't a fool, however. Was Aidan making this offer because he genuinely needed help or was it driven by his guilt over hitting her with his SUV?

Could she really afford to let that matter to her?

"It's late," he said after a moment. "You don't have to make a decision about this right now. Think about it overnight. I do think Maddie would have fun playing with my niece and nephew. Carter is just about her age. He's a real character but fun. His sister, Faith, is a few years older and one of the sweetest girls you'll ever meet. The other kids are older but they're all really decent human beings."

"I will think about it," she said, even though she already knew what her answer would be. She wasn't particularly thrilled about working for anyone connected to Caine Tech, especially not the founder and CEO, but she had to be pragmatic. For room, board and a salary like that—not to mention the chance to give Maddie a safe, comfortable, welcoming place for Christmas—she would be a fool to refuse.

The past three Christmases had been tough, all the way around. Trent had died in November three years earlier. That year the holidays had been a blur of shock and pain and sorrow. The past two years, Maddie had been in the hospital.

The chance to spend the holidays here in this lovely home where her daughter could experience a genuine family Christmas was too choice to pass up.

She climbed up from the window seat, doing her best not to wince at her various and sundry aches and pains. "We both need to try to sleep tonight. Thank you for checking on me. As you can see, I'm perfectly fine."

He rose as well, his T-shirt clinging again to those unexpected muscles. "I'm glad," he said with a slow, sexy smile that made her toes tingle.

Oh, for crying out loud, she chided herself. The man was a gazillionaire who probably had his pick of any hot-bodied bimbo he wanted. He would never be interested in someone like her, a frazzled mom wearing pajamas she bought at a big box store and wrapped in a blanket.

Even if he *were* interested, for some unfathomable reason, she certainly wasn't. Right? Not in Aidan Caine, who was brilliant and gorgeous and *dangerous*.

"Good night," she murmured quickly and hurried to her room before he could even answer.

When she slipped back into the cool covers, her daughter made a tiny sound in her sleep but didn't awaken. Eliza lay in the darkness while the storm flung snowflakes against the window, listening to the miracle of her daughter's breathing, as she had done so many times before.

While she might be reluctant to stay at Snow Angel Cove for a plethora of reasons, she would do it for one reason only. Her child.

CHAPTER SIX

SHE ACHED IN every single joint and muscle.

Even her eyelids hurt—though she had no idea why. It seemed a good enough excuse to keep them closed, even though her internal biorhythms sensed daylight.

She wanted to roll over and try to go back to sleep but even that seemed like too much effort right now.

With great exertion, she managed to wrench her eyes open, only to find a curious little face about an inch and a half away from hers.

"Mama! Are you awake?"

"Mmmph," she mumbled. Even that hurt.

"Come on. Get up. It snowed *so much* last night! You have to see!"

Maddie bounced on the bed in her enthusiasm, unleashing a whole host of new aches and pains. Eliza swallowed her groan and opened her eyes fully. Maddie beamed and bounced on the bed again.

Her delight in the world around her, how she embraced each day with excitement and joy, filled Eliza's heart with a little burst of joy, even when the rest of her hurt.

"Good morning, Miss Maddie."

"It snowed so much!" she repeated eagerly. "You have to see. Hurry, Mama, before it all melts!"

Eliza had a feeling she wasn't going to be hurrying anywhere for quite some time. She drew in a deep breath and pushed away the blanket then swung her legs to the floor.

Maddie waited eagerly while she wrapped the throw over her shoulders again and dutifully padded over to the window. When she looked out, a small laugh escaped her. Wow. Maddie wanted her to see the snow before it melted. Judging by the scene outside the window, that happy event wouldn't be until April, at the earliest.

Maybe not even until May.

The snow covered everything in heavy, deep mounds. Even the pines wore thick white coats, with hardly a bit of green showing through.

As she expected in the night, the view from the house was spectacular. The vast lake—her research before deciding on the move to the area had taught her the lake was seven miles across and fifteen miles long—gleamed a bright, vivid blue in contrast to the blinding white snow everywhere else. The raw, dramatic mountains rose up almost from the water's edge.

"Isn't it pretty, Mama? Don't you just love it? I want to build a snowman *right now!* Can we?"

Yeah, that wasn't happening at the moment, when she could barely walk. "Why don't we go look for breakfast first and then we'll see how things go?"

"Okay. I am *hungry*."

"We need to get dressed first. Can you find some clothes in your suitcase?"

Maddie nodded and unzipped her case. "Can Bob and me visit the horses today?" she asked as she was pulling out her favorite sweater which, not surprisingly, had a horse appliqué sewn on the front. "Mr. Aidan said I could if you let me."

"That would be fun. You have to do some homework first before we do anything else right? While I'm in the shower, finish changing out of your pajamas and try to finish a worksheet or two."

Maddie, predictably, made a face at that but agreed.

Eliza had decided not to enroll her into a new kindergarten class until after Christmas so her daughter didn't have so many transitions at once, especially since school would be breaking for the holidays only a week after she moved to Haven Point.

She had worried a new apartment, new schedule and new school all at the same time might be too difficult for Maddie. In this whole mess, that, at least, was one of her own decisions she didn't doubt.

While Eliza showered—oh, the wonder of those jets—and finished dressing and fixing her hair and makeup, Maddie quickly finished several of the worksheets her teacher in Boise had given Eliza to carry Maddie through the end of the year.

When she was done, Maddie entertained herself

by playing her favorite game on Eliza's tablet and watching the snow steadily falling outside.

Eliza considered it nothing short of a blessing that her daughter entertained herself so well. Maddie hardly ever complained she was bored. Give her a few art supplies or a couple of favorite toys and she could amuse herself for hours, something Eliza definitely appreciated for long waits in the doctor's office or during lengthy hospital stays.

After she was dressed—finally conceding she had done the best she could with her limited makeup tools and skills to conceal the bruises from the accident—she pulled Maddie's hair back in a ponytail and the two of them set off to try finding the kitchen again.

They walked hand in hand through the gorgeous house, with those honey-colored logs that glowed glossy and warm in the shafts of sunlight streaming through the windows everywhere.

A gas fire flickered cheerfully in the great room fireplace but no one seemed to be in sight. That huge tree looked even more barren and forlorn in the daylight.

From somewhere close by they heard someone singing "I Saw Mommy Kissing Santa Claus" in an off-key twang. Sue. Eliza followed the sound to a big, well-appointed kitchen with gorgeous professional-grade appliances, granite countertops and a work island in the middle as big as a decent-sized children's swimming pool.

"Good morning," Eliza said.

Sue whirled around from the sink. "Hello! I wondered when you two might show your faces this morning."

"Sorry we slept so long."

"No need to apologize, darlin'. You had quite a day yesterday. It's barely nine o'clock, anyway."

On a normal day, Eliza was usually up by six so she could work out, get in a load of laundry or take care of bills before Maddie awoke.

"How are you feeling this morning?" Sue asked.

She forced a smile. "Much better," she said. It wasn't a complete lie.

"Aidan told me to let the two of you sleep as long as you need."

"Did he?" She wondered where he might be, but she didn't want to ask—nor did she want to think about the heated dream she had about him.

Sue answered her unspoken thought, anyway. "He and Jim are out trying to clear the driveway. They've got the plow on the pickup truck and the tractor going, too."

She tried to picture sexy brainiac Aidan Caine driving a tractor and couldn't quite make the image jell.

"He mentioned last night that more snow was expected throughout the day." Right now the sun was shining but she knew that could change in a blink.

"Oh, yes," Sue said cheerfully. "We're supposed

to have loads and loads of it, at least for another day or two. Guess you're stuck with us."

"Yay!" Maddie said. "I like it here."

"And we like having you, Miss Maddie," Sue said. "I've got some breakfast waiting for you. I've just been keeping it warm."

She pulled a couple of plates out of a warming oven, layered high with scrambled eggs and sausages. "Have a seat, my dears. It won't take me five minutes to add some pancakes to these."

As they wouldn't be able to eat half of what she had already prepared for them, Eliza started to tell her that pancakes weren't necessary but Maddie spoke up before she could.

"Oh, I *love* pancakes!" Maddie declared. "My mama makes the *best*. Sometimes she even pours them into a heart."

Sue smiled at her. "Well, I don't know if I can handle a heart since that takes some serious skills. I'll see what I can do, though. You two have a seat and I'll set you up."

"You don't have to serve us. I can help." It seemed strange to let Sue fuss over her when they were basically fellow employees now.

"Suit yourself," she said as she fired up the griddle. "There's juice and milk in the refrigerator or coffee if you want it."

Eliza settled Maddie on one of the stools around the huge granite-topped island that dominated the kitchen space, found silverware for both of them in a drawer Sue indicated and then poured her a small glass of milk and another of juice.

"Aidan said you might be staying," Sue said after a moment.

Eliza flashed a look at Maddie and saw she wasn't paying them any attention.

"Did he?" she asked, trying for a casual, noncommittal tone. The whole job offer seemed so perfect, she still couldn't quite believe it was real.

"You would be saving my hide if you take him up on his offer, I'll tell you that much. Twenty guests, coming in just over a week and I've not even had time to decorate yet. You wouldn't believe how crazy the last three months have been, trying to make the house ready for guests. I never thought we would make it before the holidays but when Aidan sets his mind to something, nothing can sway him. Even from his hospital bed, he would call me with suggestions for this and that."

"Hospital bed?"

Sue looked horrified for a moment but quickly hid her reaction behind a cough. "Er. Forget I said that. No hospital bed for him. He's healthy as a horse. Why, he's healthier than some horses I know."

Was he? Eliza thought of those lines that looked fairly new around his mouth and the way his shirt the night before had looked a size too large. Had he been ill? And if so, why couldn't Sue just tell her? Why the big secrecy about it?

"I've met Aidan's family a time or two," the older

woman went on quickly, as if trying not so subtly to change the subject, "and you'll never meet a nicer bunch. Every last one of them."

She decided not to press her about their employer's health, for now. It wasn't her business, anyway. "That's good."

"They're just regular folk. I know you'll like them."

"That will make the job a little easier." She sipped at her coffee as Sue flipped the pancakes on the griddle.

"As nice as they are, just thinking about a whole week of preparing three meals a day for twenty people—and then having to run the rest of the house on top of that—wears me right out. I don't mind the cooking, it's the rest of it that is a struggle. If you can handle all the details of throwing a big old-fashioned house party, you'll be a real lifesaver, darlin'. For me and for Aidan."

She had wondered if he were inventing a job merely to make amends for the accident the day before. Listening to Sue, she wondered if her services might genuinely be needed at Snow Angel Cove.

"If I agree to the job, where would Maddie and I stay? I didn't have the chance to ask Aidan last night. I certainly don't want to continue taking up one of the guest suites. By the sound of it, he will need all the space he can find for his family."

"Don't you worry about that. We've got the perfect space for you and your little one." She pointed to a hallway. "Matter of fact, it's right through there. Cook's quarters."

"But you're the cook."

"This cook likes to lay her head next to my husband's—I guess I'm funny that way—and *he* likes to stay close to his horses. We're in a cozy little house just off the barn that used to be the foreman's cottage, which means the cook's quarters are completely available for you and Maddie. It couldn't be more perfect. After you finish breakfast, we'll go take a look and see if the rooms might work for you."

Sue was right. So far this job offer seemed made to order for her particular circumstances, she thought, as she and Maddie ate the hearty breakfast — complete with pancakes that were so perfectly heart-shaped, Eliza didn't know how she ever again would have the guts to make her own paltry attempts.

Maddie chattered away about her other favorite foods and other delicious pancakes she had tried, which led to a conversation about the berry pancakes she had eaten when the two of them had driven to the Oregon Coast during the summer and how she had chased a hermit crab around the beach and had looked at tide pools and touched a starfish.

Eliza would have tried to divert her attention in some way but Sue seemed to enjoy whatever conversational detour Maddie meandered down, watching her with a kind, indulgent expression.

When they both had finished breakfast, Sue took

their plates and loaded them into one of two gleaming stainless-steel dishwashers Eliza could see.

"Should we go take a look at the cook's quarters?" she asked.

She nodded and slid away from the table. Sue led the way to a door just down the hall from the kitchen. As Eliza looked around at the comfortable space with twin beds, a basic but well-equipped bathroom and even a sitting room, she had to fight the inappropriate urge to laugh.

Call her a pessimist, but she had to wonder about what fine print she must be missing. The position seemed almost too good to be true—a jaw-dropping salary, a beautiful home in which to spend the holidays and the ideal apartment for her and Maddie. It was better, even, than the slightly larger but more outdated space they would have shared at the Lake Haven Inn.

Who would have guessed that being hit by a car might turn out to be a lucky break?

She was still shaking her head at that irony when she saw movement outside the window and spotted Aidan, bundled up against the cold, heading for the outside door that led into the mudroom.

He stomped his boots off on the mat outside the door and brushed snow from his coat, then pulled off a wildly colored knit hat, leaving his dark hair sticking up in tufts. Oddly, seeing him like this, slightly wild and tousled, made him seem somehow more human and approachable than the carefully groomed executive who appeared on the business magazine covers.

"What do you think?" Sue asked.

She thought the man was too darn gorgeous for his own good. Or hers.

"It should work very nicely," she managed to answer.

"You and the little one will have all your meals with the rest of us, of course, so you needn't worry about having a kitchen of your own. As you can see, you've got a microwave and a little refrigerator in here. If you have something special you'd like to fix in the kitchen, of course you would be welcome to. I'll also set aside space in one of the refrigerators for you to keep things of your own that might not fit in here."

"Great. I appreciate that."

"When we have a minute, I'll sit down with you and find out a few favorite foods you and Maddie might enjoy."

"That's not really necessary. We can eat anything. But thank you."

They headed back out into the mudroom, to find Aidan taking off his coat.

"Oh. You're back," Sue said. "How is it out there?"

"Deep. We could barely get the door open to the garage in order to get the pickup truck with the plow. We finished clearing around the house. Now Jim is working on clearing the drive to the main road."

"I was just showing Eliza the cook's quarters."

"Have you made a decision, then?" he asked her.

Despite Sue's avowal, Eliza wasn't convinced her help was actually needed. She was almost positive he only wanted her to take this perfect position because he felt sorry for her and to ease his guilt.

Her pride urged her to tell him she didn't need or want his pity. But this provided such a better situation for Maddie than any other alternative. Snow Angel Cove could provide a sanctuary for them for a while, at least a place where Maddie could be free to enjoy the holidays. How could she let pride stand in the way of that?

She forced a smile. "Yes. If you're serious about your offer, I accept. We will stay through the holidays and help you with your family."

A fierce, satisfied expression crossed his handsome features. He didn't look particularly surprised, however. Why should he be? What woman in her right mind could refuse such an offer?

"I'll contact my assistant immediately and have her email you some forms to fill out. Nondisclosure, confidentiality, the standard employment requirements. I don't want you doing anything but resting today and even tomorrow. Shall we say you'll officially start in a couple of days? Monday?"

"I am feeling fine, I promise. There's no reason I can't start today, especially since time is limited before your family arrives."

"Don't overdo anything. I want you and Maddie to both feel comfortable here. You're welcome to use any of the facilities—the horses, the pool and spa, the game room. Sue can tell you, I like the people who work for me to feel more like family."

"You're sure you don't mind Maddie underfoot? She loves to help me and when I'm doing a task where she can't help, she's usually very good at entertaining herself."

"I don't mind at all. In a week, this place will be crawling with kids. She'll fit right in with everyone else."

For an instant, she could picture it with vivid clarity—children filling the big house with laughter and excitement, Christmas music ringing through the space, the air rich with the smells of cinnamon and vanilla and pine.

She had hoped to give her daughter a memorable Christmas but this one might turn out to be more amazing than she had ever imagined.

CHAPTER SEVEN

"GET ME THE projected specs by Friday, then make sure your team takes time with their families over the holidays. They can hit it hard again after the New Year. Yeah. Same to you."

He hung up the phone with one of his project managers then turned back to the trio of computers in his home office, almost a complete duplicate of the setup at his office at the Caine Tech headquarters and his home office in San Jose.

The furniture was the same style and arrangement in each location—one which he found most productive to his workflow—and he used the very same brand and model of office chair.

Aidan had long ago accepted that he knew what worked for him. Messing with that structure only erected mental roadblocks that wasted his time and energy.

His brothers sometimes accused him of having obsessive-compulsive tendencies. They were usually teasing when they said it but he wasn't bothered by it. A man didn't amass a fortune out of nothing without careful attention to detail and a healthy self-awareness of his own strengths and weaknesses.

Afternoon sun pierced the thick cloud cover to slant through the vertical blinds. With a flick of a remote, he turned on the gas fireplace—a unique but necessary feature of this particular one of his three offices—and dialed Louise, his very efficient assistant.

They spent a few moments going over details of a pending merger before he turned the conversation to his family's upcoming visit.

"Yes. All the arrangements have been made," she said briskly. "The pilots will pick them up at the Hope's Crossing airport on the twenty-third and will return them all Sunday evening, the twenty-eighth."

That was as long as he could manage to convince them all to stay, as Pop didn't want to be gone from the café too long and others had work and volunteer obligations at home.

"Great. Thank you. And your holiday plans are in place?"

"Yes. Ken and I will fly out to South Carolina that same day, on the twenty-third, to meet up with Stephanie, Lane and the children for Christmas and then we're all driving down to Orlando together the day after. The kids didn't think Santa could find them if they weren't in their own house."

He absently doodled on the unprinted edge of a report. "I'll keep my fingers crossed for good weather. We were completely socked in last night and this morning with a blizzard. It's still coming down here."

"You don't have to tell me, I already know we're

crazy to travel this time of year. Even without a storm, the parks are going to be completely packed over the holidays. We won't be able to move—and don't even get me started on the lines. The kids are so excited, I hope it will be worth it. Every time we Skype, they don't want to talk about anything else."

Louise's son-in-law had recently been transferred to Charleston. Aidan knew how hard it had been on his longtime assistant—and good friend—to have her grandchildren so far away. He suspected within the next few years she would be retiring to move closer to them.

"Enough about me," she said after a few minutes of discussing her vacation plans. "How are you feeling?"

His pen jerked across the edge of his doodle. "Fine," he said.

"Is the headache any better?"

"Some."

Out of a habit he couldn't seem to shake, he reached his index finger to the spot just behind his left ear. The hair in that particular spot hadn't completely grown back, it was about an inch long now, bristly and itchy. Fortunately, the scar was in a spot where his hair was long enough to camouflage.

Pop was going to tell him he needed a haircut. He was going to have to preemptively come up with a strategic response. He wasn't sure his father would believe he wanted to audition for a rock band or he was going on the road as a competitive snowboarder.

"The new medicine Dr. Yan prescribed is helping," he answered Louise now. It was partly true. The pain was a dull, constant ache most of the time instead of a piercing, howling roar.

"Why don't I believe you?" Worry threaded through her voice.

Maybe because she knew him too well. "Don't concern yourself about me," he told her. "Just enjoy the holidays with your family."

He was doodling a Christmas tree now, complete with little curlicue ornaments.

"Same to you. It's a good thing you have a good one—and a big house to host them all. Twenty houseguests for the holidays are enough for anyone. Sue is definitely going to have her hands full."

Right. That had been the main reason for his call. "Speaking of Sue, can you email me the standard employment forms? I'm hiring someone to help her run the household while my family is here."

"I can contact the employment service in the area and have someone sent over. It might take a day or two."

"Not necessary. I've already found someone."

He could almost hear her frown communicated across the line. "You hired someone on your own? Someone from the area?"

Louise was a master—mistress?—at conveying volumes with a well-placed pause. As one of the few with total knowledge of his health issues—information that had been deliberately withheld from

Caine Tech stockholders and the general public—
she had become extremely overprotective since September.

"Relax. I vetted her first, you can be sure. I spoke
with a previous employer and received nothing but
glowing reviews."

Technically, Eliza had never actually worked
for Megan Hamilton, since the poor woman's hotel
burned down first. Her loss, his gain. He decided not
to mention that to Louise.

"What do you know about her?" his assistant
asked.

Not as much as he would like. While he couldn't
put a finger on it, he sensed Eliza had secrets she
was deliberately keeping from him. "She's a widow
and single mother, new to the area. She has been
working on the management team at a small hotel
in Boise and is eminently qualified to run the household, which will leave Sue free to focus on what she
loves best—the cooking."

"If she can manage to keep Dermot out of the
kitchen."

"Maybe I'll hire a bouncer for that, too."

Louise laughed, that rich, full laugh that always
made him smile. "That's not as far-fetched as it
sounds. You might just need one."

"Better send me two sets of employment forms,"
he joked.

They hung up after a few more moments and he
scratched a few more embellishments on his doodled

Christmas tree while he thought about all the people who worried about him.

He was a lucky man.

A few months ago, he wouldn't have been able to say that as he had stared down into the abyss of human frailties.

He looked through the floor-to-ceiling windows with sweeping views overlooking the lake and the mountains—okay, there was the *big* difference between this office and those in California—and saw the snow had begun to fall again, not as hard as the day before but big puffy snowflakes.

His stomach growled loudly. When he glanced at his watch, he was surprised to discover it was after two, hours since the quick breakfast he had grabbed before he'd headed out to clear snow with Jim.

He could use a break, he decided. Without Louise there to gently remind him, he would work straight through without eating. He was surprised, actually, that Sue hadn't brought him a tray. She usually did.

He filed the paperwork—doodles and all—then rose, stretched and headed toward the kitchen.

The moment he walked out of his office, he heard a small voice singing "Jingle Bells." Maddie, he realized. What a cute kid. The heart condition, though. He felt a little squeeze in his chest as if in sympathy. That seriously sucked, though she didn't seem to let it bother her.

Maddie and her mother were decorating that behemoth of a Christmas tree. Eliza stood on a ladder hanging ornaments while the little girl worked on the lower branches.

They must have been at it for a while, since only about half of the branches were still bare. He had to wonder how many rounds of "Jingle Bells" Eliza had endured.

Maddie finished the song with a flourish. "What should I sing next, Mama? Do you want me to sing 'Rudolph' again or 'Way in a Manger'?"

"You choose," she said. Even though she faced away from him, he could tell she was smiling by the tone of her voice.

She had no business being up on a ladder, especially after she had sustained a head injury the day before. He moved forward to tell her so but Maddie spied him before she could even get to the shiny nose part of her song.

"Hi, Mr. Aidan." She beamed at him. "You have the biggest tree I ever saw. It's bigger than the one at the mall!"

The tree was about fifteen feet tall. To a little girl who probably barely topped three feet tall, the tree must seem gargantuan.

"This is a big room that needs a pretty big tree. A little one would look kind of sad in here, don't you think?"

For a moment, the dimensional quandary seemed to stump her. She looked at the tree then at the room in general, then gave a serious nod. "It would be like my American Girl doll trying to ride my pet horse named Bob. He's way too big for her."

"Right."

Eliza started to climb down from the ladder and he instinctively moved forward to spot her, which had the added benefit of giving him a front-row, eye-level view of her perfect curves. She was lush in all the right places.

He swallowed hard, suddenly forgetting all about his hunger. The kind requiring food, anyway.

"I hope you don't mind that we started to decorate your tree. Sue showed us where to find the ornaments."

He forced his mind back to safer channels. "You shouldn't be up there. You were supposed to be taking it easy today. Climbing up and down a ladder like a monkey so you can decorate a Christmas tree doesn't really fit in that category."

She made a face. "I told you I'm not very good at doing nothing."

He couldn't argue with that since he had the very same problem. His doctors still gave him a hard time about how he had tried to send off a couple of important emails just before being wheeled in to surgery.

"Maybe you just need more practice," he said—which was a good reminder for himself, too. He was hoping the time he spent here would help him relax a little more.

"You can help us if you want," Maddie offered.

"It's *your* Christmas tree. You should put at least a few of the ornaments up."

"Oh, honey. I'm sure Mr. Caine is busy with other things." A hint of a rosy blush crept over Eliza's high cheekbones.

"No, she's right." He smiled at the girl. "It *is* my tree. It's only fair I help you decorate it."

"That's really not necessary," Eliza said quickly. "We've got it covered. It shouldn't take us long to finish up here."

She obviously didn't want his help, which conversely made him all the more determined to pitch in. Blame that obstinate streak of his.

"I'm helping," he said, giving her no room to argue. "I didn't have time for lunch. Give me five minutes to grab a snack and I'll be right back."

In the kitchen, he sliced a couple of apples, added some grapes to the plate, a few peppered water crackers and some of the imported French cheese that Sue always kept on hand, then carried the plate and a glass of water back into the living room.

Maddie beamed with delight when he returned, which sent a little burst of warmth through him, as if he had stepped into a sunbeam. Her mother, on the other hand, looked less than thrilled and even a little surprised, as if she hadn't really expected him to follow through.

Who had disappointed her so badly? Her husband? Questions about the man simmered just below the surface. He wanted to ask what had happened to him but he couldn't do that with Maddie there.

"Do you want anything?" He held the plate out to both of them. Eliza shook her head but her daughter reached for an apple wedge and a piece of cheese.

"Any idea where Sue might be?" he asked.

"Lying down, I hope. She had a migraine so I urged her to take a rest. I hope that's okay."

He stared. "Okay, what's your secret? You actually persuaded Sue to stop for five minutes in the middle of the day? How on earth did you manage that?"

"It wasn't hard. It helped that she really didn't feel well. I told her she wouldn't be able to take care of anyone if she didn't care for herself first. That seemed to do the trick."

"And you don't see the irony here? The day after being hit by an SUV, you won't be persuaded out of wearing yourself out by decorating a Christmas tree."

"This is fun, not work," she said, with that appealing blush soaking her cheekbones again.

He could quickly grow addicted to teasing out that color.

The thought and the sudden fierce, simmering attraction beneath it unnerved him.

What was the matter with him? She was lovely, yes, with that soft spill of hair, those big green eyes framed by the dark fringe of lashes, the little tracery of pale freckles on her nose. But he could think of a dozen reasons why he had no business wanting to lick the very center of that plump bottom lip, to explore those luscious curves and nuzzle that soft curve of her neck.

He couldn't imagine a worse time for him to become embroiled in a relationship—or with a more unlikely woman.

Applying the same concentration and determination he used at Caine Tech, he worked hard to shove down the attraction and turn his attention to the matter at hand.

He picked up an ornament in each hand. "It's been a few years since I've decorated a Christmas tree. What do we do here?"

"It's easy," Maddie declared. "Just hang them where Mama tells you."

He laughed. "Fair enough. I await your command, then."

He told himself not to be delighted by her rueful smile.

"I'm not a control freak usually, I swear," she said. "If this were our tree, I would let her hang the ornaments any which way. Isn't that right, honey?"

Maddie nodded her head. "But your tree is super fancy so we have to be careful."

"I only thought you might be a little more discriminating, especially as you're entertaining guests for the holidays," Eliza explained.

"Guests who honestly won't care if the ornaments

on the Christmas tree are upside down or sideways or clustered all together, I promise."

"They might not care, but I do. I want Snow Angel Cove to be perfect for you and your family. That's why you hired me, isn't it?"

In light of this attraction, he was beginning to question his own motives for wanting to keep her around, but he decided it probably wouldn't be wise to mention that to her.

"All right. We're going for perfection. I can do that. From here on out, I'll climb the ladder and take the higher branches. Your job is to hand me more ornaments when I need them and to keep an eye out and be sure I'm not making a mess of things."

She made a face. "Right."

"What this party needs is a little Christmas music."

"I know!" Maddie concurred. "I can keep singing but my voice is a little tired."

"You need a break. Let me see if I can find something."

One of the first things he had insisted upon after purchasing a house was the installation of a top-of-the-line entertainment system that could stream throughout the house. He had yet to crank up the classic rock like he did sometimes at his house in San Jose.

He opened the cabinet that held the components and punched in a few criteria, then let the server search for music online while he returned to the

Christmas tree. Soon, soft, jazzy holiday music filled the great room from the built-in speakers.

"That sounds nice," Maddie said.

"Definitely," her mother agreed.

"It's unanimous, then. We're officially ready to get our tree decorating on."

He grabbed several of the ornaments and climbed the stepladder, ignoring the slight unsteadiness in his equilibrium. His own sense of balance wasn't the greatest yet and he probably shouldn't be scrambling up and down ladders, either, but he wasn't going to tell her that.

While the snow continued to fall outside the huge windows with relentless abandon and the flames in the grate danced and swayed, they worked together to decorate the tree.

Maddie chattered about Christmas and about the vast variety of angel decorations on the tree—most that Sue had unearthed in a box in the attic that had been left over from the previous owners.

As they worked, Aidan was aware of an odd feeling, so rare for him, especially lately, that he didn't recognize it at first. Peace. A soft, sweet contentment seemed to seep through him as Eliza handed him ornaments with instructions about where to hang them. At first, she was hesitant, as if afraid to overstep by telling him what to do, but it didn't take long before they fell into a comfortable rhythm.

"I need to get a drink," Maddie announced just as he finished the top branches.

"Okay. Come right back," Eliza said.

Her absence left a conversational void that even Tony Bennett's smooth version of "My Favorite Things" couldn't quite fill.

"I haven't done this in years," he said. "The Christmas-decorating thing, I mean. Probably since I left home for MIT. My roommate in college used to put up a little tree but I was too busy to bother. After college, it always seemed like too much effort, until I could afford to hire a decorator to do it for me."

That sounded pretty pitiful, when he thought about it.

"Was Christmas a big deal at your house?" she asked.

"Definitely." He thought of crazy mornings around the Christmas tree and the frenzy of gifts and ribbons and wrapping paper. The Hope's Crossing Christmas Eve candlelight ski had always been one of his favorite traditions at home, where they would all bundle up and either gather to watch or strap on skis to participate in the annual tradition, where all the lights on the runs at the ski resort would be extinguished except the small candles each skier carried down the hillside.

He usually watched with Charlotte and his mom while his brothers took to the mountain. Downhill skiing had never been his favorite winter activity. He loved snowshoeing or cross-country skiing, where he could be all alone on a trail, able to savor the hushed magic of moonlight on thick new snow or watching a nuthatch seek out the last few berries on a currant bush.

"When I was a kid, decorating the Christmas tree was the best part of the year," he told her. "We had certain ornaments we all used to fight over, each of us determined to have the privilege of hanging them. And when I say *fight,* I mean punches were thrown. Seriously."

Her laughter was every bit as magical as a dusky evening spent alone on a winter trail. "You're telling me your family actually came to fisticuffs over Christmas ornaments?"

"Usually it was Dylan, Jamie and Brendan. They were always the most competitive. As the older two, Andrew and Patrick did their best to stay above the fray and Charlotte would usually burst into tears the minute voices were raised."

His childhood had been crazy and chaotic and wonderful. He wouldn't have changed a minute of it, even if he *had* sometimes felt like the odd one out.

"I said it before but it bears repeating. Your mom must have been the most patient woman on earth."

He felt the same sharp pang he always did when thinking of Margaret Caine. "She was an amazing person. She gave us all the same love and affection and never once treated any of us differently than the others. Of course, I always knew I was her favorite. We both loved books and music and old movies. The funny thing is, when I talk with my brothers or

Charlotte, they say the same things. Every one of us thought she treated us as her favorite."

"You still miss her."

"Yeah," he murmured, hanging a little angel with beaded wings and a glittery halo on a bough.

"You must be very close to your family."

He couldn't argue with that. As far as families went, they *were* close. He loved them all dearly and knew that he could call on any one of his brothers and they would have his back.

At the same time, over the years as he had gone first to MIT and then to Silicon Valley, an inevitable distance had widened between them. He only connected in person with his family three or four times a year while everybody else saw each other almost every Sunday, when Pop would host a big noisy family dinner.

Aidan knew it was his own fault for moving away from Hope's Crossing, an inevitability, really, but it added to his own sense of...*separateness,* barring a better word.

"What about you?" he asked, turning the conversation around. "Are you close to your siblings?"

"Only child," she answered with a stiff smile that didn't fool him for a moment.

"You said your mom died when you were a teenager."

"Yes." She picked up one of the few remaining angels and hung it on the tree with brisk movements, but not before he saw her eyes cloud with sorrow.

"And your dad?"

"He remarried a few years ago and lives in Portland now. His wife has a couple of teenagers from a previous marriage so I have a couple of stepbrothers. I don't know them well, as we have always lived apart."

He sensed more to the story. What was her relationship with her father? And had she planned to spend the holidays with him before Aidan had basically blackmailed her into staying at Snow Angel Cove?

"My sister sometimes tells me I can be arrogant and insensitive. It's just occurred to me that asking you to help me with my family might be keeping you from seeing your own family at Christmas."

She shook her head. "My father doesn't have a lot of room at his place and, to be honest, his wife and I have…issues."

"*Issues*. That's a complicated word."

She sighed. "We didn't get off on the best footing. My fault, mostly."

That surprised him. He had a short acquaintanceship with her, true, but Eliza struck him as someone a great deal like his sister, Charlotte, sweet and kind and maybe a little too forgiving for her own good.

He had hit the woman with his vehicle, for crying out loud, and she still seemed eager to help him create the perfect Christmas for his family.

"Why do you say that?" he asked, genuinely curi-

ous about what she might have done to warrant en-
mity between her and her stepmother.

"He married her and moved to Portland right in
the midst of everything with Tre—my husband's
death. I was lost and grieving and really needed my
dad, you know?"

She couldn't even say her husband's name after
three years. The depth of her sorrow gave him that
same kick in his gut as he would get from a hard
topple off the ladder.

More evidence of his arrogance. A few minutes
ago he had been thinking what a lousy time it was
for him to be attracted to a woman, focused only on
himself again. Why would he even think for a minute she would return that attraction, when she was
obviously still grieving her late husband?

"I needed him here to help me with Maddie but
instead he got married after years of being a widower
and packed up everything to move to Portland with
Paula and her children. I acted like a spoiled brat, I
guess, and I'm afraid I wasn't the most gracious of
new stepdaughters to her. Our relationship since then
has been...strained. Which means my relationship
with my father is strained, too."

Her father should have been less concerned with
his own love life and raising some other man's kids
and more concerned about his own grieving daughter
who needed him. Why hadn't he bothered to put his
wedding on hold for a few months, just long enough
to help his daughter when she needed him?

People did things for their own reasons, which often eluded Aidan. Usually selfishness, if he had to guess.

Here was one perfect example of why he preferred to work with computers and code. They did what was required of them. They didn't cheat, didn't betray, didn't wake up one morning with a damned tumor that knocked them to their knees.

"What about your husband's side? Does Maddie have paternal grandparents?"

"No. My husband's parents died when he was ten or eleven. An older sister raised him. She's on the east coast. We stay in touch and she's very kind to Maddie, sending gifts and letters and so forth, but she's busy with her own children and grandchildren now, which is only natural."

So she really had no one in her corner. His family might drive him crazy sometimes and he might lament the inevitable geographic and emotional distance between them over the past few years but they were *his* and he would be lost without them.

"Don't," she said, her voice a little sharp. "You don't have to look at me like I'm some lonely little widow with no one. Nothing could be further from the truth. I have a core group of very good friends in Boise who would do anything for me. They have stood by my side through everything with Trent and with Maddie. I also have a strong network of other parents I've met through the cardiac unit at the hospital or online and we share everything."

"I don't feel sorry for you, Eliza. Far from it. I think you're amazing."

She blinked, those green eyes reflecting the lights of the tree.

Embarrassed at words he never should have said, he looked around the room. "Speaking of Maddie, is she still getting a drink?"

"Oh. I thought she came back."

She looked around the room a little wildly. They both spotted the little girl at the same moment. She had curled up on the sofa angled in front of the big fireplace and was sound asleep with her horse toy tucked in the crook of her arm, along with one of the soft-bodied ornaments from the tree, as if she had been making the angel ride the little horse.

She looked like one of the angels herself, with that wavy dark hair and her ethereal features.

"Some days, she gets tired easily," Eliza said, gazing down at her daughter with a deep love that made something hard in his chest seem to break free.

He could care about both of them entirely too easily and the realization scared the hell out of him.

He hung another ornament on a space that looked a little empty. "There. That should do it for this side."

"It looks beautiful," she said. "Absolutely breathtaking, especially in front of the windows with that amazing scenery as a backdrop."

There were a few more decorations in boxes for the tree but it was almost done. They stood for a moment, admiring their handiwork. He felt that connection tug between them again. It couldn't be only one-sided, could it?

The moment stretched between them, fragile and sweet like a spun glass angel ornament.

Widow, he reminded himself. Off-limits. And probably not interested, anyway.

Needing to distract himself, he focused on something within his control. "Think I'm going to take a minute to grab something a little more substantial than apples and cheese."

"There's deli meat in the refrigerator. I can make you a sandwich. I'm sorry. I should have offered earlier. I didn't think about it."

"I can make my own sandwich, Eliza. I can even make one for you, if you'd like."

He headed for the kitchen. To his surprise, she followed him.

"Let me do this," she said as he started to pull the cold cuts from the refrigerator.

"Forget it. You've been on your feet all afternoon. Sit down. That's an order from your boss."

"I haven't signed any papers. You're not my boss yet."

He laughed as he grabbed a loaf of crusty bread and reached for a knife. "You sound like my sister. *You're not the boss of me* was one of Charlotte's favorite phrases. We heard it all the time. With six older brothers to contend with, can you blame her?"

Her smile was as genuine as it was lovely. "I imagine she learned early to stand up for herself."

"She did. But she also knew how to listen to us when we actually *did* know best. Like now, for instance. Please sit down. You're looking a little pale, which isn't an easy feat with that nasty bruise."

Color crept over her cheekbones as if in rebuttal. After a long moment she pulled a chair out from the work island and complied while he went to work.

CHAPTER EIGHT

AIDAN CAINE DEFINITELY knew his way around a kitchen. Who would have guessed?

True, he was only making a sandwich, not lobster thermidor, but still. He didn't simply slap a couple pieces of cold cuts on bread. No, he evenly sliced bread off a loaf, added some cheese he shaved with painstaking care from a heel and even washed and shredded a couple pieces of a ruffly lettuce she thought might be arugula—not that she was a lettuce expert or anything.

She watched, fascinated at his clean, efficient motions. He didn't make a mess, he didn't waste a speck of food. He even added a little garnish of parsley to two plates. When he was finished, it was close to a culinary work of art.

It had been a very long time since a man had fixed her a meal. Trent had hated to cook. He *could* cook, he just never wanted to, probably because he had worked his way through college as a grill cook at a greasy spoon and had loathed every minute of it.

Aidan slid the plate across to her. "What else can I get you? Water? Milk? Beer?"

What sort of wine went with a roast beef sandwich? she wondered. He probably knew exactly.

"I'm great with water." She had never been much of a drinker and less so since Trent's death.

He poured some in a fresh glass for her and set it down beside her plate.

"Thank you." She felt stupid to have him wait on her, considering she worked for him, but she would have felt more stupid arguing again with him about it.

"You're welcome." He picked up his own plate and set it next to hers then took the adjacent stool.

She did her best to ignore her awareness of him, focusing instead on the delicious meal. He had added some kind of smoky mustard that made the sandwich taste like something she would find in a fancy deli somewhere.

She was hungry, she suddenly realized. Her stomach had been a little uneasy at breakfast and lunch and she hadn't eaten much. While everything still ached, she was feeling much better right now.

"It's delicious," she said.

"You sound surprised."

"I'm sorry. I guess you're a man of unexpected talents."

He raised an eyebrow and she felt herself blush. Darn it. Sometimes she really hated her fair complexion.

"My dad runs a café in Hope's Crossing," Aidan said. "The Center of Hope. He put us all to work when we were kids, insisting we all could be comfortable in the kitchen. If you want the truth, I learned most of my best business leadership skills from watching my pop over the years."

She was more curious about his family than ever, considering she would be spending the holidays with them. "Does he still have the café?"

"Yeah. He's finally cutting back his hours a little, giving his assistant manager a little more leeway to make some of the important decisions. Now that he's married again, he and Katherine would like to travel a bit, go back to Ireland and all the other places he's talked about over the years. It's tough to go anywhere when you're chained to a stove. The man is sixty-six years old and he deserves to start taking it easy. Convincing him of that is another story."

"Can you tell me a little about the rest of your family? The more I know about them in advance, the easier task I'll have anticipating what they might need while they're here."

He gave her an approving smile that crinkled the corners of his eyes behind his glasses and she had to order her unruly hormones to stand down. She took a hasty drink of water, trying not to choke on it. This was her *boss,* she reminded herself.

"I told you about my pop. You'll love him. Everybody does."

That struck her as a singularly sweet thing for a son to say about his father.

"His wife is Katherine Thorne. They're newly-weds, so expect plenty of billing and cooing. That's

what my dad would call it—you know, all the gooey
sweetheart things people in love tend to do."

She was aware of a sharp pang, one she rarely
allowed herself these days. She and Trent had done
their share of billing *and* cooing the first year after
their marriage. They had been disgustingly gooey.
Love notes written on lipstick on the bathroom mirror, picnic lunches at the park, sweet texts and emails.

She had loved her husband deeply and had spent
that first year feeling cherished. Adored, even.

And then had come her unexpected pregnancy.
They had talked about children but not yet, not until
he was more settled in his job as a financial planner.
When they discovered she was pregnant despite birth
control, everything changed.

She understood it on an intellectual level. He had
spent most of his childhood far below the poverty
line, as his older sister, barely out of her teens herself, had been forced to work menial labor jobs just
to keep them afloat after his mother died. He had
craved security above all else and discovering he
was about to be a father for the first time had sent
that need into overdrive.

By the time Maddie was born and the doctors first
diagnosed her heart condition, Trent had become obsessed with making money, however he could.

"Actually, be prepared for a lot of lovey-dovey
stuff," Aidan went on, and Eliza jerked her attention away from the difficult memories and back to
the warm, comfortable kitchen at Snow Angel Cove.

"Sure. Okay," she said.

"You'll have three sets of newlyweds in the group. Pop and Katherine, my brother Dylan and his wife, Genevieve, and our sister, Charlotte, and her husband, Spence. All of them married within the last six months."

She suddenly realized she was going to have to do a better job of keeping track of them all than just her memory.

"Sorry. You lost me. Hold on."

"I know. We can be overwhelming."

"No. I just need to grab something to write down the names."

She grabbed a pad of paper from a small desk Sue must use to organize recipes and grocery lists and carried it back to the work island.

"Okay. Start over from the top."

He chuckled. "My oldest brother, Patrick, is a banker. He's married to Christine, a pediatrician. They live in Denver and have three kids, Maggie and the twins, Josh and Jake."

She jotted down the names. "Check. Go on."

"Andrew is next in the pecking order. He's an attorney. He and his wife, Erin, live in Hope's Crossing, where she teaches at the elementary school. Their kids, Ava and Ben, are both teenagers."

What was she going to do with a house full of young people? The game room was well-equipped with a pool table, old-fashioned pinball machine and foosball. That would do, for starters. Her tour of the house earlier had also revealed a luxurious media room with a massive flat-screen television, also something the teenagers would enjoy.

She would have to see what equipment the lodge had for outdoor activities, like ice skates and toboggans.

"Brendan comes next. He's the Hope's Crossing fire chief and is a widower who lost his wife and unborn baby a couple of years ago."

"Oh, how terrible!"

"It was tough on everyone. Jessie had a heart condition that went undiagnosed until their third pregnancy. Bren has two great kids, Faith, who's eight, and Carter, who's six. Maddie's age."

"Oh, the poor things."

"They had a rough couple of years but they're finding their way. Brendan is actually dating again. He's pretty serious with a woman who worked for me for about five minutes. Lucy Drake. She'll be coming along for the holidays."

"Brendan, Lucy, Faith and Carter. Right." She wrote those down and circled them to indicate they were a unit.

"I'm next in birth order—smack dab in the middle—and just younger than me is Jamie. I don't think he'll be able to make it, so you don't have to worry about him. Then you have Dylan and his wife, Genevieve."

"Got it."

He paused, sudden shadows in his eyes. "Since

you're creating a dossier here, I should probably tell you, Dylan was badly injured in Afghanistan a few years back and almost died. He lost an arm and an eye because of his injuries."

The Caines certainly had seen their share of hardship. Cancer, heart conditions, war injuries. No family escaped pain and sorrow. Sometimes it ripped them apart but she sensed Aidan's family had drawn even closer together.

"That must have been difficult for all of you," she murmured.

"He had a pretty rough time coming back from it for a while there. I'm not sure where he might have ended up if not for Gen. She's surprised all of us—a society belle who ended up seeing past the scars and the anger to the good man still somewhere inside there."

Intrigued and looking forward to meeting the woman—along with the rest of his family—she wrote down the two names with another circle.

"And finally Charlotte."

"The lone sister who had to put up with all of you boys."

He smiled again as he rose and carried his plate to the sink. "Exactly. Poor thing. She's the other newlywed, as I mentioned. She married Spencer Gregory this summer."

The familiar name made her stare. "Not Spencer Gregory, the baseball pitcher?"

"The same. He grew up in Hope's Crossing, too,

and hung out with all of us, especially Dylan and Jamie. You a baseball fan?"

For a moment, she was back to being a teenage girl, trying to connect with the father who had been a somewhat distant, unapproachable figure, a quiet, introverted man who always seemed tired after his twelve-hour days working as a road crew supervisor.

"Baseball was one of the few places where my dad and I could connect, especially after my mom died. He was a big Portland Pioneers fan. We used to drive from our house in Lincoln City to watch them whenever we could. I saw Smokin' Hot Spence Gregory pitch his very first game in the big leagues."

She had also had a bit of a celebrity crush on him her last year of high school and into college and had followed his career with interest even after she married. The supermodel wife, endorsements, the records he continued to break.

His plummet into disgrace and scandal had come right around the time of Trent's death and had struck her like one more personal blow.

Over the past year, Spence had been vindicated, the drug-dealing charges against him revealed to be a fabrication and cover-up. He was now respected, vaunted, on track once more to be entered into the Baseball Hall of Fame.

Again, she had taken his redemption in the public eye far more personally than she should have, finding a much-needed ray of hope in watching him rehabilitate his public image.

It seemed silly, she knew. She'd never even met
the man. Now he was coming here, to Haven Point—
and he was apparently married to Aidan's sister. Oh,
she was going to be such a dork around him and
probably wouldn't be able to string two words together. Perhaps she could at least manage to tell him
how grateful she was as a true-blue fan for the many
hours of enjoyment he provided her and her father
and how happy she was that he had been able to turn
things around.

Or maybe she would just stand there like a tongue-
tied idiot when she finally met him.

"Spence has a daughter from his first marriage,
Peyton," Aidan went on. "She's now about fourteen
and good friends with Maggie and Ava."

She wrote that all down, trying not to be overwhelmed at the task ahead of her. "It's probably
going to take me a few days to figure out who's who.
Most likely, I'll make a few embarrassing mistakes
and mess up names."

"Don't worry about it. Everyone is pretty easygo-
ing. I have pictures of the whole family from Pop's
wedding. I'll print out a couple for you and tag everybody so you can start putting names with faces."

"Great idea! That would be very helpful. Thank
you."

"You're welcome."

He gave her a bright, unreserved smile, and all
her girly parts sighed, forgetting all about smokin'
hot jock baseball players.

There was just something about a man in glasses, especially one whose brilliance was off the charts. She wanted to pull them off and toss them onto the table so she could see those amazing eyes....

She jerked her attention back to the matter at hand. "Your family sounds terrific," she said. "I can understand why you're so close to them."

"Pop worked hard to keep us tight after our mom died. It wasn't always easy with so many kids, especially when we were all heading in different directions by that point. Over the years, it has become more difficult to get us all under one roof."

"What a nice gesture, then, to bring everyone here for the holidays. I am sure your family will be grateful."

She thought she saw a shadow flit across his gaze before he blinked it away. "I hope so," he said. "My motives are mostly selfish. This way I get to spend Christmas with everybody but don't have to sleep in the uncomfortable twin bed of my childhood room at Pop's house on Winterberry Road."

She didn't believe his casual tone. This holiday with his family was important to him, for reasons she didn't quite understand.

She had picked up the impression before. Somehow she sensed he needed his family around him this year—maybe because of the heartache they had all endured over the past few years or perhaps to celebrate anew the joy that had come hand-in-hand with the sorrow, as it often did.

He wanted everything to be perfect and she resolved again that she would do her best to make sure of it.

She slid off the chair to her feet. "I had better finish with the Christmas tree. Those angels aren't going to jump on the tree by themselves, you know."

He smiled and reached to clear her plate. "Angels fly, you know."

"So I've heard. I can do this, really."

He shook his head. "I've got it. Pop's number one rule in the kitchen, if you don't work, you don't eat."

"I haven't even met the man and I already like him."

"You're going to love him, I promise. All the women do. They just can't seem to resist that trace of an Irish accent. One time Jamie and I went to a party over in Steamboat when we were in high school and he convinced me to pretend we were exchange students from Ireland. It wasn't that tough since we had spent our childhoods imitating Pop's brogue. You should have seen the ladies topple at Jamie's feet."

"And yours, I'm sure."

He made a face. "Jamie has always been a natural flirt. Mom used to joke that he charmed the nurses in the hospital nursery from the very beginning. I, on the other hand, was always more comfortable behind a keyboard."

"I doubt that. I'm sure you do just fine with the ladies, working that sexy geek thing you've got going."

The faint echo of her own words seemed to circle

around the kitchen, growing louder and louder in her mind. Oh, no. Had she really just said that? Hot color soaked her cheeks. Where was the darn off switch on her mouth sometimes?

He gave a strangled sound that wasn't quite a laugh and just gazed at her for a long moment, until she wanted to sink through the radiant-heated Italian tiles of his kitchen.

"Okay, can we just forget I said that out loud? I had a concussion yesterday, remember? I'm not in my right mind."

A new awareness seemed to spark between them, sizzling and arcing like heat lightning on an August afternoon.

"Sexy geek?" He spoke the words in a low voice that made her insides shiver.

Oh, like he didn't know how that smile broke nerd girls' hearts everywhere. "It's the glasses," she said. "Not to mention the whole computer-genius thing."

Okay, she had to stop now.

"Mama? Mama! Where are you?"

In all her life, she had never been so grateful for her daughter.

"In the kitchen, honey. Stay where you are, I'll be there in a minute."

She turned back to Aidan and found him watching her with an expression she couldn't quite read.

"I've got to go. Thanks for the, um, delicious sandwich. Oh, and the primer on your family. It helps. Maybe I won't make a total fool of myself around anyone but you."

She scooped up the notebook, drained the rest of her water and hurried out of the kitchen as fast as she could manage.

CHAPTER NINE

THE STORM FINALLY started to ease again about the time she and Maddie put the finishing touches on the tree.

Her daughter clasped her hands together at her chest and gazed raptly up at the tree. "It's so pretty, Mama. The most beautiful tree I've ever seen!"

Eliza had to agree. The tree made a stunning statement in front of the big two-story windows of the great room, its greenery a vivid contrast to the stark white snow blanketing everything outside.

"You're absolutely right."

She looked up sharply at the voice and found Aidan standing at the end of the hall that led to his office, where he had retreated to take a phone call an hour earlier, shortly after they finished their quick sandwich and she had completely humiliated herself.

His hair was a little rumpled on the left side, as if he had run his fingers through it while on his phone call.

She had actually called him a sexy geek. Where was a conveniently placed snowdrift to dive into when she needed one?

"Hi, Mr. Aidan. Do you like it?" Maddie asked.

"I think it's the most beautiful tree *I've* ever seen, too. The two of you did a great job."

"You helped! We couldn't have reached the top without you."

"Not unless one of those angels swooped in and carried you up to the top."

She laughed, delighted at the image, as Eliza heard a rattling of pans in the kitchen, followed by muffled swearing.

Aidan glanced in that direction. "I guess Sue must be feeling better."

"She says she is."

"What about you?"

She still ached, she couldn't deny that. Even now, she had to fight the urge to knead her fist into her throbbing lower back, but she firmly believed staying in motion had been the best possible medicine. By this time tomorrow, she expected even those aches and pains would dissipate.

"Almost back to normal," she answered.

"Good." He gave her one of those irresistible smiles and for a moment she was once more in his gleaming kitchen with the electricity snapping and sizzling between them.

He was the first to look away. "The snow seems to have finally stopped. Feel like getting some air? I thought maybe we could bundle up and walk out to the barn to check on the horses."

"Yes!" Maddie answered instantly, before Eliza

even had a chance to think. "Can we, Mama? Oh, please!"

She didn't want to spend any more time with him than she had to but maybe the best way to deal with her mortification would be to wade straight through it. After snowfall all day, the temperature would undoubtedly be icy. A nice walk in a blizzard might be just the thing to cool down her overheated imagination right about now.

"Sure. A little fresh air would be nice. Maddie, why don't you work on straightening up in here while I go find our coats?"

"Okay!"

Maddie eagerly scurried around underneath the tree picking up extra hanging wire and stray clumps of paper towel someone had used to wrap around some of the ornaments in storage.

She was such a sweet girl, always so earnest and ready to please. With a heart full of gratitude, Eliza hurried to the guest bedroom. She hadn't had time to move their things to the cook's quarters off the kitchen yet but planned to do that before dinner.

She shrugged into the wool peacoat she'd bought on clearance two winters before and picked up Maddie's pink-and-purple parka. When she returned to the great room, she found Maddie and Aidan, heads bent together as they looked at something on the Christmas tree.

She paused and watched them, a funny little ache in her chest. The only men in Maddie's life were her doctors and Eliza's dear friends Sam and Julio, a gay couple who had lived in the apartment across the hall.

"This is my favorite ornament on the whole tree," Maddie declared.

"It's a nice one," he answered, "but why is this particular ornament your favorite? There have to be hundreds of angels on the tree."

"Because it's a boy angel, just like my daddy. See?"

He bent his head to see it better and Eliza couldn't help craning her neck for a closer look. She remembered hanging that one earlier. The porcelain angel had looked antique to her so she had been extra careful with it and had let Maddie look but not touch. It did indeed have slightly masculine features, she recalled, though they looked nothing like Trent's.

"Mama says Daddy is watching over us from heaven. Whenever I have to go to the hospital, she tells me he's there helping the doctors know what to do."

"I'm sure he is," Aidan murmured. He must have sensed her presence because he looked up and met her gaze. His eyes were filled with compassion and a warmth she didn't want to see.

Something inside her seemed to soften and stretch like caramels left out in the sun.

Don't read anything into it, she warned herself. He only felt sorry for the poor widow with the sick little girl.

"Here you are, honey," she said, her tone more abrupt than she intended as she handed Maddie her coat. She didn't look at him as she helped her daughter stick her arms through the sleeves and then her hands into the mittens.

"Let's go through the mudroom. My coat is there," Aidan said when Maddie was bundled up. He led the way toward the kitchen, where Sue was rolling out what looked like pastry dough.

"It smells de-lish-ous in here!" Maddie exclaimed. Eliza had to agree as the comforting smell of carrots and onions and chicken seeped into the air.

"Oh, trust me, it will be," Sue declared. She seemed to be back to her old self. Her features had lost that wan, pinched look of earlier when her migraine had attacked. "I'm making my famous chicken pot pie. Seemed just the thing for a snowy day and it's always been one of Aidan's favorites."

"Yours is even better than my pop's, but if you tell him so, I'll deny it to my dying breath."

She rolled her eyes. "As if I would ever say such a thing to that sweet Dermot!"

"What did I tell you about my pop and women? Doesn't matter if they're seven or seventy," Aidan said to Eliza, startling a smile out of her.

"I'll have to get his recipe when he's here," Sue said, pretending not to hear the exchange. "Never hurts to try something a new way."

"Why mess with perfection?" Aidan countered as he headed into the mudroom. He emerged a moment later, shrugging into the sheepskin-lined leather ranch jacket she had seen him in earlier.

Sexy Geek with a side of cowboy. How was a girl supposed to resist that?

"Are you ladies ready?" he asked.

"Yes! I can't wait to see the horses!" Maddie declared.

When they walked outside, the air didn't feel as cold as she might have expected, maybe because of the cloud cover and because the wind had died down. The lake shone blue, a vivid contrast to the snow all around. From here, she could clearly see the shape of the nearby cove, just like its eponymous snow angel.

Through her research on the area before deciding to take the job at the inn, she had learned that Lake Haven rarely froze completely because of its depth and because of all the geothermal activity in the area feeding warm water into it. The minerals in the water gave it the lovely color.

Whatever the reason, it made for a beautiful scene in the twilight.

From here, she could also see lights begin to twinkle from the clustered buildings of Haven Point up the shoreline. In the fading remains of a stormy winter day, the pretty little town looked warm and inviting.

The walk hadn't been cleared since the snowfall resumed in the afternoon and walking through it took effort. Maddie struggled for only a moment before Aidan picked her up and settled her on his shoulders, much to her glee.

She said something to him Eliza couldn't hear and they laughed together. The sound warmed her even more than her wool coat.

She inhaled deeply of air scented with pine and snow and resolved to simply enjoy the moment. Whatever her reservations about working for Aidan Caine—the tangled past she doubted he even knew about, her pride that balked at taking a job offered out of pity, this silly schoolgirl attraction—she couldn't deny that Maddie seemed happy here.

When they reached the barn, he opened a small door next to the huge double doors and set Maddie down inside before reaching a hand out to help Eliza over a patch of ice. He wore leather gloves but she could swear she felt the heat of his skin through them.

She quickly pulled her hand away and looked around the cavernous space.

Through her thirty-one years on the planet, she had spent very little time inside of barns. If someone ever asked her to design the perfect barn, however, she would have pointed him in the direction of this aging building at Snow Angel Cove.

Made of weathered wood with a traditional gambrel roof, the barn smelled of hay and horses and dust. A mouse-fat calico tabby sidled out of view as soon as they spotted it but a black-and-white border collie wandered immediately over to them, long, busy tail wagging.

"Oh," Maddie exclaimed, shrinking away from the creature. She loved horses but dogs, on the other hand, freaked her out a little.

"It's okay," Aidan assured her. "He won't hurt you. This is Argus. He's the king of the barn."

"Really?"

"Well, he thinks he is, anyway. He bosses everybody around. But he's really gentle. I promise, he won't hurt you."

Her daughter didn't look completely convinced but because her middle name should have been Spunky, she petted the dog's head with ginger care then giggled when the dog licked her, his tail wagging even harder.

"Mama, I think Argus likes me."

"Looks like it." She knelt down to pet the dog, too, and was rewarded with a nuzzle and a lick.

"Did he come with the ranch?" she asked.

"No. He's Sue and Jim's baby. Goes everywhere with them."

"Do you have a dog?" Maddie asked.

"No. But my whole family does." He gave Eliza a rueful look. "I forgot to mention when I was giving you the guest rundown that they'll be bringing a miniature herd when they come. Dylan would never travel without his dog, Tucker, a black-and-tan coonhound, Andrew has a chihuahua named Tina and Lucy and Brendan each have little mutt purse pooches who are less than a year. Daisy and Max. I hope you don't mind."

"Not at all," Eliza assured him. She loved dogs and always had. When she was a girl, she'd had a Labrador retriever named Frisbee. She had adored that dog and grieved deeply when he died at thirteen, just before Eliza went off to college. She had dreamed of having a half-dozen pets when she had children—of which she had wanted a half-dozen more.

Life as a single working mother with an ill child had forced her to put that dream on hold. Maybe when they were settled somewhere permanently, she would consider it.

They spent a few more moments showering love on Argus until one of the horses made a raspberry sort of sound that made Maddie giggle.

"That's Cinnamon," Aidan said. "The gentlest horse in here. I got her specifically with Carter and Faith in mind."

He had bought a horse strictly for the rare visit from his nephew and niece. She knew that shouldn't touch her heart but she couldn't seem to help it.

Which was the real Aidan? The tough businessman who ground up his competitors and sprinkled them on his espresso or the softie who bought a horse for his niece and nephew who might only visit him here a couple times a year?

"Oh," Maddie breathed, her eyes wide as she approached the stall containing the red horse. Roan,

Eliza thought it was called, though what did she know? She had absolutely no knowledge of horses, other than what she had seen watching *Gunsmoke* and *The Rifleman* reruns with her dad.

"She's beautiful. The most beautiful horse in the whole wide world."

Her daughter was obviously in love. She had her hands clasped together at her collarbone like the heroine of a melodrama and was gazing at Cinnamon with a rapt expression.

The horse was pretty, Eliza had to admit, with kind, gentle eyes. Even she could tell, though, that she was by no means the most elegant horse in the barn. Most of the half-dozen other horses she could see were muscled and strong, especially a big black with a flowing gray mane.

"Bob says they're all nice horses but he likes Cinnamon the best," Maddie declared.

"Would you like to make friends?" Aidan asked. "I brought a couple of carrots from the kitchen. You can feed her some."

Her daughter looked torn. "Bob doesn't like carrots. How do I feed her?"

He took her hand and led her closer to the horse, then handed her the carrot. "Nothing to it. You just hold it out for her and Cinnamon will do all the work."

"She might bite me, though."

"Not this old girl, I promise."

Eliza held her breath as Maddie hesitated for

only a moment then offered up the carrot. Cinnamon lapped it out of her hand in one bite, with a grateful whinny.

Maddie giggled. "It tickles, Mama!"

"I'll take your word for it," Eliza said.

"I've got another carrot if you want a turn."

Despite Aidan's confidence that the horse wouldn't bite, those teeth were *big* and she wasn't at all eager to put her fingers within reach.

"I'm good. Thanks."

"Okay, Maddie. Looks like you get to be the designated carrot-delivery girl. Here you go."

He gave her another one and this time she held it out with more confidence. She even found the courage to pat the horse's neck and was rewarded with a gentle head butt that made her giggle again.

"See? She likes you."

"I like her, too," Maddie announced, which wasn't really news to anyone.

He chuckled. "I need to check on a couple of the other horses. We have one who's going to foal in the next month. Are you two good staying here with Argus and Cinnamon?"

Eliza nodded. As he walked down to the far end of the barn, she tried not to watch him go, focusing instead on her daughter introducing Imaginary Bob to her new friend while the other horses whickered for attention and the somehow comforting scents of hay and horses swirled around them and dust motes floated in the air like gold flakes.

CHAPTER TEN

AIDAN TOOK HIS time checking on Jemma, their foaling mare, talking to her, making sure she had the special feed mix the vet had recommended.

He knew his efforts were completely unnecessary as Jim did an excellent job managing the horses, but it gave him a good excuse to keep a little distance between him and Eliza and to work on trying to rein in this crazy attraction he hadn't been able to shake all day.

This stupid season—this time for family, for connection—was seriously messing with him, especially this year, when he had almost lost everything.

He didn't want to be so drawn to her and her cute little girl.

Yes, Eliza Hayward was a lovely woman—soft, curvy, with an air of delicate vulnerability he found intensely appealing.

She made him want to take care of her, to tuck her close and protect her from the hardships of life—an impulse he knew was completely ridiculous, not to mention chauvinistic and also unnecessary. He had only known her a day but he already knew Eliza Hayward had a fierce independent streak and seemed to be doing a fine job of managing life on her own, including raising a child with health challenges.

He admired many things about her, including her willingness to jump right in where she saw a need—specifically decorating his Christmas tree.

He had never been so immediately and forcefully drawn to a woman. Even BethAnn the Betrayer had taken a few months to pierce through his natural defenses and gain his trust—and that had happened when he was a naive college student living far from the security of home and still raw and grieving from his mother's death.

He wasn't that dumb, hungry kid anymore. Beth-Ann had taught him to be cautious and vigilant, especially when it came to women who appeared sweet and needy on the outside but could be cold, calculating, soulless bitches beneath the fluttering eyelashes and shy smiles.

Eliza had secrets. He hadn't missed the shadows in her eyes or the way she carefully evaded certain topics, like her husband. In all likelihood, she was exactly as she appeared—a widow who had sustained some tough breaks lately.

Or she could be a con artist who had manipulated him and the events of the past twenty-four hours to her best advantage.

He couldn't quite believe that one, but he would be a fool to let the magic and wonder of Christmas overshadow his own hard-won common sense.

He hadn't been a fool in a long, long time.

Okay, he might have made a few irrational decisions during the summer—like purchasing three hundred acres on an Idaho lake, along with six commercial buildings and a factory he didn't know what the hell to do with. But that had been a fluke, a medically induced anomaly. He was all better now, back on track, clearheaded and completely rational.

Maybe this attraction to Eliza—this *yearning* he also didn't know what the hell to do with—was simply an unexpected side effect of that brush with mortality. Maybe she represented the world he had consciously given up when he set out to create the dynasty that would become Caine Tech.

Whatever the reason, he needed to keep his distance from her until his family arrived. After that, he would be so busy keeping all the Caines happy and entertained, not to mention avoiding Pop's entirely too perceptive gaze, to have time to do something crazy like fall for a woman he barely knew.

He fed Jemma one of the apples he had also filched from the kitchen. "Here you go. There's a good girl," he murmured to her and received a nuzzle in return.

With a wish that all females could be so uncomplicated, he headed back to Eliza and Maddie. Eliza was on the bench in the middle of the barn petting Argus, who was clearly infatuated, while Maddie carried on an in-depth conversation with Cinnamon about Santa Claus and whether the horse might be able to talk on Christmas Eve, along with the rest of the animals.

He remembered his mother telling him and his brothers that old folk belief, that the magic of Christmas extended to animals being able to talk only on Christmas Eve. One year when he was about seven, he and Brendan had stayed up past midnight trying to get their big yellow Lab, Chester, to say something besides *woof.* Chester hadn't been the brightest bulb on the tree under the best of circumstances and apparently Christmas Eve hadn't suddenly endowed him with any particular linguistic skills.

"Are you ladies ready to head back to the house?"

Eliza nodded. "Come on, Maddie. Let's put your mittens back on."

"I don't want to leave yet. Cinnamon is my second best friend now, after Bob."

"You can visit her another day," Eliza promised.

"Can I ride her sometime?"

"We'll see," Eliza said as she finished putting on the mittens. "Okay. We're ready to go."

He opened the door for them and immediately snowflakes swirled inside.

"It's snowing *again?*" Maddie exclaimed. She sounded not quite as excited about the continuing storm as she had earlier in the day.

"Looks like it," he answered.

Eliza lifted her face up to the flakes. "I can't believe this. At least another two inches of snow fell in the half hour we were in the barn."

"It's supposed to taper off tonight."

Maddie gamely trudged through the heavy snow for a few feet, until he reached down and lifted her up and onto his shoulders again. She didn't weigh much, probably not even fifty pounds.

"Look how pretty it is," she said, her voice soft and almost reverent. "The snowflakes look like little angels with parachutes."

"If that's the case," her mother said from beside them, "you've got an angel on your nose."

Maddie giggled and lifted her hand from his head. He couldn't see her but he assumed the wriggling he felt behind him came from her wiping it away.

"There. Is it gone?"

Eliza smiled softly at her daughter. Snowflakes tangled in her eyelashes and her pale pink beanie and the little pale freckles on her upper cheekbones. She was so lovely and he had a feeling she was completely oblivious to it, which somehow made her all the more appealing.

"That one is gone. You've got about four more all over your face."

"Ack! Get off me, angels! Get off," Maddie exclaimed with more giggles, which made Eliza smile.

He loved that about kids, he thought, as he led the way up the path to break a trail for Eliza. They had such a clear insight into the magic and wonder around them, a perspective that adults surrendered when worry over mortgages and car payments took over their imaginations.

When they neared the house, an unfamiliar beat-up pickup truck was parked under the porte cochere. He frowned, wondering who was crazy enough to brave the poor roads and snowy conditions. The pickup had a snowplow on it, half full of melting snow, and giant studded tires. Whoever was here must have plowed their way up the hill to Snow Angel Cove.

"Expecting somebody?" Eliza asked when they neared the house.

"Not that I know of. I suppose it could be someone with a delivery for Sue."

"Great service, if it is."

"Let's find out."

He opened the door leading into the mudroom and heard the sound of female voices coming from the kitchen. He swung Maddie off his shoulders to more of her giggles—man, a guy could get addicted to the sound of a kid laughing—then hung up his coat and the wool hat his physician insisted he wear against the elements. Eliza helped Maddie out of her coat and mittens and hung them and her own outerwear on a hook near his.

When Aidan went into the kitchen, he found Sue in the sitting room off the kitchen, along with the auburn-haired doctor from the emergency room and the woman who had come out of the store to help Eliza after the accident.

They were sipping coffee, a tray of pastries on

the table between them, and seemed on the best of terms with Sue.

"Dr. Shaw!" he exclaimed. "And Mayor Shaw."

They must be related, he suddenly realized as the surname finally clicked. He hadn't made the connection until right then because they looked nothing alike—the doctor with her pale skin, green eyes and auburn hair and the incoming mayor with the dark hair and complexion that spoke of some sort of Hispanic or Native American heritage. They did share a similar bone structure and their mouths were the same, but the resemblance ended there.

"I'm not mayor until the first of January," she said. The laughter in her dark eyes faded and she gave him a polite smile.

"How did you make it up the hill to Snow Angel Cove?" he asked them.

Dr. Shaw's smile was slightly warmer though still not quite cordial. "Best investment I ever made, trading a year of waived office deductibles for Maisy Perkins and her kids in exchange for that old pickup. My nurse and office assistant both told me I was crazy, since Maisy herself is a hypochondriac and out of her six kids, two have asthma and two have brittle bones. Joke's on them, right? Already this winter I've used that old pickup to get to the hospital more times than I can count when my own car was stuck, not to mention saved a fortune plowing the parking lot of my office. Hi, Eliza. Hi, Maddie."

"Hi, Dr. Shaw," Maddie said, skipping forward.

"Guess what? I have a new best friend named Cinnamon. She's a red horse."

"Do you?" The doctor smiled kindly down at the little girl, no more immune to her charms than any of the rest of them.

"Hello," Eliza said. "You're sisters. I should have realized."

"We are," the physician said.

"Half sisters, actually," McKenzie offered. "Same father, different mothers. And a long story."

To him, her smile was the temperature of Lake Haven—colder maybe, since the lake never quite froze over—but to Eliza, her smile was as warm and welcoming as a mug of hot cocoa, with whipped cream on top.

"Devin was saying she wanted to check on you and I offered to tag along."

"And here we are," Dr. Shaw said. She reminded Aidan of a much calmer version of her sister, who seemed to vibrate with energy—along with the antipathy toward him he couldn't miss, even though he didn't quite understand it.

"I've been dying to see inside this place since Mr. Caine here took it over. We played here a lot when we were kids, when the Kilpatrick family used to own it. I hardly recognize the place now. With all the building permits that were railroaded through the town council the last few weeks, I knew it had to be spectacular and I was absolutely right. It's just stunning."

He didn't miss the caustic edge in her tone. What

beef did the mayor have against him? Yeah, he had caused an accident in front of her store but she had said herself the road conditions were at least partly to blame.

"I'm sorry you went to so much trouble," Eliza said, a delectable hint of color on her cheekbones. "Especially *unnecessary* trouble. I am really doing much better, as you can see for yourself. A phone call could have saved you time and effort."

Dr. Shaw studied her carefully. "I'm glad to see you've got a little color back. Yesterday you were so pale, I thought you were trying to camouflage yourself into the snow. Staying here at Snow Angel Cove appears to agree with you."

Eliza cast a sideways glance in his direction and he was almost positive her blush intensified.

"It's a lovely home and Sue is a fantastic cook, as I'm sure you have figured out."

McKenzie, in the act of choosing another of Sue's delicious lemon bars, grinned. "You know it, sister."

"I love it here," Maddie declared. "Did you know Mr. Aidan has *six* horses? And one is a pony named Cinnamon who is just the right size for a girl who will be six years old in February?"

"I did not know that," Devin said. She smiled at the girl, though her gaze seemed sad somehow.

"We just went to see them and Cinnamon ate a carrot right out of my hand. It tickled."

"Guess what?" McKenzie said. "I have a horse,

too. His name is Darth Vader and he's my best friend, too. Next to my sister, anyway."

Both women seemed charmed by Maddie, which wasn't surprising. She seemed to have that effect on people.

"I wish I had a sister," she said wistfully. "Even a brother, I guess, if he wasn't a pain."

"I've got five of them and I'm usually more than willing to give a few away," Aidan offered.

"I want a *baby* sister or brother," she said. "Your brothers are probably old like you."

McKenzie Shaw and Sue both chortled at that and Eliza groaned.

He was only thirty-seven and until that moment he thought he was in the prime of his life—the past few months notwithstanding—but he suddenly felt like he should be looking into buying a Jazzy and investing in denture cream.

"Sorry," Eliza murmured.

"You're the one under pressure to procreate, not me," he said.

Her color returned in a delightful pink tide. "Why don't you have a cupcake?" she suggested quickly to distract her daughter.

"How are you really feeling?" Devin asked. "I worried about you all night."

"Oh, I wish you hadn't. I'm fine. A little achy but that's all."

"Would you mind if I perform a quick exam?

That's the real reason I came, because I wanted to check your condition for myself."

He liked the doctor more and more for her diligence.

"Please?" she pressed.

Eliza sighed. "It's completely unnecessary, but since you've gone to so much trouble, I suppose I can't say no."

"Is there somewhere private we can go?"

She gestured toward the hallway leading to the cook's quarters. "Back here to the rooms I'm moving into. There's a comfortable sitting room there."

"Perfect."

As soon as they walked into the other room, Sue rose. "I need to take those chicken pot pies out of the oven if I don't want them to burn."

"Can I help?" Maddie asked.

"No, but you can keep me company," Sue said. "Come on, kiddo."

They headed hand in hand toward the oven. Though they were only fifteen feet away, it felt like a football field as he was now virtually alone with the prickly new mayor.

"Would you and your sister care to stay for dinner?"

"No," she said abruptly.

The polite thing would probably be to make casual, meaningless conversation. He didn't have much patience these days for doing the polite thing. "You don't like me very much, Mayor Shaw. Care to explain what I've done to offend you in the twenty-four hours I've been in town?"

She looked guilty for a moment before she sighed. "Transference, Mr. Caine. Plain and simple."

Against his better judgment, he was intrigued. The situation didn't seem plain *or* simple to him.

"I don't like you or not like you," she went on. "How can I? I don't even know you. I'm sorry if I'm acting otherwise. I'm just…angry at the person who sold you half of my town."

"Ben Kilpatrick."

At the name, she made a face as if she had tasted something particularly nasty in Sue's lemon bars.

"Yes, Ben Kilpatrick."

Her animosity toward his old friend was startling. Nearly everybody liked Ben—or respected him, anyway. He was one of the hardest-working men Aidan knew.

"I love Haven Point, Mr. Caine. This has been my home my entire life. I know you haven't spent very much time here but when you do, you'll see it's a magical place, a good town full of kind, decent people who are struggling to survive."

"What I've seen of it would certainly back you up on that."

"It's a nice enough town now, but you should have seen it a dozen years ago. This was a dynamic community with a thriving economy—thanks in large part to the Kilpatrick legacy. After Big Joe Kilpatrick died and Ben inherited his estate, everything started to fall apart."

Ben never talked about his family. He ignored direct questions and subtly and skillfully deflected the indirect ones. "Why do you say that?"

The mayor frowned. "Before Big Joe was even in the ground, Ben closed the boat manufacturing plant that was our biggest employer around here. Two hundred people lost their jobs in a single afternoon and we've never recovered from the blow."

That must be the large empty factory building he had bought when he wasn't quite in his right mind. He had walked through the facility a month ago and wondered what the hell he was going to do with it.

"Ben turned his back on this town and everything we stand for," McKenzie Shaw went on, her features growing more and more animated—and angry. "While he was off doing Lord knows what in California, he let Snow Angel Cove—his beautiful family home that his grandfather had built by hand—fall into complete disrepair. You've done wonders with it, by the way. I'll give you that. The place really does look great."

"Thank you." At least she was no longer giving him the skunk-eye. He would have to warn Ben not to make any unexpected visits to town unless he wanted to be hauled out to the middle of the lake and dropped in.

"What he did to this house was a crying shame. What he did to Haven Point was criminal. He owned half the commercial buildings in town. As an absentee landlord, he did nothing to upgrade the infrastructure or even do basic repairs like plumbing or electrical work. One by one, businesses either moved into better facilities on the outskirts of town, relocated to Shelter Springs or folded completely. The rest of us are barely holding things together. Now that the inn has burned down, we're down to a couple of restaurants, my flower shop, an insurance office, the bank, the copy shop and a few gift stores. It's pathetic."

She didn't seem to expect a response from him, just went on as if she had been rehearsing this speech since the election.

"I love this town, Mr. Came, and I understand we need investment and smart planning. As the new mayor of Haven Point, I am more than willing to work with you, whatever you decide to do with your property here. I would beg you not to simply sit on it and do nothing. Oh, and if you think you're going to come in and build some big tourist trap resort that will suck all the personality and life out of my town, I will fight you with every last breath in my body."

"You don't want tourists?" he asked, surprised at her vehemence. His hometown, Hope's Crossing, had a booming economy *because* of tourism.

"Short-term visitors are fine in moderation. Sure. We welcome and embrace them. Lake Haven is breathtaking and the Redemption Mountains offer endless recreational opportunities. People have been coming here for the benefits of the mineral hot springs since Native Americans first stumbled onto them generations ago. They're necessary and important to the area but we can't survive on tourism alone. We need long-term employment, jobs that pay enough to support families."

She had gone from looking at him like he was Satan's favorite cousin to gazing at him with a completely unwarranted hope, as if he could step in and solve all the town's problems.

He had bought a vacation home to escape the pressures and demands of his frenzied life in California, for crying out loud—and he hadn't been thinking very clearly when he did it. He wanted a place where he could fish and ride horses and be with his family, not another project.

He was trying to come up with a diplomatic way to tell her so when Eliza and Dr. Shaw returned.

They were smiling together and neither of them looked particularly worried, which he had to assume meant the doctor hadn't found any unexpected problems in the impromptu examination.

"Since I know you're only going to hound me to tell you after they left," Eliza said to him, "I'll save you the trouble. You'll be relieved to know, everything checks out."

He glanced at Dr. Shaw, who nodded. "She is in amazing condition for someone who was hit by an SUV yesterday."

"Barely tapped," Eliza muttered.

"Thank you for coming out all this way to make sure," he said, ignoring that. He still broke into cold chills whenever he thought of it. "I appreciate your dedication. I asked your sister if you would like to stay for dinner. She declined but I will repeat the invitation. We would love to have you."

The two sisters exchanged an unspoken communication. "We can't," Dr. Shaw said reluctantly. "I have a few other patients I wanted to check in on during the storm. Thank you, though. And thank you, Sue, for the coffee and delicious treats."

"I enjoyed the visit," Sue said. She came over carrying a white paper bag. "I wrapped up some of the nibbles for you to take with you."

"Wow! Thanks!" McKenzie Shaw exclaimed, looking far too fresh-faced to be on the brink of assuming the town's mayoral position.

"You're welcome. You two be careful out there."

"We will. Can I use your ladies' room before we hit the road?" McKenzie asked.

"Certainly. I'll show you where it is," Eliza said. She led her toward the front of the house to the guest powder room.

"Mr. Caine, could I speak with you for a moment?" Dr. Shaw said when the other two women were out of earshot.

Was he about to get another lecture on his responsibilities to the town? He sighed but didn't know how to avoid it. "Certainly."

She glanced over to the kitchen where Sue was

pouring Maddie a glass of juice. "Somewhere private?"

He raised an eyebrow. "Of course."

He led the way through the house to his office. "Actually, I'm glad for the chance to speak with you, Dr. Shaw. I know Eliza said she was fine but do you still have any areas of concern about her physical condition we should know about?"

"You know I can't tell you anything more, Mr. Caine. Confidentiality laws and all. If it sets your mind at ease, I can let you know I told her I see no reason to schedule a follow-up."

He felt as if a weight the size of one of his horses had just been lifted from his shoulders. "That helps. Thank you."

"I asked to speak to you because I wanted to ask how *you* are."

He picked a pen up from the desk and idly twirled it through his fingers. "Fine. I was completely unhurt. Shaken up, maybe, but physically fine."

"I'm not talking about the accident," she said, her voice quiet.

His fingers tightened on the pen. "I don't know what you mean," he lied.

"Don't you?" Though she spoke the words quietly, he saw firm knowledge in her eyes. "I saw the incision at the hospital yesterday when you ran your fingers through your hair. It's quite well hidden by your hair but not completely concealed. Tumor?"

He could bluff here and lie to her. It would be the

safest route because of the secrecy that had been so carefully maintained for the last three months. What would be the point? She wasn't a stupid woman.

"Before I say anything else, I must demand absolute discretion from you. You cannot mention this conversation to anyone. By some miracle, we have managed to keep it a secret from the media and I intend to keep it that way."

"I would lose my medical license if I casually chatted about my patients' medical history, Mr. Caine. And before you tell me you're not my patient, you live in my town now. That makes you mine, whether you ever come into my office or not."

In her way, she was as committed to Haven Point as her sister, the mayor, he realized. "I appreciate that. I'm sure you understand that I cannot be too careful in my circumstance."

"I do. So *was* it a tumor?"

He had kept this a secret for so long, he found it difficult even to form the words. "Yes. Benign meningioma."

"Ah. Benign. That must have been a relief."

He thought of those two weeks of hell when he hadn't been sure. The entire time as they waited for tests, he hadn't been able to shake the dark memories of his mother's lingering, horrible cancer death. He just figured he would buy a one-way-ticket to Africa, wander into a veldt somewhere and let the lions have at him.

In those two weeks, everything in his life had

come into sharp, raw focus and he had come to the stark realization that though he had achieved incredible material and professional success, he still had hollows and spaces inside him he didn't know how to fill.

"A relief. Yes. It started growing quickly and affecting function, which is how it was discovered in the first place, so the decision was made to remove it in September."

"What sort of residual side effects have you seen in the last three months? Headaches?"

"Sometimes." He considered *headache* a relative term for those moments when he wanted to rip his scalp right off his skull.

"Blackouts? Seizures?"

"You mean did I pass out when I was driving yesterday and endanger innocent pedestrians?" He didn't bother to keep the testiness from his voice.

"I didn't say that."

He knew that hadn't happened. He remembered each instant of the accident with vivid clarity, something he wouldn't have been able to do if he had passed out.

"Since the surgery, I haven't had any. Beforehand, yeah. The tumor was kind of a tangled mess. It made life…complicated."

"I can imagine."

She was quiet, green eyes filled with compassion. With that calm, trust-inducing bedside manner, she must be an extraordinarily good physician, he thought. He feared she would be one of those doctors who burned out quickly from caring too much for her patients.

"I've been cleared to drive again for the last six weeks."

"I'm sorry I pressed you about it but I'm very glad you confided in me. I assure you, I will keep what you have shared with me confidential. I'm sure you have a strong support system around you and probably amazing physicians back in California but I understand how isolating a serious medical condition can be." She handed him a card. "This is my cell number and my email. Please know you can contact me at any time if you have any concerns or questions while you're in the Lake Haven area."

"Thank you."

He opened the office door for her and after a pause, she walked out and rejoined her sister and Eliza, who stood admiring the Christmas tree in the great room.

"Everything okay?" McKenzie asked with a curious look at her sister.

The physician gave her a casual smile. "Yes. I was just telling Mr. Caine here about the Lights on the Lake Festival and urging him to take his family while they're here."

"The Lights on the Lake Festival?" Eliza asked.

"Yes. It's a week from today," McKenzie said. "It's great fun. You'll love it! It's a huge celebration in town where all the boat owners in Haven Point and Shelter Springs decorate their watercraft with Christmas lights and sail in a big parade from their marina to ours, three miles. There's a big gift boutique, food vendors, music and then they light off fireworks over the lake."

"In the cold?" Eliza asked.

"Everybody bundles up, warm and cozy, and the town puts little kerosene heaters all over downtown. I promise, you'll have a great time."

"You said it's next Saturday?"

"Yes."

"My family isn't coming until the following Tuesday. The day before Christmas Eve."

Too bad he hadn't known about it earlier or he could have scheduled his family visit differently— though with all the complicated schedules, he wasn't sure they could have pulled it off, anyway.

"Oh, that's a shame," McKenzie said. "It's a can't-miss event. But you all should definitely come. I promise, you'll love it."

"Sounds fun," Eliza said. "Thank you for the information. And thank you especially for coming out in the storm to check on me. It was very kind of you. Both of you."

"We take care of each other here on the lake," Dr. Shaw said. "You'll see that after you've been here a few months."

Eliza looked regretful. "I'm afraid I won't be here that long," she answered. "I'm only staying here through the holidays to help Mr. Caine with his guests."

"I understand from Megan Hamilton that you were supposed to start as her new manager today, until the place burned down yesterday," McKenzie Shaw said.

Eliza made a face. "Yes. Obviously, yesterday was not the best day of my life."

"No kidding! I'll keep my eyes open to see if anybody else might be hiring in the area," she offered.

"Thanks. I appreciate that."

"Oh, you're welcome. We love when new people move in," McKenzie said. She gave him a quick look. "Well, usually."

He didn't laugh but was surprised to find he wanted to.

"Kenz, we better go," her sister said quickly.

"Yeah, you're right. Places to go, people to see. You know how it is."

They both hugged Eliza, who seemed surprised and touched by the gesture, then headed out into the softly falling snow.

CHAPTER ELEVEN

SHE COULDN'T SLEEP.

Eliza lay in the comfortable bed listening to Maddie's soft breathing and gazing out through the slats of the blinds to the pearly glow of the moonlight on the snow.

She really hated these nights, when her mind raced in a hundred directions and she just couldn't get comfortable.

By all rights, she should be snoozing away. This just might be the most comfortable bed she had ever slept in. The mattress was the ideal firmness—not too hard, not too soft. The sheets were high-end Egyptian cotton, at least thousand-thread count. The quilted comforter was warm and cozy without being oppressively heavy.

So why was she wide awake at—she checked the readout on her phone—3:00 a.m.?

Okay, maybe she had a few reasons. So much had happened to her in the past few days, she really hadn't had a chance to process everything—new job, new responsibilities, a new place to live, the intricacies of forging new working relationships. Underneath, as always, was the unrelenting fear that she wouldn't be able to take care of this fragile child who depended on her for everything.

She gazed out at that slice of moonlight. For now she had a job, they had a more-than-comfortable place to live, and she had the rare luxury of time to figure out her next step—of course, she also had a great deal to do in the next week and a half.

She had taken a complete tour of the house earlier with the list of family members Aidan had given her, trying to figure out which room would work best for each of them. She found the bedroom suites empty shells containing bare-bones furniture but little else— naked beds, empty dressers and blank walls.

The public rooms of the house—the great room, the media room, the game room—were furnished and decorated, though all of them could use a little more warmth and holiday cheer.

What she had seen of Snow Angel Cove reminded her too much of an elegant hotel, she thought again. That was all fine when someone wanted to *stay* in an elegant hotel but Aidan's family was coming to enjoy Christmas together in his *home*. They didn't need fancy amenities as much as they needed all the comforting touches that made a place feel like a home—and she had her work cut out for her to deliver it to them given the time constraints.

She wouldn't be able to do that work if she didn't get some sleep. She flipped her pillow to the cooler side and rolled over but even that didn't help her find a comfortable position that eased the ache in her wrist and her back.

Between her discomfort and her racing thoughts, she probably wasn't going to be able to sleep anytime soon. The last time she took pain relief had been hours before, at lunchtime. Maybe swallowing her stubbornness along with some ibuprofen would be a good first step.

With a sigh, she pushed the comforter down and sat up. Good plan.

She pulled on fuzzy socks and her robe then found the baby monitor she had dug out of one of the boxes Jim and Aidan had brought in after dinner. She hadn't had time to unpack all of them—and wasn't sure she would, anyway, since they would only be here for a few weeks—but she had found this while looking for Maddie's favorite cozy blanket before bedtime.

Some little burst of mother's intuition had prompted her to include it in the boxes she had brought along to Haven Point instead of leaving it in their storage facility with the rest of their things. She had thought maybe it would come in handy if she were required to work the front desk after hours at the Lake Haven Inn and needed to leave Maddie sleeping for a while in their attached apartment.

Whatever the instinct, she was grateful to have it in this big house where she might not be able to hear her daughter wake up otherwise.

How many times over the past five and three-quarter years had something similar happened to her? One memorable time, she had been compelled to double-check a prescription she had picked up a dozen times before at the pharmacy, one she usually didn't think twice about. She vividly remembered the cold fear cramping in her stomach when she discovered the pharmacist had made a grave error and given her a much more highly concentrated medication than Maddie's usual dose.

It could have been a deadly mistake. If she hadn't followed that sixth sense to check the bottle before giving it to Maddie, the overdose probably would have killed her daughter.

She liked to think Maddie had more than a few angels looking out for her.

After turning on the monitor, she slipped the receiver in her pocket then used the flashlight app on her cell phone to first find the bottle of ibuprofen in her purse and then guide her path through the boxes in the sitting room and out of her rooms toward the kitchen.

The instant she walked into the kitchen, she realized she wasn't alone. Flames danced in the sitting area's gas fireplace, sending out warmth and light enough to outline the shadow of someone sitting on the sofa. She felt just an instant's fear at the unexpected before she recognized Aidan.

Was he asleep?

She started to tiptoe back to her room, not wanting to bother him, but again that instinct stopped her.

"Are you...okay?" she asked.

Her employer shifted to face her and in the shaft of snow-brightened moonlight filtering in through the window, she caught an expression of raw pain on his features before he quickly contained it.

"Fine," he said, his voice tight.

That was a bald lie if she had ever heard one. She hesitated. It was none of her business. He was her boss, that was it, and she sensed he was also a very private man. She should just turn around and go back to her room, leaving him in peace.

Unfortunately, she wasn't very good at doing what she should.

She took a step forward and then another. "I don't believe you," she said calmly.

The rough sound he made wasn't quite a laugh, but close. "Who said you had to?"

His blue eyes gleamed silver in the moonlight and flames, his mouth set in grooves of pain. He had his elbow up on the back of the sofa and was resting his head on his hand as if his neck couldn't bear the weight of it.

"What is it? Headache?" It seemed the logical choice, given his posture.

He made that rough sound again. "Something like that."

"Can I get you something for it?" She held out the bottle in her hand. "I was on my way to take a couple of ibuprofen. I only came out for a glass of water."

"I have medicine for it. I was just…delaying the inevitable."

He reached out and flipped on the lamp beside the sofa and she saw the prescription bottle on the table at his elbow.

"I'll get you some water," she offered. Without waiting for a response, she crossed to the cupboard by the sink for two glasses then filled them from the filtered water pitcher in the refrigerator before returning to his side.

"Thanks," he said when she handed him one. "You know you don't have to wait on me."

"It's only a glass of water. I didn't exactly offer to wash your feet with my tears."

He made that same rough, not-quite-a-laugh sound, sending shivers up her spine. She did her best to ignore them. She was *not* going to give in to this unwelcome attraction, especially right now. The man was in pain, for heaven's sake.

"Go on. Take your medicine so you can feel better. You're not proving anything, except your own stubbornness."

"That sounds like something my mother would have said."

"You can consider me your surrogate mother, then."

He gave her an unreadable look. "Yeah, that's not about to happen."

The words seemed to shiver between them like the echo of sleigh bells on the night air.

After a moment, he shook out a couple of pills from the bottle and washed them down in one gulp.

"There. Now your turn."

Apparently, they were bonding over pain medication. These few days were turning into the most surreal of her life. Under his watchful eye, she took out a couple of ibuprofen and swallowed them back. The cold water tasted delicious and she took several more swallows.

"There. Happy now?"

"Getting there. Tell me the truth. Are you having a lot of pain from the accident?"

"No, not really. Just a bit achy. I thought a couple of ibuprofen would take the edge off. What about yours? Migraine?"

He was silent for a several moments and she thought he wasn't going to answer her. She had the impression he was having one of those personal debates with himself like she always did.

Finally, he seemed to reach some kind of internal decision. His sigh sounded weary and a little self-conscious. "The truth is, I had brain surgery eleven weeks ago. I still have some residual headaches once in a while."

She stared at him, quite certain she hadn't heard him correctly. Of all the things she might have expected him to say, she never would have anticipated that answer.

"Brain surgery! You're not serious?"

"I could be wrong, but I don't believe most people would throw those particular words out as some kind of a joke."

She sank down onto the easy chair next to the sofa. "Why did you... I mean...are you... Is everything okay now?"

He lifted one palm. "As far as the docs can tell. I had a brain tumor. Benign, thank God, though they weren't sure of that at first."

A brain tumor. Dear heavens. She tried to imagine how terrifying that must have been for a man like Aidan: successful, powerful, used to being completely in control of his own empire. His genius was legendary, even to someone outside of the tech world. Trent had been a huge fan, naturally, and used to rave about Aidan's cutting-edge ideas. He *was* Caine Tech—brilliant, creative, innovative.

And apparently he had a brain tumor.

"After they figured out it was benign, they wanted to leave it alone but it started growing at a rather alarming rate so they decided it was best to remove it."

Eleven weeks. Not even three months. How had he concealed it so well? She hadn't seen so much as a scar. "Have you had the headaches since the surgery?"

"At first they were constant but the last month they've eased to once or twice a week."

She still couldn't imagine that, after her own experience the past thirty-six hours with pain.

"Besides the headaches is everything...okay?"

"You mean is my cognitive function impaired? Am I having hallucinations or seizures or anything? You're the second one to ask me that today. I'm fine. I've had a little memory loss from right before the surgery and right after but that's the extent of it. The doctors tell me my recovery has been nothing short of miraculous. I wouldn't have even mentioned it if you hadn't come in tonight and caught me in an unguarded moment."

"I'm sorry I bothered you."

He waved off her apology. "No need to apologize. You have every right to be here."

"Does anything help? A warm compress? A cold one?"

"I'm fine. Usually I just need to sit in a dark room for a while."

She rose again. "In that case, I'll get out of your way."

"You don't have to leave. I'm already feeling better. You were right, I shouldn't have been stubborn about the medication. I don't like some of the side effects but the headache is worse than a few minor inconveniences. Sit down if you'd like."

He wanted her to stay. Though he didn't specifically say so, she saw a certain shadow of loneliness in his eyes, a sort of wistful hesitance in the invitation.

She paused, torn. A winter night, a flickering fire, a gorgeous, fascinating man. All in all, a dangerously irresistible combination.

How could she possibly walk away?

She sank back into the easy chair with an odd feeling of inevitability. "For a few moments. I really need to at least *try* to sleep tonight. I have it on good authority my new employer is a harsh taskmaster."

"I'm sure he's not as bad as his reputation."

"I will have to judge that for myself, I suppose."

In light of the information he had just shared with her, a few more pieces of the Aidan Caine puzzle seemed to click into place. "Your brain tumor is the reason you've invited your family to Snow Angel Cove for the holidays, isn't it?"

He sipped at his water instead of answering but she knew suddenly she was right.

Like many people facing a personal crisis, he was turning to those who had loved him all his life—for comfort, for support, perhaps simply for a connection to the familiar.

The insight made her heart ache a little for him, even as she was aware of a tweak of envy that he had such a huge circle he could gather around him.

"I hate to mention this, but I'm going to have to insist you don't say anything to anyone else about what I just told you," Aidan said.

She bristled, that moment of soft compassion giving way to annoyance that he would think she was the sort of person who might run to the tabloids with this sort of juicy tidbit. "I never would! Even if I hadn't signed a nondisclosure clause with my employment paperwork, I wouldn't share your personal information with anyone, Aidan."

"I'm sorry. I'm sure you wouldn't. I just had to be clear. It's a very closely guarded secret. If it became public knowledge before I'm a hundred percent back to normal, the Caine Tech shareholders could panic. We're in the middle of some very intricate negotiations to purchase two other companies right now and I don't want to unnecessarily complicate matters."

Again, that compassion squeezed her chest. The poor man. She couldn't imagine the sort of pressure on him, where he had to be so guarded about his personal life.

On the other hand, she was keeping secrets from him about her own history and about Trent's death, so perhaps she wasn't in a position to judge.

"I won't say a word," she promised.

He sipped at his water and gazed at the flickering fire. The gas fireplaces were far more convenient than those that burned wood for fuel and were cozy enough to warm a room, but something was definitely lost without the crackle and hiss and the aroma of burning fruitwood.

"I also must insist you not mention anything about my brain tumor to my family members while they're here."

It was a good thing she was firmly sitting down or she would have stumbled, with her typical style and grace. "What? You mean your *family* doesn't even know?"

He gave a shrug that wasn't really an answer at all.

She stared at him, appalled. "Let me get this straight. You seriously had major surgery—someone drilled a hole in your skull and stuck a knife into your *brain,* for heaven's sake—and you didn't bother to mention this little fact to your family?"

"Technically, they removed a piece of skull and used a laser, then put the skull back. But yeah. My family doesn't know."

"I don't understand. I had the impression from the way you spoke of them that you're all quite close."

"We are."

"And you didn't think they might want to know that you had a brain tumor removed?"

She couldn't seem to wrap her mind around it—and her brain was completely intact, thank you very much. From all he had told her, his family was filled with wonderful people who gathered around each other in times of need. He had talked about his brother the wounded soldier and his other brother who had lost his wife with deep love and compassion—and yet when he needed that same hand of support, he had shut them all out.

"What good would it have done to worry everyone? Doctors first found the tumor the week before my pop's wedding. They weren't sure then whether it was benign or malignant. I couldn't ruin things for him with that kind of news. And then we decided to go for the surgery while Pop was on his honeymoon. Again, I certainly wasn't going to call him on his cruise and tell him to rush back to sit at my bedside when it was completely unnecessary."

"Okay, I suppose I can give you that one. But what about the rest of them? Good grief, you have enough siblings for a basketball team with a couple of alternates! You don't think a single one of them would have come to help you out?"

He winced a little at her raised voice—apparently his headache wasn't completely gone. She was sorry for that but not sorry for her sentiment.

"It was my call and I made it. My family can be overwhelming and I didn't want everyone fussing around me. A few trusted members of my household and corporate staff knew and that was plenty."

She frowned, sensing something else at play here. He had purposely isolated himself from his family. Why? He obviously loved them. She would have thought he would automatically turn to them during what could have been a life-threatening health condition.

None of it was her business, she reminded herself.

"You can disagree with my decision," he went on, his voice stiff. "But if you are unable or unwilling to promise you can keep this information to yourself while my family is here, I am very much afraid I can't honor our employment agreement."

She gaped at him. "Let me get this straight. You're basically threatening to fire me before the paperwork even goes through if I so much as *think* about telling your family about the major brain surgery you neglected to mention to them."

"That's about the size of it, yeah."

Oh, good grief. She threw up her hands. "Fine. Mum's the word, then. I already told you I wouldn't tell anyone. If that includes your family, so be it. Am I allowed to tell you I think you're completely wrong? You obviously care a great deal about your family or you wouldn't be going to so much trouble to have them all here for Christmas. I fail to see the point of even *pretending* to have a loving relationship if you shut them out when you need them most."

"Duly noted. Now can we talk about something else?"

She *should* make some excuse and go back to bed but their disagreement seemed to have had an energizing effect. She didn't feel tired at all, though she would undoubtedly pay the price in the morning.

"Sure. How is your headache now?"

"Better. Thanks. In case you wondered, coddling me isn't in your job description."

She was quite certain nagging him about his family wasn't in there, either. "Consider it a bonus. I like to give my employers extra bang for their buck," she said.

"Do you?" he murmured.

She could detect absolutely no innuendo in his voice but for some ridiculous reason, she could feel her face heat, anyway. She was suddenly aware again of the intimacy of the situation, the two of them virtually alone except for her sleeping child, in a darkened house, in front of a cozy fireplace.

"And you can see how well that's been working out for me." She tried for glibness.

"Temporary setback. You'll get back on track."

His confidence in her warmed her more than the gas fireplace.

The lines of strain seemed to have eased around his mouth, she saw with relief. Now he just looked lean and dark and compelling, especially with his hair a little messy and evening facial hair shadowing his features. Maybe it was the surroundings or the memory of him out with his horses but he didn't look like the perfectly groomed executive right now, more like a sexy, slightly disreputable outlaw.

"Tell me how you became a hotel manager."

"Assistant manager," she corrected. "I was working my way up to manager, remember? Unfortunately, my one big shot at glory is now a pile of ash and rubble down by the lake."

He smiled a little, as she intended. "Assistant manager, then. Why hotel management in the first place?"

She settled deeper in the comfortable chair, her mind retracing the steps that had led her to this moment. "I told you my mother died when I was in high school, right?"

He nodded. "How did it happen?"

"She worked the front desk at a small seaside motel owned by her good friend, just for a little spending money. It was only about a mile from our house and in good weather she liked to ride her bicycle to work. One night she never came home. My dad went out looking for her and finally found her mangled bike and my mom about thirty feet away. Hit-and-run driver. The police never found him. They said she died instantly."

He flexed a hand as if he wanted to reach for her. "I'm so sorry."

The pain of that original loss had never quite left her. Her life up to that point had focused on clothes and makeup and boys and studying hard enough to earn a scholarship, since her dad repeatedly lectured her they couldn't afford tuition otherwise.

Her mom had been a constant source of encouragement, her biggest cheerleader. She had been funny and warm, someone everyone in town liked.

"After she died, her friend who owned the motel knew money was an issue for us. She hired me to help out during the summers and after school. I think at first I did it because it helped me feel closer to my mom but then I realized I really enjoyed it. I did check-in, housekeeping, took reservations, even learned a little about repair and maintenance. Wherever she needed help, she turned to me."

"You must have done a good job."

"I don't know about that. I guess. I do know that even though I was still in high school, the owner put a great deal of trust in me and I didn't want to let her down. It was the very best on-the-job training I could have received."

Eliza had fantasized about taking over the Sea-swept Inn eventually, but then the economy in the area took a hit and Karen had been forced to sell.

"After I graduated from high school, I was able to get a scholarship and obtained a degree in hotel management. I always wanted to open a small inn somewhere."

Nothing big, just something she could dabble in while raising her family, too. How many times had Trent promised that when all his plans became reality, he would be able to buy her any inn she wanted? Countless. Like so many other plans they had made together when things were good, those dreams had died along with him.

"When my family arrives, you should talk to Lucy, my brother Brendan's fiancée."

"Oh?"

"This summer, she turned one of the historic silver-dynasty mansions in Hope's Crossing into a bed-and-breakfast. I stayed there during my dad's wedding and was really impressed."

"It sounds lovely."

"Yes. The thing is, Lucy is relatively new to the hospitality industry. I think it's safe to say she's still trying to figure things out. With your years of experience, you could probably give her all kinds of great tips."

She couldn't deny she was flattered. "Of course. I

don't know how much insight I can offer but I would love to talk shop with her."

"Lucy is a marketing genius. Knowing her, by now she probably has network connections throughout the industry, including people who might be looking to hire someone with exactly your skills. I can have her put out some feelers for you, if you would like."

She couldn't afford to turn down his help. "Thanks."

"I'm assuming you want to stay in Idaho."

"If possible. Maddie's doctors are all in Boise. I don't want to have to start over somewhere new."

"That makes sense." He was quiet for a long moment. "How is she, really, if that's not too intrusive a question? She seems perfectly healthy to me."

"Right now she is. We've had a really good year. There's a chance that will continue indefinitely. Some children with atypical cardiomyopathy never end up needing a transplant. Their condition is managed with a pacemaker and medication."

"I hope that's how things go for you and Maddie. She's a great kid who deserves a normal, happy childhood."

She smiled, touched by his words. "I agree. That's been my prayer for her from the day the doctors first suspected her condition."

"You're a good mother. She's lucky to have you."

His quiet words seemed to seep into her own heart, past all her fears and inadequacies, warming a tiny space that had been cold and alone for so very long. "Thank you."

"I mean it. I know it can't be easy to have a child with health issues, especially when you're on your own."

"I'm not some kind of a saint, Aidan," she said, her voice low. "Don't make the mistake of thinking that. Sometimes the strain and worry over her seems more than I can bear by myself. I cry myself to sleep some nights, wishing with all my heart that we could have that normal childhood you were talking about. Sometimes I'm so damn angry at God or fate or whatever for making my baby have to suffer. Other times, I just want to pick her up and run away to some tropical island somewhere and pretend everything is fine."

She had never told anyone that before. Not even Trent. By the time he died, their relationship had been so strained, she'd kept most of her deepest emotions locked away for fear of completely unbalancing the precarious load that had become their lives together.

Why she had confided in Aidan, she didn't quite know. Something about the night and the fire and the snowfall seemed conducive to sharing secrets.

She shouldn't have said anything. She barely knew the man—*and* he was her employer. He didn't need to know how tangled and chaotic her psyche could be.

"You're probably wondering what kind of hot mess you've hired."

He smiled a little and she was happy to see no trace of the pain that had etched his mouth earlier. "Actually, no. I was just thinking that while I truly regret the circumstances that led to meeting you, I can't be sorry I did."

His low words and the expression in those vivid blue eyes seemed to shiver through her. He wasn't looking at her like he thought she was crazy. She saw admiration and respect and something else, a spark of something hot and hungry that sent nerves suddenly jumping through her stomach like butterflies doing the *paso doble*.

She caught her breath. She was imagining things. She had to be. It was only a trick of the firelight. Aidan Caine, gazillionaire tech genius and all-around geek hottie, couldn't possibly be interested in *her*, the perpetually stressed single mother he had rescued literally off the street the day before.

"I should go. It's late and I have a busy day ahead tomorrow."

If she didn't leave, she would make a complete fool of herself over him. Hadn't she just told him how she wanted to escape her problems and pretend they didn't exist? He was the ultimate fantasy, the gorgeous and insanely wealthy man who would swoop in and rescue her from the stress and angst of her life.

And the whole brain-tumor thing, knowing he had walked through the valley of the shadow and all that. It brought out all her nurturing instincts and made her want to cradle his head to her breast and take care of him.

She could just see herself falling hard for him—and ending up battered and bruised emotionally. *Not* what she needed.

He rose as well. "Sorry I kept you up so late."

"You didn't. I...enjoyed talking with you."

The flames flickered over his features, making him look rakish, slightly dangerous and infinitely appealing. She swallowed, trying to will herself to move toward her room but something seemed to hold her in place.

"Good night," she murmured, at the same moment he said her name. Only her name, and then he murmured something that could have been a curse or a prayer and the next moment he stepped toward her and lowered his mouth to hers.

CHAPTER TWELVE

YES. THIS.

Eliza caught her breath at the first touch of his mouth on hers, firm, minty, delicious. He smelled so good, leather and sage and perhaps a hint of peppery citrus.

Some little voice in her mind whispered this was a lousy idea but she shoved it hard into a corner, tossed a big pile of mental debris on top of it and turned back to relishing his mouth against hers.

The attraction she had been fighting since she walked into the darkened kitchen—okay, let's be honest, since she opened her eyes the day before and found that lean, compelling face gazing down at her—seemed to simmer through her, frothy and bright.

He kissed like a man used to taking what he wanted from the world, with single-minded concentration—as if he wanted to tease out every secret, every fantasy.

She was completely unprepared for the riot of sensations he evoked. How could she be otherwise? Nothing in her very limited experience could have prepared her for *this*.

She had been so alone for so very long. The chance to lean into someone else's strength, even for a moment, seemed like a wonderful gift wrapped up in shiny paper with a diamond-studded ribbon around it.

If she had her way, she would stand here in the dimly lit room the rest of the night indulging herself in the decadent kiss, like a child stuffing sweet after sweet in her mouth, even though she knew they would make her sick later.

She might have, if the wind outside hadn't suddenly picked up, moaning under the eaves like some kind of warning siren.

She froze as that voice of caution suddenly managed to make itself heard again. What on earth was she doing? She was kissing Aidan Caine—*really* kissing him, tongue and all.

Okay, that sealed the verdict. She had absolutely no sense of self-preservation.

With one grand burst of self-control, she eased away from him, trying to catch her breath and reorganize the wild frenzy of her thoughts into some semblance of coherence.

He gazed at her for a long moment, his eyes a deep and vivid blue, and then raked a hand through his hair.

"For the record," he said, his expression a bemused sort of regret she didn't want to see, "that's not part of your job description, either."

She drew in a ragged breath, willing her racing

pulse to slow so she could think straight. Why, oh, why hadn't she listened to that warning voice? She should have slipped back into her room the moment she walked out into the kitchen and found him there.

"That's probably a good thing," she managed to say in a deceptively casual voice, "unless you want to have job applicants lined up from here to Boise."

His laugh had an edge of surprise to it, as if he had expected some other sort of reaction from her.

"I mean it. I don't want you to think I expect anything from you. I won't forget again that you work for me."

And that quite effectively put her in her place.

"Neither will I," she murmured. "Now if you'll excuse me, I really do need to try to sleep."

"Good night."

She didn't have far to go to her rooms, which was probably a good thing since she felt so shaky and off-balance. Wouldn't it be a lovely end to this strange encounter if she tripped over a side table or something and went sprawling at his feet?

Much to her relief, she managed to make it to her room without completely embarrassing herself— more than she already had, anyway.

Once inside, she closed the door behind her and sank into the wingback chair. She couldn't seem to catch her breath and she could hear each rapid beat of her pulse in her ears, each surge of blood through her veins.

What in heaven's name had just happened?

That kiss.

She could still taste him on her lips—minty, male, completely delicious.

She buried her hot face in her hands. She was *such* an idiot. She remembered her own eager response, the clutch of her hands around his back and the way she had kissed him with that wild urgency and she wanted to die.

She had just tangled tongues with *Aidan Caine,* for the love of all that was holy.

What was the matter with her? She hadn't even *thought* about another man in three years, too busy scrambling to care for Maddie's needs, to keep the financial wolves at bay, to rebuild their lives. Romance had been the last thing on her mind.

She had been too damn busy to think about how lonely she was, how she missed a man's arms around her and someone else's steady strength to lean upon.

She dropped her hands and gazed into the darkened sitting room. When had she *ever* had someone else to depend on, except the early few years of her marriage? Since her mother's death, she basically had been forced into emotional self-reliance. Her father had never been demonstrative and losing the wife he loved and depended upon hadn't suddenly turned on some magical switch.

Trent had been wonderful in the beginning. The perfect boyfriend. She wouldn't have married him if she hadn't been sure she could lean on him. She could honestly say the first two years of their marriage had been everything she wanted.

But gradually things began to shift. The minute that plus sign showed up on the pregnancy test, it seemed as if everything had changed.

Financial success became the only thing that mattered to him, to the point of obsession—and not just financial success, but *instant* financial success. He had pursued one get-rich-quick scheme after another. Day trading, direct sales, real estate flips.

If someone else had made a dollar at something, Trent had been determined to make a thousand.

After Maddie was born with a heart defect, achieving success had become almost a compulsion.

She would have been thrilled with a steady paycheck, decent health insurance, but he wouldn't listen.

"This is it, babe. The big payoff. I swear it."

How many times had he said those words to her? At first, she had been stupidly proud of him for working so hard to support their family. Gradually, that had become the only thing that mattered to him. Not her, not Maddie. Just adding more zeros to their bank balance.

His last grand idea had actually been a good one, surprisingly enough. He had come up with the concept for a revolutionary new productivity app and had begun working with a developer friend of his from college.

He had been determined to sell the idea to one of

the big Silicon Valley companies—and of course, Caine Tech had been his first choice for their forward-thinking products and phenomenal success rate.

Somehow through a friend of a friend, he had finagled a meeting. Not with Aidan, she knew that. Trent had called her after leaving the company, ranting about how he had been fobbed off on a couple of lower management flunkies who didn't have the imagination or brains to see the genius of his idea.

After a few moments, the rant had turned despondent and she had spent a few moments trying to play the supportive wife while inside she had been completely exhausted and wondering how much longer she could do this.

He had told her he was going to stop off for a drink. Just one, he'd said, because he deserved it after that complete waste of time.

Two hours later, he was dead in a single-car accident—or at least she hoped it was an accident. She would never know if he had hit that barrier intentionally or just been too impaired after *six* drinks.

For a man obsessed with providing for his family, Trent had been remarkably shortsighted. He had racked up thousands in debt—and had missed their life insurance payment three months before his death.

She released a long breath now, trying not to think about that terrible chapter in her life. She had grieved for her husband and the life she had once imagined

for them together and his death had reinforced that
Eliza could only truly depend on herself.

Long after Eliza returned to her room, Aidan sat
in the dark kitchen trying to analyze what the hell
had just happened.

He wanted to blame a hundred different things.
The warm, seductive intimacy of the quiet kitchen,
the pain medicine he hated that seemed to make him
act in strange ways.

The hard truth of the matter was that he had *ached*
to kiss her, quite fiercely. As he looked back on the
past few days, he realized this attraction had been
simmering inside him almost since the beginning.

The attraction part he fully comprehended. Eliza
was a beautiful woman, with that silky spill of honey-
streaked hair, the green eyes flecked with gold, the
little smattering of freckles across her nose. Hers
was a soft, understated beauty, fragile and sweet and
deeply appealing.

This aching hunger inside him might be a normal,
perfectly understandable physiological reaction to
a beautiful woman— especially considering he had
been living like a monk for the last three months.

Acting upon it was a completely different story.

She worked for him! He had a firmly held personal policy not to become entangled emotionally
with the people who worked for him. He tried not to
be cold or harsh about it, only resolute.

While he cared deeply for long-term employees

like Sue and Jim, Louise, a few others in his trusted circle, he had learned not to combine romantic relationships and business. They created a toxic mix for everybody involved, as he had learned from bitter experience early on when a few overambitious women had tried to take advantage of him—including one miserable lawsuit he would prefer to forget.

Eliza worked for him, which automatically made her completely off-limits to anything like heated kisses in the early morning hours. Yes, her employment was temporary and maybe a bit unorthodox but that didn't change the underlying philosophy.

Beyond that, Eliza was not his usual sort of woman. He typically was drawn to sophisticated, urbane women after the same sort of relationship he wanted—casual, easy, uncomplicated.

A young widow with a medically fragile child—however adorable Maddie might be—didn't strike him as someone who would be amenable to a quick fling.

The reminder served as the same bracing shock he would have gotten from sticking his face in the snow.

So. Lesson learned. He had to avoid intimate conversations with her in seductively quiet rooms. He could do that. Now that he was aware of his attraction to her, he would just have to be careful to keep out of situations where it might become an issue.

He had always been able to compartmentalize easily and had learned to shove aside the unimportant in order to focus on higher priorities.

He knew people thought him cold and emotionless. Even his siblings accused him of it. He wasn't. He felt things just as deeply as everyone else—maybe even *more* deeply—but his long and difficult grieving process after his mother's death had one good side effect in that he had learned through it how to put aside fears and hurts and loss and distill his concentration toward meeting his goals.

He considered his single-minded focus one of his greatest strengths—and he would simply apply the same principle to the quandary of Eliza Hayward.

Forgetting that intense kiss wouldn't be an easy task but he would just have to force himself to try in order to return things between them to a professional level.

She would only be here for a few weeks. How difficult would it be to shove down his inconvenient attraction for that time, especially since he would no doubt be distracted once his family arrived?

CHAPTER THIRTEEN

"ARE YOU SURE you don't mind running to the grocery store for me, too?" Sue asked Friday.

Eliza shrugged into her coat. "Not at all. It's right on my way after I pick up the new lamps."

"I told you, Jim can do all of that for you. I'm not sure you should be carrying those big boxes to the car. I know you say you feel fine now but I still worry about you."

The other woman's concern warmed her heart. After several days of working closely with Sue, Eliza had come to consider her a dear friend.

"I'm perfectly fine, I promise." She still had a lingering twinge in her wrist and shoulder but even that was fading. "I have to go to the pharmacy, anyway, for Maddie and to be honest, I'm looking forward to finally seeing a little more of Haven Point."

The past week had been so busy, she hadn't even had a chance to leave the ranch. It was hard to have cabin fever in a vast twelve-thousand-square-foot lodge complete with all the amenities of a small resort but a change of scenery would certainly be welcome.

"You said you needed cream of tartar?" she asked.

"That's right. How can I make snickerdoodles without cream of tartar?"

"Excellent question. I'll be happy to pick some up for you. How much do you need?"

"Better get me at least four of the biggest spice containers they have. Aidan has always loved my snickerdoodles and he assures me his family will, too."

"Because you make the best snickerdoodles in the whole wide world," Maddie declared from her elbow.

Sue smiled down at her, rubbing her head. The two of them had become fast friends, too, these last few days. Sue clearly adored Eliza's daughter and treated her like a beloved granddaughter. Her quiet, darling husband did the same.

In their many conversations over the past few days, Eliza had learned that Sue and Jim had found each other late in life, too late to start a family. Sue had confessed that being with Maddie made her ache for the children and grandchildren she never had.

"Wait until you try my cut-out sugar cookies, darlin'," she said now to Maddie. "I promise, you'll be in cookie heaven."

Maddie giggled. "There's no such thing!"

"You say that because you haven't tried my cookies yet."

Eliza smiled. "Okay, cream of tartar. Anything else?"

"Let me check."

Sue pulled down the notebook she used to organize menus and shopping lists for the party. "I think that should be everything. Aidan is supposed to be bringing some of the specialty items I can't find locally."

"And he's coming home tonight?" she asked, trying for a casual tone even as her pulse hitched up a notch.

"Tonight or tomorrow. When he called this morning, he still didn't know when his meetings would be done."

Against her will, Eliza's gaze shifted to the sofa in the kitchen sitting area, where they had shared that stunning kiss.

Try as she might, she couldn't seem to shake the memory. She had started to avoid sitting down on that particular sofa because she could swear the clean, deliciously masculine scent of him still drifted in the air.

After six days she should be over this ridiculous and completely embarrassing crush she had developed—especially since she hadn't even *seen* the man since that kiss.

The day after their early-morning conversation and embrace, he had made himself scarce, spending his time either outside helping Jim clear away the fresh snow or holed up in his office on phone calls. She knew, because every time she walked past his office toward the other rooms she was working on in that area of the house, the muted murmur of his voice through the closed door seemed to shiver through her as if he had trailed a finger down her spine.

The next morning, Tuesday, she found out after breakfast that he was gone, ostensibly to handle urgent, last-minute negotiations for a company Caine Tech wanted to acquire.

She was grateful he was gone, she told herself. Without his presence, some of the fine-edged tension under her skin seemed to dissipate and she could really go to work making his house into a warm and welcoming haven.

"Looks like we're running low on baking powder," Sue finally said. "Why don't you pick up more of that and maybe some of that local artisanal cheese they carry in front of the store?"

"Got it. Cream of tartar, baking powder and cheese. Okay, find your coat, Mads."

"Why don't you leave the little one here?" Sue suggested. "I can sure use a little help decorating the sugar cookies."

Maddie's eyes widened. "Oh, can I, Mama? I want to decorate sugar cookies! You know I love putting on the sprinkles."

She smiled. "That *does* sound like fun. You always have been an extrasprinkles girl, haven't you?"

"Can we make some angels with silver wings?" Maddie suggested to Sue.

"I do think I might have a cookie cutter in the shape of an angel. We'll see what we can do."

Though Eliza was torn about leaving her daughter, she didn't feel like she could deprive her of this fun. "Thank you," she said to Sue. "I know you have plenty to do without babysitting, too."

"Are you kidding? I'm not babysitting her, she's helping me. Anyway, I love the company. Take all the time you need. There are a few nice shops in town you should check out while you're there, especially if you need anything else on your Christmas list."

Christmas. It always seemed like such an abstract concept until it started getting this close. The holiday was just around the corner, only five more days— this was Friday and Aidan's family would be arriving the following Tuesday, the day before Christmas Eve.

She still had so much to do but as she walked through the house on her way to the garage, she couldn't help admiring what she had accomplished so far.

She was far from an interior decorator but she did know the little touches that warmed up a room and made a guest feel welcome. A beautiful home wasn't necessarily a gracious one and she wanted his family to remember how comfortable they felt at Snow Angel Cove.

To that end, she had made sure every bedroom had extra blankets, house slippers and fuzzy socks in various sizes, water carafes for the bedside tables, little baskets full of designer toiletries she had ordered rush delivery from the same supplier she had used at the hotel. She had carefully selected books and magazines for each room according to what she knew about his family and had worked late into the night making basic instruction manuals that explained in simple terms how to work the electronics, the wi-fi passwords and the gas fireplaces.

To make each room more festive, she and Maddie had spent a wonderful afternoon cutting boughs and glossy red winterberries from the abundant forested areas around the house and then arranging them on mantels and in containers on side tables. They had used extra to make wreaths to hang on some of the doors. Each room also contained a small four-foot Christmas tree, decorated with the individual guests in mind.

Would he like the little touches or would he think she had overstepped?

She supposed she would find out when he returned. If he had been here, she could have asked his opinion and at least had a little direction. Sue had approved of everything she had done, so Eliza had to hope she was on the right track.

If he hated everything, she could strip the house back to the cool, impersonal shell it had been four days ago.

A few moments later, she was pulling her SUV out of the garage and driving toward the town of Haven Point, some two miles away, feeling strange to be without Maddie.

The setting was spectacularly beautiful, with those commanding snow-covered mountains rising almost directly up from the other side of the brilliant blue lake.

With all this splendor to distract the eye, she didn't know how people kept from driving off the road. Somehow she managed to make it to Haven Point without incident and drove down the appealing main street that curved around the lake.

She felt a pang as she passed the burned-out remains of the inn. How was Megan doing? she wondered. And what was she planning to do with the inn? She made a mental note to check in with her before she left Lake Haven.

She could have made a good life here with Maddie. Maybe they would have attended that charming little church on the lakeshore, with its Gothic stained glass windows and honey-gold brick. Maddie might have gone to the elementary school that rested on a hill overlooking the town and the lake. Eliza might have been on a first-name basis with the old-timers she saw talking to each other with elbows propped on the hood of a pickup truck in front of the feed store.

Maybe here she could have found the sense of belonging she and Maddie both needed.

In a perfect world, she would have been able to find another job here but she had scoured the online classified section of the community's weekly newspaper and had come up with nothing but a few part-time, minimum wage retail jobs and a live-in companion to an elderly woman that specified Absolutely No Children, with several exclamation points.

She would figure something out. She had a couple of promising leads back in Boise already from some email inquiries she had sent out.

It only took a moment to pick up the two extra bedside lamps she had ordered for one of the guest suites that somehow didn't have any, then she drove back to the small commercial center of Haven Point.

From what she could tell, McKenzie Shaw's shop would be her best option for a few last-minute Christmas gifts.

She parked down the street and walked toward Point Made Flowers and Gifts, which was housed in a historic-looking redbrick building.

Chimes rang out like jingle bells as she pushed the door open. She was immediately greeted by a welcoming warmth and the cozy smell of cinnamon and apples, scents that conjured up home and hearth and old-fashioned Christmases.

Oh, this looked like just her kind of place, packed to the brim with clever little hard-to-find items. Oddly, the store appeared to be empty—except for a ginger-colored dog who rose to greet her.

The dog—a standard poodle wearing a bandana printed with gleaming green-and-gold Christmas ornaments—walked gracefully over to her, planted its haunches a few feet away and held up a hand just like a department store greeter.

"Hello. Are you in charge today?" she asked the dog, who seemed to give her an uncanny sort of grin.

Okay, strange. Where was McKenzie?

"Hello?" she called.

A moment later, a door in the back of the store popped open and McKenzie peeked her head around the frame. "Oh. I thought I heard the bell. Hi, Eliza! Great to see you! Welcome to Point Made."

"Thanks. I'm in love with your shop."

"Oh, thanks! I'm pretty crazy about it, too."

"I finally found a minute to get away from Snow Angel Cove for a bit and take care of a little of my Christmas shopping."

"This is the place for it. No Maddie today?"

Eliza shook her head. "I left her making sugar cookies with Sue."

"Lucky girl. A sugar cookie would be *fabulous* right about now."

"I'll have her save you a few and we'll drop them off next time we come to town."

"That sounds like an excellent plan." McKenzie gestured to the big poodle. "I see you've met Rika. Short for Paprika."

"Yes. She was very polite and greeted me with a handshake."

"She runs the place with an iron paw, don't let all that charm fool you."

Rika grinned at her owner then plopped down in a multicolored patch of sunlight coming through a display of stained glass sun catchers in the window.

Feminine laughter spilled out from the open doorway and what sounded like a good-natured argument. The mayor glanced back at the room and then at Eliza. "I'm so glad you stopped by today! What luck. You're just in time for lunch!"

"I am?"

"Yes. Take off your coat and come grab a bowl of soup. Some of us in town get together regularly for a potluck lunch. It's sort of an informal service club where we work on projects like crocheting afghans for the children's hospital in Boise or sending care packages to members of the armed forces from the area. We call ourselves the Haven Helping Hands. I know, really lame name. I wanted to call it the Pointer Sisters but I was vetoed. Apparently that's already taken."

"I like the Pointer Sisters. The musical group and the name, for what it's worth."

The incoming mayor beamed. "Thank you! I knew I liked you for a reason. Come on back. We've got tons of soup."

For just a moment, Eliza was torn. She should probably hurry to finish her shopping and return to Maddie. She also wasn't sure she *wanted* to meet more people and find more reasons to love Haven Point when she couldn't make her home here, after all.

On the other hand, Maddie was in excellent hands with Sue and it had been so very long since Eliza had socialized with other women outside of work. It also seemed rude to refuse after McKenzie and her sister had been nothing but kind to her.

"I can only stay a moment."

McKenzie beamed and led the way to a work-room that looked at least as large as the display area of Point Made gifts. Boxes were stacked around the edges of the room. At a long table in the middle, about a dozen women of various ages—from barely twentysomethings to a couple of women who looked to be in their sixties or early seventies—were eating and chatting.

Megan Hamilton was one of the first to spot her. "Eliza! Hi! I am so glad to see you. How are feeling after your accident?"

She smiled at the woman she had wanted for an employer. "I'm doing well. Thank you."

"I've been worrying about you and Maddie. I was so glad when Kenz told me you found work and are staying in the area through the holidays—even if the job is with Aidan Caine."

At the name, the entire room full of chattering women fell as silent as if Megan had just belched the alphabet.

All eyes fell on her and Eliza squirmed, not sure what to say.

"You work for Aidan Caine?" a plump, well-dressed woman with dark hair and warm brown eyes asked.

"Ye-es," Eliza said warily. Why was everyone staring at her?

"Is he as gorgeous in real life as he is on You-Tube?" one of the twentysomethings asked.

"I swear, I've watched his Ted Talk like a hundred times, just so I can swoon a little at the place where he takes his glasses off for a minute while making a point."

Eliza wasn't sure what to say. She had signed a confidentiality agreement. Did her opinion that he was even *more* sexy in person violate that agreement? She decided the wise course would be to remain quiet.

"What do you do there?" The question came from a tired-looking woman wearing a gray sweater that was fraying at the sleeves.

She wasn't sure whether she could talk about that, either. "My official job title is housekeeper. A little of this, a little of that. Do you all live here in Haven Point?"

As she hoped, the question seemed to turn the conversation away from tricky areas. "Oh, I should introduce everybody," McKenzie said. "Hang your coat over there and then grab a bowl of soup out of the slow cookers there—they have little signs that say what's in them. After you're settled, I'll tell you everyone's names."

She wasn't going to remember more than a few, but she supposed that didn't matter. In a few more weeks, she wouldn't meet these people again.

McKenzie was very good at ordering people around, which was probably a good skill for a mayor, Eliza thought in amusement as she obediently grabbed a bowl from a slow cooker marked White Chicken Chili, added a slice of thick-crusted bread and found a seat between the flower shop owner and Megan Hamilton.

"Okay, everybody, this is Eliza Hayward. She was supposed to start work this week for Megan but of course the inn fire has changed everything. Five minutes after she found out the inn burned down, she was hit by a car right outside here—driven by Aidan Caine himself."

"Oh, my word," a matronly woman with a silver-and-black bob exclaimed. "But you're okay?"

"It was just a tap," she assured her. "I'm really fine, nothing broken, just some scrapes and bruises."

"And now you work for Caine?" a woman with a poodle perm and a sour expression demanded.

"Only for a few weeks. He found out about the inn fire and that I was now unemployed and homeless because of it and insisted on my daughter and I staying at Snow Angel Cove for the holidays to help him out."

Poodle Perm snorted. "He can afford it. What else is he spending his money on? Not fixing up the buildings he owns in town so we can bring some real businesses in, that's for sure."

McKenzie frowned at the woman. "I'm sure he will. Give the man a chance, Linda."

"We don't have time for him to sit around on his ass looking gorgeous," she retorted. "Our holiday sales are down fifteen to twenty percent from last year. At this rate, my boutique won't be open by summer. Everybody is shopping at the new big box store in Shelter Springs, not here."

"How many times do I have to tell you, Mom?" the blonde twentysomething said. "Sales will pick up when you stop offering stuff that was out of date when *you* were in high school."

"My clients favor the traditional, classic items."

"Sure. For their funeral clothing."

The conversation devolved from there into what sounded like a familiar disagreement that had McKenzie rolling her eyes at Eliza. "Sorry," she said. "Don't mind the great Fremont family feud. Samantha wants to drag her mom into the twenty-first century, kicking and screaming if she has to. Let me introduce you to everyone else."

She went around the circle and introduced the women, the rest of whom seemed friendly and interested in her. Eliza knew she wouldn't remember half of them, though she had tried to use some of the memory devices to remember the names of guests at the hotel.

"This seems like a fun organization. How often do you get together?" she asked, when McKenzie had introduced everyone.

"A couple times a month, always on Friday," the mayor said. "We charge five dollars for the potluck lunch and give the money we raise to the food pantry. Usually we have a quick lunch and then a craft or something. Today we're just relaxing because we've been working like crazy making things for our booth tomorrow at the Lights on the Lake Festival."

"Oh, you mentioned that the other day. What is it, again?" she asked, innocently enough.

The volume in the room escalated as a dozen women answered her at once.

"Whoa. Slow down. Give the girl a break," said the woman with the salt-and-pepper bob—Maria, she remembered.

"The Lights on the Lake Festival was started by boat owners around here years ago. Since the lake usually doesn't freeze until late January, if at all, boat lovers decided to decorate their watercraft with Christmas lights and have a parade along the lake-front the Friday before Christmas. The whole thing exploded from there and now it's part gift bazaar, part food and music festival, part holiday celebra-tion. I've been the chairperson three years in a row. It's a wonderful time for all."

"It sounds lovely."

"Be sure to check out our booth. We're selling all kinds of gifts we've made through the year. All proceeds benefit the Lake Haven Library and their literacy program."

"Maddie would love the boat parade," Megan Hamilton said. "It's really magical to see all the boats with their lights sparkling on the water at sunset."

"Tell me what's going on with the inn," she prompted.

Megan sighed. "It looks like we're going to rebuild but it's going to take six months to a year. It's too bad you can't work for Aidan until I'm ready to reopen."

Eliza thought of that stunning kiss she couldn't shake from her memory and wasn't sure she agreed. Another few weeks of working for him and she would probably be more than a little in love with the man—exactly what she *didn't* need right now.

The conversation turned to holiday travel plans people had and when the group would meet again. She loved listening to the interaction of these women who were obviously a tight-knit group but were willing to open their ranks to her, a newcomer who wouldn't even be here in a few weeks.

At one point, one of the ladies cornered her to tell her a little more about the history of the area, a subject she found fascinating.

A short time later, the informal lunch started to break up.

"I've got to finish my errands and get back to Maddie," she said to McKenzie. "I'm just going to walk through your store for a few minutes to see if I can cross a few gifts off my list."

"Sure! Don't worry if you can't find what you want. Just come to the festival tomorrow and walk through the booths, especially our Helping Hands booth."

"Absolutely."

Under the watchful eye of Rika—who was probably a very formidable deterrent to shoplifters—she wandered through the displays of handmade and specialty items in the store. She ended up finding a pretty silk scarf and some delicious pear-scented handmade soap for Sue—along with buying ten more bars for the bathrooms at Snow Angel Cove—and a local author's book of cowboy poetry for Jim.

She couldn't come up with anything for Aidan. No surprise there. What could she possibly buy that might be meaningful to a man who had his own private jet, for crying out loud?

After Eliza paid for her items, McKenzie surprised her with a hug. "I'm so glad you came. I'm still keeping an eye out for a job around here. We want you to stay."

She smiled back, gave the dog a rub on the curly scruff just above her bandana and headed out into the cold wind that blew off the lake.

A quick trip to the pharmacy and grocery store later, she was loading bags into the back of her SUV when her cell phone rang.

"Hello?"

"Eliza, darlin', it's Sue. Tell me you haven't left town yet."

"I haven't left town yet," she answered dutifully. "I just finished at the grocery store and was about to head back."

"Oh, perfect! Listen, Aidan just called. His plane landed early and he needs a ride out to the ranch. We didn't expect him until later and Jim is still in Boise buying a new part for the tractor and I'm up to my elbows in frosting. Do you mind swinging past the airport there on the west side of the lake and picking him up?"

For all of about ten seconds, she couldn't answer. Her heart raced and her palms suddenly felt clammy.

Oh, for Pete's sake. She had to get a grip here. Yes, the last time she had seen the man he had kissed her senseless but she was a grown-up here. That was no reason for her to panic just at the thought of seeing him again. She worked for him and lived in his house! She couldn't avoid him forever.

"Um. Sure. I can do that."

"Thanks, hon. There's a sugar cookie in it for you when you get back, assuming your little girl doesn't eat all eight dozen of them first."

She heard a giggle in the background that warmed her heart.

"Everything going okay?" she asked

"We're having a great time and don't need you back anytime soon. If Aidan hadn't called, I would have told you to go see a movie or something."

"Thanks. Give her a hug from me."

"You bet. You can find Aidan at hangar twelve in the airport. It's the newest and biggest one, on the north end of the back row of buildings."

"Okay."

She blew out a breath. She could handle this. Yes, she had been ridiculously obsessed with that kiss. Just because he had left town shortly after—as if

he couldn't wait to get away from her—didn't mean
things had to be awkward between them. Right?

She sighed and backed out of the parking space,
then headed in the direction Sue had indicated, trying to keep her suddenly clammy palms from slip-
ping on the steering wheel.

The airport—really only a cluster of metal hangars and one taller concrete building that must serve
as the air traffic control center—was located on a
wide stretch of land just below the foothills with
broad views of the lake and the surrounding mountains.

She found the newest hangar easily and had just
pulled up in front when Aidan walked out wearing
a tailored peacoat with a worn tan leather laptop bag
strung over his shoulder and carrying a small duffel.
He looked distracted and tired and rumpled, his hair
tousled with deceptive casualness that still managed
to hide any trace of his scar.

And he looked sexy, she added silently.

Very, very sexy.

His eyes widened when he spotted her and she
thought she saw a quick flash of something else in
his expression, a heat that made those dancing butterflies in her stomach take to the floor again.

No, she was probably imagining it, she told herself as he lifted a hand in greeting and headed to the
passenger side of the SUV.

When he slid inside, the air seemed to shiver with
the luxurious scents of leather and the black pepper

and sandalwood of his soap—she knew it was his soap because she had discovered it in his shower a few days earlier when she was checking the towel supply there.

She hadn't meant to snoop but just walking into the en suite bathroom of the master bedroom at Snow Angel Cove had been an intoxicating sensory experience.

Now, having that familiar scent in the enclosed space of her vehicle sent all her pheromones into ecstasy until she sternly ordered them to cut it out.

"Hi," he said as he settled his duffel and briefcase behind the passenger seat. "I guess you're my ride."

"Sue just called and asked me to pick you up," she said quickly. "Apparently Jim is tied up out of town and since I was in Haven Point running errands, anyway, I told her I didn't mind."

"Thanks. I appreciate it. Sorry if I made you go out of your way, coming out to this side of town."

"You're paying for my time," she was compelled to remind him. "If you want a dozen doughnuts from my favorite shop in Boise, individually hand-delivered in twelve separate trips, it wouldn't make a difference to me."

He didn't quite smile but she thought some of the exhaustion seemed to seep out of his features. "I like maple bars. For future reference."

"Good to know. I'll keep that in mind."

For the next few moments, she concentrated on driving around the hangars toward the exit.

"How was California?" she finally asked when she pulled onto the main road that would lead them back to the lodge.

"Rainy, when I left. How have things been here?"

"It's been beautiful weather since you left. Today was even above freezing. A little of the snow is even melting, though I understand we're supposed to have a small storm Sunday. It should clear out before your family's travel day on Tuesday."

"That's good."

"Sue has been cooking up a storm. Your family is going to eat very, very well, I can promise you that. Maddie and I have almost finished preparing all the bedrooms. We've only got a few more things to do and should wrap up tomorrow."

"You work fast."

"It's a beautiful house. Making it a little more comfortable for your guests has been a joy."

"Good."

He seemed to settle farther in the seat and even closed his eyes for a moment. Did he have another headache? She wanted to ask but didn't want to bring up any reminders of that fateful night.

"You've been running errands, you said," he finally said after a moment.

"Yes. I ordered a couple of lamps for one of the guest rooms that didn't have them and then Sue asked me to pick up a few things at the grocery store."

"It seems like shopping opportunities are few and far between in town. The town must close up in the winter, not like my hometown. Winter is the busiest time of year back home, though high summer is beginning to draw as many visitors."

"I've seen pictures of Hope's Crossing. It's very pretty."

"You've never been there?"

She shook her head. "My family lived in Grand Junction for about six months when I was in elementary school but we didn't do a lot of sightseeing to other areas of Colorado."

"Why only six months?" he asked as they drove over the bridge that spanned the Hell's Fury River and headed around the east side of the lake toward Snow Angel Cove.

"My father was on a temporary job for the summer there. He was a road construction supervisor and we moved around a lot. I went to nine elementary schools in seven different states by the time I graduated sixth grade."

"That must have been tough on a kid."

"Yes." An understatement. "When I was thirteen, he got a more stable job as the county road supervisor on the central coast of Oregon so we stayed put through my high school years."

"What was your favorite place to live?"

She had to think about it. "Well, I did enjoy Lincoln City. We lived for four months on the Big Island in Hawaii. I loved waking up and smelling the ocean, being able to ride my bike down to the beach and play in the baby breakers. I even surfed a little.

There is something so…comforting about the water, you know?"

"Something we have in common. It's one of the things that drew me to Lake Haven. It's not quite the same as the ocean but a mountain lake offers its own kind of calm."

She thought of the lunch she had shared with the women in town and the bits of conversation she had picked up. "I think it only fair to let you know, you've put the whole town on edge."

He looked startled. "I have?"

"I stopped at Mayor Shaw's gift store earlier. Apparently a group of her friends gets together a few Friday afternoons a month for a buffet lunch. This happened to be one of them and they invited me to join them."

"That's nice. Haven Point seems like a very friendly town."

She wished again that it could have become *her* friendly town. All those years of moving around as a child had given her a deep desire to settle in a place where she and Maddie could belong. This would have been idyllic.

She had to stop wishing for the impossible. First a job that now didn't exist and then a man who might have kissed her once but certainly wouldn't make that mistake again.

CHAPTER FOURTEEN

SHE WAS NERVOUS.

As Eliza drove, Aidan couldn't help noticing the way her fingers would tighten and release on the steering wheel or the fine tension in her shoulders, the curve of her jaw, the way she pressed her lips together.

Was it because of that kiss?

He certainly hadn't been able to stop thinking about it. The entire time he was enmeshed in the last-minute negotiations for a software company he didn't even care about, he had been remembering the softness of her skin, those delectable little sounds she made, the sweetness of her mouth.

She was even lovelier than he remembered. He wanted to kiss her all over again. Even the headache pressing in against his skull wasn't enough to distract him from the aching need.

He dragged his attention back to more appropriate channels and tried to focus on what she was saying.

"Haven Point is a friendly town, from what I've seen," she said. "You should probably know, however, that the people of this friendly town all seem to be waiting with bated breath for you to make a move."

"Make a move?" For a crazy moment, he thought she was talking about kissing her again.

"Yes. You're now the biggest landlord in town. Did you know that? From what I gathered at lunch, you hold the title to a huge chunk of the available commercial space. It could reasonably be said that you own this town."

"That's an exaggeration." Yes, he knew Ben's holdings included several commercial buildings in town, along with the family's now-closed boat manufacturing plant.

Ben had been desperate to sell after years of trying to keep up with the property tax on his family's holdings in the town he now hated, for reasons he had never shared with Aidan.

He had been eager to unload the property and after one exploratory visit, Aidan had jumped at the chance. Okay, he might have been influenced by a brain tumor pressing in on critical decision-making parts of his brain, but his attorneys still assured him it had been a sound investment.

"It's not much of an exaggeration, from what I hear," Eliza went on. "At least not according to the leading ladies in town—the Haven Helping Hands. Yes. Lame name. They know. They all seem to think you have the power to make or break this town."

He rubbed at the side of his head where his scar

itched like crazy. "That's ridiculous. I don't have plans to make any changes in the immediate future. I just want to get through the holidays with my family."

"What about *after* the immediate future? I got the impression during the conversation over soup that everyone is worried you're going to let their downtown dry up and become a ghost town, like some of the empty towns on the north side of the lake. Or worse, they worry you'll bring in a ski resort—or five or six—until the whole lake area becomes just another Aspen or Vail—or Hope's Crossing—and loses all its character."

He frowned. "Hey. Hope's Crossing drips with character and charm. You should visit some day. It's a great place. Becoming a hot tourist destination doesn't automatically suck all the personality and sense of community out of a town."

She shifted her gaze from the road to him and then back again. "So you *are* planning to bring in some kind of big resort?"

"I didn't say that. I honestly don't know what I'm going to do yet. It hasn't been at the top of my priority list."

"Maybe not, but it is for the people of Haven Point. You might fly in for a weekend here and there but these women live here all the time, have their businesses here, raise their families. The local economy is obviously struggling. You've probably seen it yourself. Half the shops on Main Street are shuttered during what should be the busiest shopping season of the year."

And people thought *he* was going to sweep in like some white knight and make all the difference? The guy with the hole in his brain?

He wanted a place he could come to relax, not a new set of problems and more people who wanted him to fix them all.

"Why is this so important to you?" he asked.

She looked surprised that he would ask. "It's a nice town," she said after a moment. "I'd like to see it stay that way. I had an earful in the forty minutes I spent at the mayor's shop. Apparently back in the day—when people used to flock here by the thousands to take the miracle waters at the old Shelter Springs resort, before the waters all but dried up— this town was once completely dependent on tourist income. At one point the population was almost equal to Boise, or so Linda Fremont told me. She's apparently the self-appointed town historian. In the 1920s, the springs slowed to a trickle and the town started to die with it. This area has been struggling ever since. Your friend closing his family's boat factory was the last straw, apparently. People want to know what you plan and I can't say I blame them," Eliza said.

He had seen the shuttered buildings on Main Street but hadn't given it much thought. Really, the only thing he wanted in town was Snow Angel Cove but he supposed he was going to have to figure out what to do with the other buildings and the closed factory.

"As soon as I work up some kind of a game plan," he said slowly, "I'll schedule a town meeting or something to take input and spread the word. Will that help?"

"Yes! Oh, what a fabulous idea, Aidan. A town meeting would help everyone feel invested and involved. If you alienate the whole town from the beginning, you'll have a very hard time finding support later when you're ready to make changes."

"How do you know so much about community dynamics?"

"I don't. I just know from working in management and trying to motivate a team how important it is for everyone to feel like they have some skin in the game, you know?"

"You're right, which is why stock shares are an important part of the benefits package for all my employees."

"Whatever you decide, you definitely want to do whatever you can to get McKenzie Shaw on your side. She is not only the new mayor of Haven Point but I get the impression she's also a natural leader. It wasn't hard to see that she's the driving force behind the service group and though she's young, she's a firecracker. And watch out for a woman named Linda Fremont, the one I mentioned before. She is one of your tenants. She seems a little sour and not afraid to share her opinions. Her daughter Samantha seems pretty reasonable-minded, though."

"I will keep that in mind. Thank you for the suggestions. Very valuable insight."

Out of nowhere, Eliza blushed. "Sorry. It's a habit. I try to read people so I can determine how best to meet their needs as my guests. Sometimes I go overboard."

He was willing to bet she had picked up that habit while she was a young girl trying to make new friends in move after move to a new town.

"Don't apologize. It's a skill I envy. I'm much better at analyzing data and working with code than I am with personal relationships. They give me a headache, if you want the truth."

"Or maybe that's from the brain surgery you had three months ago."

He laughed, surprised and delighted somehow that she could joke about it. Most people in his world who actually knew about the surgery treated it as some dark, mysterious, rather embarrassing off-limits subject, as if he had a huge hairy wart on the tip of his nose. "Good point."

She cast him a sidelong look as she pulled up to the security gate and pressed the remote in the car so the gates swung open. "Did you try to see anybody about your headaches while you were in California?" she asked.

Her concern felt like a soft blanket tucked around

his shoulders, warm and comforting. "Yeah. The neurosurgeon gave me another med to try."

"Good. I hope you're able to enjoy the holidays with your family without too much pain."

"I should be fine."

She pulled her SUV in front of the house, shifted out of gear then turned to face him, her eyes serious. She was so lovely, prettier than a Christmas ornament, with those bright green eyes, and the little smattering of freckles over the bridge of her nose, he wanted to just gaze at her all day, his headache be damned.

He hadn't been able to stop thinking about that kiss. No other woman had ever jumbled him up inside like this. The whole flight back from California, he couldn't seem to shove down the anticipation bubbling through him, the feeling that he was, at long last, coming home to her.

"You know you're going to have a tough time keeping this from your family, right?"

"That's your opinion," he said, his voice more terse than he intended as he reminded himself he wasn't coming home to her or to Maddie. Eliza was his employee and Maddie was his employee's daughter. That was all.

She didn't seem to be deterred by his cold tone. "Think about it. Unless your family members are stupid or just completely oblivious, they're going to suspect something is wrong."

"Why would they?"

She gave him an exasperated look. "You had brain surgery, for heaven's sake! You have headaches that just about knock you to the ground. You've got a four-inch scar on your head that all the hair product in the world can't completely hide, once somebody knows where to look. With a house full of people, someone is bound to notice *something*."

He frowned. "I know what I'm doing when it comes to my family."

"I don't get the big secrecy, especially keeping something this big from your family—the people you're supposed to turn to when times are hard."

"It's not your job to understand anything." The headache sharpened his voice. "For the next week, your only job is to keep my family happy. That includes not divulging my confidential medical issues."

She recoiled a little as if he had smacked her and pressed her mouth together. "I overstepped. I'm sorry. You're right, your family dynamics are your own business."

"Eliza—"

She shook her head. "I'm going to pull into the garage but this is probably the most convenient place for you to get out."

She put a little more emphasis on the last two words than strictly warranted, not quite making them an order but close enough.

He gazed at her for a long moment. He wanted to tell her he was sorry for his abruptness but he wouldn't apologize for the motive behind it. He *didn't* want his family to know about his surgery. He had told her so. It would cause unnecessary drama and would make him the object of concern to his father, unwanted compassion to his sisters-in-law and deplorable pity to his brothers.

"Fine. Thank you for the ride."

"Just doing my job," she answered with a polite smile, in a perfectly pleasant voice he hated.

Aidan climbed out of the vehicle and headed into his house. Yeah. Give him an uncomplicated computer any day over people and their messy, tangled feelings.

THROUGH THAT EVENING and the next day, Aidan could tell she was avoiding him. She had plenty of excuses. The house. Her responsibilities. Her daughter.

An awkward tension seemed to crackle through the house like static electricity and he didn't know how to ease it. She was polite enough but not the warm, sweet woman whose company he had craved while he was in California.

He and Jim spent Saturday morning at a ranch twenty miles to the west with the horse trailer and the flatbed pickup, arranging for the loan of a large ten-person sleigh and a couple of sturdy draft horses so he could take his family around on Christmas Eve.

After unloading the horses and the sleigh, he headed inside to take off his hat and his coat in the mudroom. His stomach growled at the delicious scents coming from the kitchen—fresh bread mingling with some kind of hearty smelling dish. Vegetable beef soup, if he had to guess.

"Sue, my dear, I don't pay you nearly enough," he called out.

He heard her whiskey-rich voice laughing. "Da— er, darn right you don't," she answered.

Maddie must be in the kitchen with her, he thought when he heard Sue temper her typical salty language. He was smiling as he walked into the kitchen, until he found Eliza *and* Maddie at the table with bowls in front of them.

Maddie beamed at him. "Hi, Mr. Aidan."

"Hey, kiddo," he said with a smile.

Her mother's smile lacked both warmth and sincerity. What would she use as an excuse to escape his presence this time?

"We're almost finished," she said with some predictability. "We'll be out of your way in just a moment."

At her stiff tone, he mentally uttered the curse word Sue had swallowed back, and a few juicier imprecations along with it. He didn't like this stilted, cool Eliza. He wanted the one who freely offered advice, who was sweet and appealing, who kissed with her whole heart.

"Don't hurry off," he said. "I would enjoy the company."

Her mouth tightened and he realized that as her employer, he had just basically ordered her to stay and entertain him. Here was a grand example of why becoming involved with people who worked for him was a lousy idea.

"We're having beef and barley soup," Maddie announced. "It's very good, except I don't like barley."

Sue snickered, unoffended. "Next time I'll keep it out for you, except it will be plain old beef soup, then."

He went to the sink and washed his hands then pulled a bowl out and served himself from the big stockpot on the stove, then cut off a large slice of Sue's fabulous honey wheat bread.

He deliberately took a seat next to Maddie and across from Eliza.

"What have you been up to today?" he asked the girl.

"Helping my mama," she answered in a matter-of-fact tone. "We're making this big house into a real home instead of a fancy shell."

Now that sounded like she was parroting words she had heard from someone else. He glanced at Eliza and saw that delicate blush creeping over her cheekbones.

He managed to hide a smile at the last minute. He shouldn't enjoy seeing her a little embarrassed at her daughter's openness but after the way she had avoided him for nearly twenty-four hours, he would take amusement where he could find it.

"Do you know what? That's exactly what this place needs. You're both doing a fantastic job, too. I could tell the difference the moment I walked in yesterday. I especially love the pine boughs on all the fireplace mantels and the glittery pinecones in some of the rooms. Did you have anything to do with that?"

"Yes!" she exclaimed, looking delighted that he had noticed. "I helped spray paint them. It wasn't hard at all, just a little messy."

"You did an excellent job. I'm very impressed at your spray-painting skills."

"Look. The paint is almost gone from my fingers where I pushed the spray thingy."

She held up her pointer fingers and he did indeed see a little residue of metallic paint.

Sue chortled at that. "Hey, look at that. Guess you're not the only one at Snow Angel Cove with the golden touch, boss."

"Are you good at spray painting, too?" Maddie asked.

"Not as good as you," he assured her. She beamed at him and he was happy to see her mother seemed to have relaxed a little during the conversation. She even unbent enough to smile a little.

"How are the new additions to the barn?" Sue asked.

"All settled in. You'll have to go down and visit them. They are a couple of fine-looking gentlemen."

Maddie giggled. "That's silly. Gentlemen live in the house, not the barn!"

"These gentlemen are two new horses who are

visiting for a few weeks. They're going to help me with a surprise."

"What surprise?" she asked.

"I can't tell you yet. You'll have to wait until later this week. But you can come down to the barn and meet them."

"Now?" she asked eagerly. "Bob would like to meet them, too."

"We have some things to do this afternoon, honey. Maybe later," Eliza said.

"When Jim and I stopped for gas this morning, everybody was sure talking about the big boat parade tonight."

"Boat parade?" Maddie frowned. "How do they do that?"

Eliza answered. "Everyone in town decorates their boats with Christmas lights and then they float from the marina in town around the edge of the lake to Shelter Springs and then back to Haven Point."

"Christmas lights and boats? Oh, can we go see, Mama?" Maddie sounded breathless with excitement at the idea.

"It's so cold out. Who wants to watch a parade in the wintertime?"

"I think it sounds wonderful. I think we should all go together."

"That is an excellent idea, Sue," Aidan said. "Now I'm sure I don't pay you enough."

"Can we, Mama?" Maddie pressed.

Eliza looked torn. She obviously didn't want to

spend more time with him but he guessed she also didn't want to disappoint her daughter.

"Sure," she finally said with a smile. "That sounds like fun."

"According to the sign I saw in town," he said, "the boats leave the marina just after sunset, at about six o'clock, which means they would probably hit the downtown area about ten or fifteen minutes later. Let's leave at five-thirty, to be safe. That should give us time to park and find a good vantage point to watch the parade go past. We can all grab dinner in town somewhere and try to squeeze in a little shopping, too, if you want."

"I *love* shopping," Maddie informed him. "And I love parades, too. And boats, except I've never been on one."

He was rapidly coming to adore this sweet little girl. She made him smile, which he was discovering he didn't do nearly enough of. She made him want to do crazy things, like rent a boat, decorate it with Christmas lights and take her for a spin around the lake, just to make her happy.

Maybe next year.

Except she wouldn't be here next Christmas and neither would her lovely mother. He swallowed the bite of bread he had just taken, wondering why it suddenly tasted like horse feed.

He forced a smile. "Well, I love to eat so it sounds like the Lights on the Lake parade is something we definitely can't miss. It's a date, then. We'll all meet back here and go together."

"I cannot *wait!*" Maddie exclaimed.

Her mother didn't look nearly as enthusiastic, but Aidan figured he would have all night to make Eliza glad she had agreed to go.

CHAPTER FIFTEEN

"You have your mittens, right?"

"Yep." Maddie thrust out her hands to prove it. "And my hat and my scarf and I have on two pairs of socks under my socks. I'm going to be warm enough to bake beans."

Eliza gaped at her. "Where on earth did you hear that?"

"That's what Jim said yesterday when I helped him feed the horses. I asked if they were cold in the wintertime and he said their hide keeps them warm enough to bake beans."

Her daughter was going to come out of this sojourn at Snow Angel Cove with quite an education. Eliza had to smile. Both Jim and Sue treated her with such kindness. She was going to miss them both so much when the holidays were over and she and Maddie moved on.

Aidan's family would be arriving in just a few days. A little burst of panic fluttered through her. Twenty-something strangers, and she was charged with making sure they all enjoyed themselves—and she had to help Aidan keep a fairly significant secret from them, information she didn't believe should be withheld.

She had to put it from her mind. No need to panic. She had played host to plenty of strangers while working at the Diamond Street Inn. This wasn't any different, only perhaps on a more intimate level.

She had more immediate concerns, anyway—like how she was going to get through the evening in her employer's company without turning into even more of an idiot around him.

How could she have been stupid enough to argue with him about his own family? She still didn't think it was right for him to keep his brain surgery a secret from them, but he was absolutely right. That decision was his alone to make and her job was simply to honor his wishes, as she would do for any other employer.

At least the disagreement had served as a much-needed reminder of her place here at Snow Angel Cove. She was his employee, not his advisor or his confidante—or anything else that might involve heated kisses she still couldn't shake from her memory.

"All right. Let's do this." She gave the ends of Maddie's purple-and-pink scarf a little tweak, picked up her purse and walked with her daughter out into the kitchen, which she had quickly realized was the real heart of Snow Angel Cove.

Aidan sat alone in the sitting area in front of the

fireplace, reading something on his ubiquitous tablet. When he spotted them, he closed the cover and rose.

"Are you two ready for a boat parade?"

"Yes!" Maddie beamed.

"Let's go. I brought the ranch Suburban around the front of the house."

"Are we picking up Sue and Jim at the foreman's cottage?" she asked.

He shook his head. "They already left. Jim needed to pick something up at the farm implement store before it closed so I told them to go ahead. We'll try to meet up with them."

She drew in a sharp breath. That changed *everything*. She had been counting on the older couple to provide a buffer between her and Aidan. Now she was going to have to be alone with him except for Maddie, at least during the short drive to town.

"Let's go! I can't wait to see the boats!" Maddie exclaimed.

He smiled down at her. "Okay, Miss Maddie. You've got it."

Whatever her disagreements with the man and her self-protective instincts, she couldn't deny he was wonderful with her daughter. How was she supposed to keep any emotional barriers in place around him when he could be so sweetly patient with a five-year-old girl?

This ridiculous crush was one thing. Yes, it was mortifying—especially if he ever figured it out—but she could at least tell herself it was just a normal physiological reaction to a gorgeous-looking man who happened to kiss like he had written a doctoral thesis on effective technique.

It would be a disaster of a completely different nature if she let herself fall for him.

Eliza let out a breath. She couldn't seem to shake the idea that she was standing next to a railroad track watching a train race merrily along toward the inevitable plummet into the abyss.

She couldn't do this. Her mind raced, searching for some way to jump the track before it was too late and everyone onboard was doomed.

She could always say she wasn't feeling well, that her head was pounding or her stomach hurt. She could fake-sneeze a few times and pretend to be coming down with something.

At the thought, she rolled her eyes at herself. How pathetic. What kind of mother would deprive her child of a greatly anticipated treat, a festive holiday event, because she didn't trust herself to control her wayward feelings?

Couldn't she simply enjoy herself for the evening without falling head over heels for the man?

Absolutely. She hadn't taken enough time over the past few years to simply have fun.

"Let's go," she said, resolving to live in the moment and not worry about a million things at once. "We should probably hurry if we want to make sure we have a good spot to see the boats."

"Great. Let's go."

Maddie chattered from her booster seat in the backseat the entire drive to downtown Haven Point about everything and nothing. Eliza tried not to think how surreal it was that the CEO of a Fortune 500 company didn't seem the least bit bored.

Aidan actually seemed to be enjoying her daughter's conversation about everything from the movie she watched that morning about two cute elves to a book Eliza had read her the other night to a robot toy her friend Rodrigo in her Boise kindergarten class was going to ask Santa Claus to bring him.

The lake gleamed a brilliant blue in the fading sunlight as they reached the outskirts of town.

"Oh, look at the big Christmas tree at that house, Mad," she said, pointing out the window, just as her daughter was gearing up to start into a conversation about how she went to see Santa Claus at the mall, only he wasn't very fat.

Maddie allowed herself to be distracted. "It's pretty," she said. "But not as pretty as ours. And not as big, either."

She winced a little, wishing she could remind Maddie the Snow Angel Cove tree wasn't theirs. They had their own smaller tree in the sitting room of the cook's quarters that would be more than sufficient for their needs.

Maddie had become rather territorial about Aidan's house. She wondered if he noticed. Eliza had even reminded her that morning they wouldn't be staying there long, only through the holidays. "I know,

Mama," she had answered. "But when we have a house, I want it to look just like this one and I want to have a barn with six horses, too."

She didn't have the heart to tell her daughter they would most likely end up back in a crowded apartment building, probably without much of a yard at all. They certainly wouldn't have a barn with room for six horses.

"Why don't you see if you can find a snowman wearing a purple scarf before we arrive at the parade," she suggested. Sometimes little distractions like this were the only parenting ploy that kept her sane.

"A purple scarf like mine? Does it have to have pink flowers, too?"

"Any shade of purple will do, flowers or not," she answered.

Maddie immediately turned her attention outside the vehicle, frowning in concentration as she looked.

"Sorry," Eliza murmured to Aidan, pitching her voice low so her daughter couldn't hear from the backseat.

"For what?" he asked in the same low tone.

"Maddie likes to talk. I'm not sure if you noticed."

He gave her a half smile. "I don't mind. I have a few nieces and nephews, remember? Maggie and Ava could probably give lessons in chatter to all comers. Little Faith isn't much for conversation but her younger brother, Carter, will talk both ears off and your eyeballs, too, if you give him the chance. Maddie will fit right in with all the craziness."

She didn't anticipate her daughter spending too much time with his family, though she imagined some interaction would be inevitable.

"She is entirely too comfortable with adults, probably because she has spent so much time in the hospital, around doctors and nurses."

"She's a delight, Eliza. Full of life and joy. You should never apologize for raising a child who rushes out to embrace life the way she does."

His words seemed to resonate right into her heart. "You know, you're right. I should remember to appreciate those moments, especially in contrast to those moments when she's too sick to say much. Thank you for the reminder."

He gazed at her, a warm light in his eyes that gave her a strange ache in her chest. "You're welcome."

"I can't see a purple scarf *anywhere*," Maddie exclaimed dramatically.

"I'll help you look," Eliza said.

"Too late. We're here," Aidan said. "And look at that. This must be our lucky night. A perfect parking spot."

He skillfully parallel-parked between a minivan and an SUV with Oregon plates. It really was the perfect spot, close to what looked like the main viewing area.

"We *are* lucky," she said. "I can't see your name

on it but maybe the Chamber of Commerce saved it just for you. A sign of their goodwill and all."

He gave a short laugh as he opened the door and walked around to the passenger side of the vehicle to let them out.

He reached a hand out to help her over an icy patch on the sidewalk as she climbed out and she tried to ignore the little spark as his skin brushed hers.

He gazed at her with that strange light in his eyes that made the butterflies twirl again.

"Do you have gloves?" he asked. "It's cold out here."

She swallowed. "Yes. Right here."

She pulled them out of her pocket while he opened Maddie's door and lifted her out onto the sidewalk. While she adjusted Maddie's scarf again, Aidan pulled out a black wool hat with red stripes and planted it on his head.

"I like your hat," Maddie said.

"Thanks, bug."

He smiled that devastating smile of his. To Eliza, he added, "I'm not much of a hat-wearer but the neurosurgeon recommended it out in the cold as I continue to heal. My sister, Charlotte, made this one for me. I believe she is a better candy maker than she is a knitter but I still like it."

She shouldn't be so charmed that a man who could probably afford to buy an entire hat factory would

wear a slightly lopsided beanie because his sister
made it.

"Where can we see the boats? Is it time?" Maddie asked as Aidan pulled a couple of blankets out
of the backseat. She was practically jumping up and
down with excitement

"Almost. We'll go find a good spot." He pointed
toward the long, skinny parkway that ran through
most of the town along the lakeshore. "Looks like
that's where most of the action is taking place."

They headed toward a much bigger crowd than
she had yet seen in Haven Point. Maddie huddled
a little closer to her side as they walked past the
charred pile of rubble that used to be the inn.

Eliza sighed. It was only a small sound but it must
have been loud enough for Aidan to hear. He took
her arm to help her over the curb and gave it a comforting little squeeze before he released it.

"I'm sorry things didn't work out as you planned
when you came to Haven Point."

"Things rarely turn out the way we intend, do
they?"

"True enough."

"That's not always a bad thing," she observed.
"Sometimes the unexpected is better than what we
might have otherwise known. For instance, you probably never imagined when you were in high school
that one day you would be running your own company, did you?"

"No, and if someone had told me, I never would

have believed it. In retrospect, I guess it wasn't that much of a stretch. I always knew I had serious skills when it came to tech things and I fooled around on computers from the time I was little."

"A Geek God, even in elementary school."

He laughed. "Something like that. My parents always supported me—Mom, especially. Whenever Pop would grouse about me spending the money I earned working at the café on a faster processor or a beefier hard drive instead of saving for college, Mom always managed to calm him down."

"I would say that was a good gamble on her part, since all that computer time probably helped you get the full-ride scholarship to MIT."

He raised an eyebrow. "Have you been reading my press bio?"

Oh, crap. She could feel herself blush and hoped he would attribute it to brisk color in her cheeks from the cold, "My daughter and I are living in your house. You don't think I would do a little homework about you before I agreed to put my child and myself in a situation I might come to regret?"

A Google search didn't constitute cyber stalking. Exactly.

"Find out anything else interesting?"

Her blush intensified as she thought of the pictures she just might have looked at more than once, where he had looked gorgeous in a well-tailored tuxedo at some charity event in L.A., with a sexy, skinny model-type on his arm.

Fortunately, she was spared from having to answer as they neared the park when she heard someone calling her name.

She turned and spotted Barbara Serrano, one of the ladies she had met at McKenzie's shop, bundled onto a lawn chair next to a man who wore a scarf in exactly the same garish colors as Barbara's.

Eliza gave a small wave. Barbara returned it with a beaming smile as she rose and headed toward them.

"Hi! You made it! Oh, I'm so glad. You can't miss the Lights on the Lake! I was just telling Tom—that's my husband over there—this is my favorite night of the whole year. We're lucky. The weather's perfect for it this year, even above freezing. Two years ago, we had to cancel the whole thing because of a blizzard. Be glad the last storm we had hit early in the week instead of now. I was worried for a bit there. And who is this? You look just the age of my granddaughter Lacy."

"Hello. Pleased to meet you. I'm Madeline Elizabeth Hayward and I am five years old."

Barbara grinned at Maddie's formal self-introduction. "Hello, Madeline Elizabeth Hayward. I'm Barbara Renee Serrano."

Apparently her daughter had better manners than she did. "I'm sorry. Barbara, this is my daughter Maddie and this is, er, my employer, Aidan Caine. Aidan, Barbara and her husband own Serrano's, up on Main Street."

He smiled. "Hello. I'm happy to meet you. I've heard good things about your restaurant."

"Have you?"

She wasn't exactly cold to him but the friendly welcome she had given Eliza and Maddie was now nowhere in evidence.

"Serrano's is obviously popular with the locals. Every time I drive past, the place looks like it's hopping. That's always a good sign. It reminds me a lot of my father's café in Colorado."

Dropping that little tidbit of information, that his father had a café, pushed just the right button. The wariness in Barbara's gaze seemed to fade. "Next time, pull in instead of driving past. See what all the fuss is."

"I will do that. Thanks. Actually, I'll bring my father over the holidays when he comes to town. He loves to see what other successful restaurants are doing right."

This time she even gave him a smile. "We've got a booth over at the fair, where we're selling chili and fry bread. Old family recipe. All profits go to the Lake Haven Public Library."

"Sounds great," Eliza said. "Thanks for the tip."

"Oh, and make sure you stop by the Helping Hands booth for any last-minute shopping."

"We will definitely check it out. Thanks."

Maddie tugged on Eliza's coat. "When will the boat parade start, Mama? We haven't missed it, have we?"

"You haven't missed a thing," Barbara said cheerfully. "Now, you watch closely. My son and grand-sons have their little pontoon boat all decked out with red chili pepper lights and a big snowman."

"We'll watch for it."

"And on the very last boat," Barbara informed her, "you just might see a special visitor."

"Who is it?" Maddie asked, eyes wide.

"I'll give you a hint. He likes to dress in red and hang around with reindeer."

"Santa Claus?" Maddie breathed.

"Bingo," Barbara beamed at her.

"Barbie, where's the hot chocolate?" her husband called.

"Check my bag. I know it's there."

"I did. I can't find it. I bet you left it on the kitchen counter."

"I didn't leave it on the kitchen counter." She sighed. "I better go before he dumps my whole bag in the snow. Enjoy the parade."

"Thanks. You, too," Eliza said.

After she walked away, Aidan pointed toward the lakeshore, where waves licked at the rocks. "Looks like there's a bench open over there."

With all these people around, nobody had claimed the perfect spot, with a great view of the lake and even one of those portable propane heaters nearby? Had people deliberately left it available for him?

"What are the odds that you would find an empty bench tonight, amid all this chaos? I'm telling you, that kind of luck is unnatural."

He chuckled a little but his expression grew quickly serious again. "I'll remind you, you're speaking of luck to a man who just had surgery to remove a brain tumor. Plenty of things have gone my way in this life. But not everything."

It would be easy to think his world was perfect, without stress or challenge, but she definitely knew better. "Point taken. But tonight, you have to admit, you're lucky."

He smiled at her and Maddie, a warm light in those eyes that seemed to match the lake, glowing silver now in the dying rays of the sun. "Right now, I feel like the luckiest man in town."

She had expected him to use one of the blankets and give the other one to her and Maddie. Instead, he folded one for them to sit on and wrapped the other blanket around all three of them, enfolding them in a cozy little nest.

Oh, this was dangerous, for a woman already in danger of falling hard for him.

Easy, girl.

She tried to ignore the heat coming from him and the delicious scent that reminded her forcefully of that kiss.

"Tell me this," he said as they waited for the boat parade to start. "How is it you've spent less time in Haven Point than I have but you seem to have made friends with half the town?"

"That's a bit of an exaggeration. I've only met the

people I told you about, at the mayor's store yesterday. Everyone has been very kind."

"Not to me. I'm getting the skunk-eye from half the people here."

She looked around and saw he was right. People obviously knew exactly who he was. What would they think of her snuggling in a blanket with him?

She didn't have time to worry about it.

"Look, Mama!" Maddie, sandwiched between them, suddenly pointed. "Can you see the boats way down there? I think it's starting!"

She looked in the direction Maddie indicated and saw a glitter of lights on the horizon, growing larger by the moment.

"I do. Look at that!"

Maddie clasped her hands together. "Here they come! Here they come!"

By the time the boats actually approached their spot on the bench, Maddie was practically jumping up and down with excitement.

"Oh. Oh, they're so beautiful! It's like a fairy lake! Like Rapunzel and the lights in the sky on her birthday," she exclaimed, citing one of her favorite Disney animated movies.

Eliza's gaze met Aidan's and they shared a smile. She couldn't seem to look away and after a moment she could feel her smile slide away. She wanted him to kiss her again. Right now, even with Maddie squished between them.

She jerked her gaze back to the lake, horrified

at herself, and tried to focus on the progression
of boats, large and small, all bedecked with lights
and ornaments. Some were humble-looking fish-
ing boats, others were grand cabin cruisers. A few
regal-looking sailboats cruised along, too.

The light display was elaborate, with animated
snowmen, fish wearing beanies, even a couple of
surfing reindeer. It wasn't long, perhaps only twenty
boats, which was probably a good thing, given the
cold Idaho winter night.

On the last boat, Santa stood on the deck waving
to the cheering crowd as he sailed off out of sight.

"Oh," Maddie said. "That must be the last one. I
can't see any other lights."

"That was wonderful, wasn't it?"

Maddie nodded vigorously. "That was the best
parade I ever saw," she declared. "I didn't want it to
end. Can we come back next year and see the boats
again?"

Aidan seemed to tense beside her. She didn't
know how to answer her daughter without casting a
pall on the delightful evening.

She hated all over again that she hadn't figured
out a way to give her daughter the stability and roots
she wanted for her.

"I don't know where we will be next year, honey,"
she said, choosing her words carefully. "If we're
close enough to this area, we certainly will try."

A muscle seemed to flex in Aidan's jaw. "Wherever you might end up after you leave Haven Point,

I want you to know, you're more than welcome to come back for Christmas next year and stay at Snow Angel Cove. I hope you do. Even if I'm in California, the house is open to you. I'll make sure of it."

"Yay! I want to see that parade again. I loved, loved, *loved* it."

"You know, I did, too," Aidan said, smiling down at her. "Thanks for keeping me warm, you two."

He looked around. "Looks like everybody is leaving. I guess the show really is over. Should we head over to the booths and grab some of that chili your friend was talking about?"

"Great idea. We should try to find Sue and Jim, too."

If they found the other couple, perhaps she would be able to remember Aidan was her boss and that this wasn't a memory-making family outing.

CHAPTER SIXTEEN

In his entire life, Aidan had never been the recipient of so many charged glances.

It seemed as if every time he looked up from the cleared path ahead of them, he would meet the gaze of someone who would quickly look away again. Sometimes they appeared simply curious and a few were even friendly but others wore expressions of anxiousness and even outright anger.

When he made the deal to assume ownership of the land and property from Ben, he hadn't even considered how that decision would ripple through the small town as if a meteorite had plummeted into Lake Haven.

This was their town. He was an outsider. No wonder they were concerned about what his plans might be. Eliza was right. He needed to do *something* with the property he owned. The town meeting should probably take place sooner, rather than later.

He wasn't used to being accountable to anyone except his board of directors and stockholders. Even then, he owned the outright majority of stock in his own company and could usually make his own decisions about most things.

This was different. These people were invested in Haven Point and its surrounding communities. They had a stake in whatever he decided to do.

A tired-looking young woman with a bundled-up baby in her arms gave him a tentative smile as the man walking beside her picked up a boy who looked to be about three and hefted him onto his shoulders before he took the hand of a girl about Maddie's age.

The father wore a John Deere cap and his ranch coat had a grease stain on the arm. The little boy's coat was too big and his boots were bright yellow, probably passed down from his older sister.

As the fourth boy in a family of seven, Aidan had known his share of hand-me-downs. He hadn't had a brand-new, never-been-worn coat until he bought his own as a teenager, with money from working at Pop's café. His family hadn't been poor but they hadn't been wealthy, either, not with all those mouths to feed—and a father known for his openhanded generosity.

Aidan wasn't Dermot's son for nothing. His father had taught all of his children that each had an obligation to leave the world a little better than he—or she, in Charlotte's case—had found it.

He had the ability to make a huge difference in Haven Point, for good or for ill. It was a humbling realization.

Ben Kilpatrick was a good friend and someone Aidan respected and liked, but his inaction here had hurt the community's economy and morale.

If Aidan could help this little family somehow, along with all the others who were watching him so carefully, he had to try. It wasn't right for him to do nothing with the resources he now owned. Aidan had taken over Ben's properties and therefore also his responsibility. Like it or not.

"Oh, look." Eliza burst into his mental discussion. "There's the Serrano's chili booth."

This, at least, was something he *could* make a decision about. "Let's eat first and then we can spend a little time shopping, if you want."

"Sounds good."

He settled her and Maddie near one of the propane heaters then headed over to grab some food for them. He stood in line for only a few moments before he reached the counter, just as Barbara arrived to help take orders.

"Well? What did you think of our little celebration?" she asked.

"Very festive. Maddie and Eliza had a great time."

"She's a cute one, that girl."

"She is." With more courage than most adults, he thought.

"Too bad the two of them can't stick around town a little longer. Eliza seems like a woman who could use a friend or two."

Whenever he thought about Eliza and Maddie moving on and out of his life, he felt a weird little tug in his chest.

Before he could answer, he was jostled from behind. He turned around to find one of the men who had given him a less-than-welcoming look earlier.

"Sorry," the man said, with no trace of apology in his eyes. A strong whiff of alcohol wafted from him. "Didn't notice you there."

Tension rippled through Aidan. Thanks to his brothers, he had plenty of experience with barroom brawlers. Though they weren't anywhere close to a barroom, he sensed the man was half drunk and just stupid enough to think he could piss Aidan off enough to take a swing at him.

"No worries," he answered. He could certainly take care of himself—again, thanks to his brothers— but he didn't want to cause trouble with Eliza and Maddie a few yards away.

"What do you want, Jimmy?" Barbara asked, with enough wary impatience in her voice to make Aidan quite sure this was the town rabble-rouser

"What the hell you think I want? Chili! I want chili and some of that fry bread. Otherwise I'd a gone to another booth, right? Put some hustle in it, would you? I'm starving and I've got to get back to work."

"You'll have to wait your turn. It will be a few minutes before we have a new batch of fry bread."

"What about that one?" He pointed to the fluffy pieces of golden bread draining on a rack.

"Those are for Mr. Caine and his party."

"The rich bastard can wait. Some of us who actually have to work for a living ought to have first dibs."

Barbara glared at him. "Two more minutes. That's all, then the new batch will be done."

"I don't want to wait. I want one of them that are already finished. Let *him* wait."

"He was here first. Don't be a jerk, Jimmy. You want me to tell your ma you were harassing Mr Caine here?"

"Go ahead. She won't care. She hates his guts, too, thinking he owns the whole town just because he has a fancy house and a big old airplane."

Aidan managed to rein in his temper. "Don't forget the ninja security force that follows me around specifically to deal with assholes."

The guy looked around as if he didn't know whether to believe him or not. "I'm just kidding." Aidan forced a smile. He had figured out early in the game that confusing and disarming opponents was a far more effective strategy than outright warfare. "Here. Your lunch is on me. Barbara, give the working man here one of those pieces of fry bread over there. We only need two."

Jimmy looked like he didn't know how to respond as Barbara quickly complied and served up a bowl for him and then three more for Aidan, obviously anxious to defuse the tension.

"What was that about?" Eliza asked when he carried over their tray.

"Just meeting a few of the locals," he answered.

"It's a nice town, don't you think? Everybody is so friendly."

Not quite everybody. "Yes. And the food looks good, too."

They finished eating and then walked through the booths for a little while. He bought several things he didn't need or want, especially from booths whose proprietors were friendly to Eliza or Maddie.

A short distance from the gift show, the town council had set up a little Christmas village filled with animatronic elf figures hammering, sawing or nailing Christmas toys.

Aidan paid the dollar admission for each of them and then they wandered through. It was worth the dollar and more, the way Maddie's eyes lit up with excitement at each new animatronic figure. They spent a good twenty minutes inside the little village but as they passed the last elf, he saw Maddie yawn for the second time in as many minutes.

"It's getting late. We should probably head back to Snow Angel Cove."

"No! We haven't seen the petting zoo yet."

"We might have to catch that another night, honey," Eliza said gently.

Her patience and love for her daughter warmed him. He was coming to admire so many things about Ms. Eliza Hayward. Her resilience in the face of adversity, the wry sense of humor she tried to hide, but especially the loving care she took of her child.

"I don't want to go back." Maddie's lower lip trembled enough to turn even the hardest heart into dough.

"I know." Eliza smiled sympathetically. "That must be so disappointing for you."

She was a genius of a mother, with a real knack for showing compassion for her daughter's perspective without giving an inch.

"It is!" Maddie declared.

"It's been a big day and I'm pretty tired. I'm a little cold, too. Some hot cocoa by the fire and the Christmas tree back at Snow Angel Cove sure sounds nice," Aidan said. The second part, at least, was the truth.

"I am a little cold, too, I guess." She yawned again, a huge, wide, ear-popping stretch of her mouth, and he had to smile. At this rate, she wasn't going to make it home, forget about hot cocoa.

"Let's go find our warm car."

As he expected, Maddie fell asleep in her booster seat before they even hit the outskirts of Haven Point. One minute, she was chattering away about the parade and about seeing Santa Claus and the cute doll with the curly hair like hers she had seen at one of the booths—which he had sneaked back and purchased, though neither she nor her mother knew. In the middle of a sentence once again extolling her favorite boat in the parade, her eyelids drooped and her words trailed off.

He glanced in the rearview mirror at the sudden silence. Her head lolled to the side and her mouth was slightly open. She was completely adorable and he would have to possess a heart of tungsten carbide not to be crazy about her.

"Looks like she's out," he murmured.

Eliza shifted around to look behind the seat. He loved the way her eyes turned soft at the sight of her child.

"She runs hard all day, then usually collapses. She's always been that way."

"Her medical condition doesn't seem to get in the way of her energy level."

"She's usually pretty good at pacing herself. I think it must be some natural-born instinct. She knows when something is too much for her to handle—a talent I sometimes wish I shared."

She added the last slightly cryptic comment in a bit of an undertone and he had to wonder what she meant.

"I wonder where Sue and Jim ended up," she said after a moment. "We never did run into them."

"There was quite a crowd tonight. I guess we missed them somehow."

"I'm glad we came," she admitted. "Thank you for the invitation. Maddie enjoyed herself immensely."

He shifted his gaze from the road briefly, just long enough to wish he could pull over and kiss her.

How had this woman and her child become so important to him after only a week in his life, especially when he had been gone for half of that?

"What about you? Did you enjoy yourself?" he asked.

"Yes." When she finally answered, her voice was small, as if she didn't want to admit it.

"You're allowed to have fun, you know."

"I have plenty of fun," she said, bristling a little.

"How?" he asked, genuinely curious. He wanted to follow and tug and unravel all the tangled little pieces of her. "What brings you joy, besides Maddie?"

She made a small sound of amusement. "That's like asking someone how he breathes without air. She's everything to me."

"But you're a woman first, before you're a mother. What does the non-maternal side of you enjoy?"

"You don't ask the easy questions, do you?"

He shrugged and waited for her to think through her answer.

"I love to run, when the weather is good," she finally said. "It's tough to do that with Maddie. It was easier with a regular jogger when she was smaller. Last summer I bought an oversize one and we still go, though I don't know how much longer she'll fit."

She was right, her world was inexorably tied to her daughter's. He wasn't really surprised. He had seen it in his siblings with their children. His three older brothers were all excellent fathers, patient and loving—which surprised the hell out of him, considering how they had all tormented each other growing up.

"What else?" he asked.

She was silent, gazing out through the windshield,

her face in lovely profile. "On cold winter nights like this one, after Maddie's asleep and the house is still, I love to read curled up on my sofa with a warm throw and a cup of tea. It's a total indulgence. I love finding treasures at garage sales for next to nothing and repurposing them into something wonderful for our apartment. I love fresh-cut Christmas trees—who doesn't, really?—and summer evenings that stretch out forever and crunching through dry leaves on a mountain trail that smells earthy and musty with autumn."

He smiled, enchanted with her. "I do believe that is the most you've ever said about yourself since we met."

She shifted, clearly uncomfortable. "Because I'm basically a boring person."

He would firmly disagree. She was one of the most fascinating people he had ever met, made up of textures and layers and subtleties.

"What about you?" she asked. "What brings you joy? And since you wouldn't let me say Maddie, I'm making the same rule for you. You can't answer the obvious, your family."

Since that was exactly how he intended to answer, he had to regroup. "Fair enough. If you want the truth, I've had a little more time to think about this very question these last few months, especially in those few weeks before the doctors knew the tumor was benign. The possibility of everything ending

long before you expect it to tends to distill everything in your life to the essentials."

She made a tiny sound, just an exhalation, really,
and reached a hand out to squeeze his arm, a sponta-
neous comforting gesture that just about slayed him.

Too quickly, she returned her hand to her lap. He
suspected if he could see her in the dark, she would
be blushing.

He cleared his throat. "Okay. To answer your
question. What brings me joy. I also love running—
something we have in common. During the initial
weeks after my recovery when I wanted absolute
privacy, I leased a place on the coast between Car-
mel and Big Sur. After I worked up to it for a few
weeks, I discovered I love to run on the beach there
just as the sun is coming up behind the mountains."

"That sounds lovely. What else?"

This was tough for him. He was an inherently private person. Not shy, exactly, just…self-contained.
His brother Jamie would spill his life story to any
girl he met in a bar but Aidan would guess that even
Louise and his other close associates didn't really
know the heart of him.

"The horses, naturally. I guess that's obvious. I
bought an entire ranch and half of a town, apparently,
so I can have a place for them. I don't know what it
is, but just being around them calms me. It takes me
back to my childhood and summers I would spend
with my grandparents."

His mother had loved horses, too. She had always stabled a horse at one of the ranches outside of Hope's Crossing and had gone riding in the mountains around town. Her mental vacation, she used to tell them. Of all the Caine children, he was really the only one who shared that love with her.

"I love a good basketball game, playing it or watching it."

"Are you any good?"

"Not really. Doesn't stop me from enjoying it. I'm the unathletic one of my brothers."

"Somehow I doubt that," she murmured.

Heat swirled between them, not all of it coming from the vehicle's ventilation system.

"What else brings you joy?" she asked, rather quickly.

"Hmm. I love sleeping on good sheets and that first sip of coffee in the morning and fine-aged Scotch. I love going to the opera, but if you tell my brothers, I'll deny it with all the breath left in my body."

She laughed softly. "Secrets and more secrets. I'm not going to be able to open my mouth when your family is here."

He smiled and realized he was quickly becoming crazy about her, too. He had a sudden disorienting, unsettling urge to reach for her hand, to drive through the quiet, peaceful dark with her fingers tucked in his.

Did she sense the connection between them? The fragile threads that seemed to curl and twine around them?

He pushed away the impulse, curled his own fingers against his thigh and forced himself to continue the conversational thread.

"That's about it. Though—and this is probably going to sound arrogant as hell—I have to admit that I love what I have created with Caine Tech. It's not really the material things that success has afforded me. I never sought that, though you won't hear me complain about having them now. You were right earlier, I have been incredibly lucky in my life in some areas. Beyond all the perks of that success, I love knowing that a device or an app I created is making someone's life easier—*many* people's lives, more than I ever imagined. It's an incredible rush. Indescribable, really. Sometimes I still can't quite believe it's real."

He also couldn't believe he had spilled something so intimate with her. "I don't think I've articulated that to another person before."

"Thank you for being willing to share it with me," she murmured.

"You're probably sorry you asked."

She shook her head. "Not at all. How could I be? You're a fascinating man, Aidan. More so now that I see a little of the man behind the Geek God legend."

To his embarrassment, he could feel himself flush at the mortifying nickname from an in-depth article one of the newsmagazines had done on him. Brendan and Dylan still called him that when they wanted to rile him, usually when they were head to head on the basketball court.

Fortunately, he was saved from having to respond when they pulled up to the house. He glanced in the mirror and saw Maddie hadn't stirred.

"Will I wake her up if I carry her in?"

"I doubt it. She can sleep through just about anything."

He scooped up the little girl. She made a tiny sound, snuggling against him, and he felt an odd little catch in his throat.

All this time, he had told himself he didn't want the chaos or stress of kids. Let other people with more patience, time and inclination deal with propagating the species, he had always figured.

Just went to show how stupid he could be about some things. What the hell was he thinking? This was just about the sweetest thing he could imagine, to have a little creature turn to you in full trust for warmth and security in a crazy, messed-up world.

Eliza opened the door to the cook's quarters. The room smelled like her, like vanilla bean and citrus and summer flowers all mixed together. She had made the space their own over the past week, he was happy to see. Toys were piled in a big wicker basket next to the comfortable easy chair and a little Christmas tree stood on a table in the corner with presents underneath. She had piled throw pillows on the sofa and even hung a picture of a lovely cottage by the sea with a mother and daughter walking along the shore, hand in hand.

She was so good at making a space warm and inviting. He had walked through the guest rooms the other night and loved all the welcoming little touches she had created for his family.

"Where would you like me to put her?" he whispered.

She pointed to the bedroom and he followed her. Here, too, the space was theirs, with a pink comforter on one bed and another bright blue comforter splashed with purple-and-yellow flowers on the other.

"Give me a minute to get the bed ready," she murmured.

She pulled back the comforter and then gestured to him. The girl didn't stir as he carried her in and set her down. Eliza quickly pulled her boots and coat off in silence and handed them to Aidan, pointing to the other room.

He carried them into the little sitting room and waited while Eliza presumably changed Maddie into pajamas and tucked her in.

He should probably go but he found himself deeply reluctant for the evening to end.

When she walked out of the bedroom and closed the door behind her, she looked a little surprised to see him still there.

"I didn't know where you keep these." He held out the coat and boots in his hands.

"The mudroom. Sorry. I should have told you."

"Oh. Right." He felt stupid for not figuring it out. "I can take them."

She walked out into the kitchen and then to the mudroom, where she hung her coat and Maddie's while he did the same with his own.

"Thank you again," she said. "We both had a wonderful time."

He didn't want the evening to end. Not yet. "It's still early. We were supposed to end the evening with hot cocoa by the fire, remember? You haven't had anything until you've tried my pop's famous real chocolate cocoa."

"That was a bribe for Maddie's sake and she's sound asleep," she pointed out.

"What would I have to offer to bribe you to stay?"

"Oh, I'm fairly impervious to bribes or blackmail," she said, with rather adorable primness.

"Fine. I'll just ask you, then. I'm not ready for the evening to end yet. Will you have some of my pop's hot cocoa with me?"

CHAPTER SEVENTEEN

SHE SHOULD REFUSE. If she were wise, she would bid him good-night, escape into her rooms and close the door firmly behind her.

Clearly, she wasn't very wise.

The bald truth was, she shared his sentiments. She wanted to spend more time with him. The night had been wonderful. Whether it was foolish or self-ish or both, she just knew she wasn't ready to close the door on the evening quite yet.

He had been so sweet to both of them all night: teasing and funny, protective and kind. With Mad-die, he had been extraordinarily gentle, taking de light in the simple pleasure of Christmas lights on the water simply because the little girl had loved it.

That quiet conversation in the enforced intimacy of the SUV seemed to echo between them, remind-ing her all too forcefully that for almost six years—and especially the past three on her own—she had dedicated everything she was and had ever been to her daughter. She had made every choice with Mad-die in mind, first and foremost.

As Aidan so eloquently reminded her, before she

was a mother, she was also a woman—something she had lost sight of along the way.

Foolish it might be, but this man made her feel glittery and bright and *alive.*

Yes, she knew this wasn't anything approaching the beginnings of a relationship. She wasn't a complete idiot. They were attracted to each other, certainly. Crazy as it might be, she was still at least woman enough to sense a man's interest.

Aidan Caine was attracted to *her,* an idea she found stunning and intoxicating at the same time.

Physical desire between them was one thing, a natural—if shocking—human reaction, but the idea of anything beyond that was simply laughable. The barriers between them might as well be as formidable and unbreachable as the raw-spined Redemption Mountains.

She fully understood all that. Even so, what would be the harm in spending an hour in conversation with him? Maybe, if she were honest, sharing another one of those intense and magical kisses, if the opportunity presented itself?

"I didn't realize I was presenting a decision of such enormity. It's only hot chocolate, Eliza. With maybe a little Irish whiskey in it, if you'd like."

Heat soaked her cheeks and she sincerely hoped he couldn't see it, that he never suspected she was contemplating sharing more than a drink with him. "I'm sorry. I was woolgathering."

She let out a breath, feeling as if she were about

to take a giant leap off the top of his barn. "Yes. I would love some hot chocolate. Thanks. Just cocoa, though, please."

She had enough trouble feeling intoxicated when she was with him.

He gave her that astonishing smile—bright, un-fettered, genuine—that seemed to turn him into an-other person.

"Coming right up, then. People travel across oceans and continents for some of Pop's hot cocoa. Okay," he amended, "for Pop's cocoa and the world-class skiing in Hope's Crossing."

"You really don't have to go to any trouble. Sue has been stocking up on gourmet cocoa mix. There are several flavors in the pantry that would suit me fine. I'm not picky."

He shook his head. "You won't say that after you have Pop's cocoa. It will spoil you for anything else."

His words had an unfortunate ring of truth. She was very afraid spending this Christmas season at Snow Angel Cove would spoil her for any other hol-iday.

"I need to go take off my boots and check to make sure Maddie went back to sleep."

"Great. I'll get started, then."

She hurried into her rooms. After switching to ballet flats and checking on Maddie, who was sleep-ing soundly, she hurried to the bathroom. Hoping he didn't notice, she ran a brush through her hair, scrubbed her teeth and reapplied a little lip gloss.

When she walked into the kitchen, she found Aidan wearing a black apron and standing at the big six-burner stove, stirring the contents of a small saucepan with a wooden spoon.

"Something smells delicious," she said. A lesser woman might get drunk on the smell of rich chocolate alone.

And him.

"It tastes better than it smells. Trust me. We're almost there, just a few degrees shy of full boil."

The chocolate or her hormones? She let out a breath and took a seat at the work island in order to watch him work. She thought again how comfortable he was in the kitchen. She almost found that more sexy than the whole Geek God thing he had going.

"And there we go," he said, removing the pan from the burner. "Now the finishing touch."

He reached into a small spice jar, pinched something between his fingers and scattered it over the pan, then shook a little salt from a shaker onto his palm before adding it to the contents of the pan.

"You added salt and what else?"

"Just a tiny bit of cinnamon. A quarter teaspoon is all you need. I would tell you that's the secret ingredient but the real secret to this masterpiece is shaving in the fine chocolate—at least seventy percent cocoa—to the light cream and whole milk."

"Wow. That sounds…insanely decadent."

"Pop would sometimes add just a dollop of some Kilbeggan or Baileys to give a little extra kick. Not at the café, of course, just at home. After we were of age, of course. I think it works fine without."

He poured some of the thick concoction into two mugs, then presented it to her with a dramatic flourish.

He then *really* impressed her by rinsing out the pan in the sink. A man might cook like a dream, but cleaning up after himself—especially when he paid people to do that for him—kicked everything up a notch or two or ten.

"Shall we go in by the fire?" he asked after he hung the apron up on a hook inside the pantry door.

Oh, this was a mistake of fairly epic proportion. She could see no graceful or polite way to back out now, after he had gone to so much trouble for her. Best to just weather through it and make her escape as soon as she could manage it.

She nodded and headed into the great room. He had turned on the fire and the lights of the tree. The room's perfectly proportioned elegance struck her again, as it always did. The warm golden timbers, the smooth stones of the fireplace, the massive floor-to-ceiling windows and the little touches she had added combined to make it comfortable and cozy, despite its grand size.

When she first came here, the room had felt like the lobby of some old lodge in a national park. Crater Lake or Grand Teton, maybe. Beautiful, certainly, but a little too formal for someone's home.

Now it was just right.

She settled in the armchair closest to the fire, leaving the sofa for Aidan. When she was finally comfortable, she took a sip of the hot chocolate and just about had a culinary orgasm on the spot. She might have even gasped out his name.

"Oh, my word," she exclaimed. "That just might be the best thing I have ever tasted."

He laughed, obviously gratified—as well he should be. "I'm glad you like it. Make sure you tell Pop when he gets here. He'll be tickled, both that I fixed it for you and that you enjoyed it."

"*Enjoy* is a gross understatement."

She sipped at it again and her taste buds burst into song. It was like an explosion of deliciousness, chocolate and cream with just that hint of cinnamon to add a little bite.

A light snow had begun to fall through the big window and with the flames dancing in the grate and the tree lights twinkling, this seemed the perfect ending to a really good day.

"I wonder what happened to Sue and Jim?" she mused.

"Oh, I meant to tell you. I called her while I was shaving the chocolate. Apparently she twisted her ankle after the parade so they cut the night short."

She set down her cup on one of the coasters she had set out in all the rooms. "Oh, no. Does she need anything?"

"I doubt it. She said she was heading straight to bed. She figured a good night's sleep would help."

"I hope it's not serious."

"She didn't seem to think so. Wouldn't that be a nightmare? A house filled with twenty people and no cook? The good news is, Pop is something of an expert on feeding a crowd so at least we wouldn't starve, but I really want him to be able to rest and enjoy the holidays, if he can."

From the sound of it, Dermot Caine sounded like a man who loved feeding other people. She wasn't sure an enforced vacation from his passion was exactly what he needed, but it seemed presumptuous to disagree.

"I can certainly pitch in if necessary. I'm not exactly an expert in the kitchen but I take direction well."

He smiled with a warm look in his eyes that felt as rich and heady as the chocolate sliding down. "Let's hope it doesn't come to that, but thank you for the offer. I imagine my sisters-in-law and Charlotte would probably be there helping out, too. Usually the Caines suffer from having too many cooks in the kitchen instead of a dearth of them."

"Your family really does sound wonderful. I can't wait to meet them all."

"I hope I haven't built them up too much. Like any family, we have our issues. My brothers can combine to be a huge pain in the ass, if you want the truth. Between Katherine, Charlotte, Lucy and my sisters-in-law, they'll all probably take one look at you and want to find you another husband."

The thick hot chocolate she had been swallowing seemed to clog in her throat. "A…husband?"

"Genevieve, in particular, thinks she's a matchmaker of some renown."

"Oh."

She couldn't think of a single thing to say to that so she took one more small sip of hot chocolate. Even without any Irish whiskey, the stuff was rich and just sweet enough to sparkle through her bloodstream, leaving her feeling vaguely tipsy.

"Don't worry," he said gently. "I'll tell them to back off, that you're still grieving for Maddie's dad."

She blinked. "Am I?"

"You don't talk about your late husband. I don't even know his name. I assumed the loss is still too raw, that you loved him too much. Am I wrong?"

She set her mug down, the flavor a little bittersweet now. Her feelings for Trent were such a mixed-up jumble, the answer to that question was far from simple. "His name was Trent," she said, her voice low. "Trent Hayward."

She waited for some spark of recognition, maybe, but he had no reaction other than sympathy. What else did she expect? He had probably never heard of her husband.

"I *did* love him. He was a…good father. He loved Maddie and wanted the very best life for her he could provide."

Unfortunately, she could see now that never would have been enough for Trent. Even if he had somehow miraculously managed to strike it rich, he never would have been content. He always would have wanted more and more.

"I'm sorry. If it's not too painful, can I ask how he died?"

This was it. She had to tell him. He had asked directly and she didn't feel right about lying to him.

"He was killed in a one-car accident. He had been drinking, something he usually didn't do, and struck a concrete barrier on the 101."

"Oh, El. I'm so sorry."

She pressed her lips together at the way he said her name, like an endearment. Suddenly she wanted to tell him all of it.

"He was out of town on a business trip San Jose, California."

He sat back, brow furrowed. "Really? Wow, that's a coincidence."

Not at all. She sighed. "It was...a very difficult time. Arranging for his body to be flown back, dealing with the police investigation."

"Investigation? It was a one-car accident. That couldn't have been too complicated."

She felt cold suddenly, even though the fire merrily cranked out heat.

"Not really. Just lingering questions. There was no indication he braked before the accident."

He watched her in the firelight, that blue-eyed gaze intense. "Do you think he killed himself?"

"I don't know. The hard truth is, I never will. He

was a good man but toward the last few years of our marriage, things were strained. He wasn't happy. I have to believe it was something inside of him. He couldn't be content. I do know his business trip didn't go well and he was…upset about it. He wanted so much to be a good provider for Maddie. He was trying to sell this brilliant idea for a new app he thought would be the answer to all our problems."

His gaze sharpened. "An app?"

"Yes. But apparently Caine Tech wasn't interested."

"Caine Tech?" His jaw dropped and he uttered an oath, looking vaguely ill.

She shrugged. "Trent wanted to deal with the best. That's you. He met with a couple of your minions. I don't know their names. He said they didn't even listen to the whole idea before they shut him down. The meeting lasted all of ten minutes."

"Eliza. I had no idea, I swear."

She liked it better when he called her El. Or even Ellie.

"I know you didn't. Believe me, I know. None of it was your fault. Oh, I might have blamed you and your company for a while. It was easier than facing the truth, that my husband had a problem that was rapidly spiraling out of control. Not drinking, he rarely did that. But he was obsessed with money and success and refused to see everything he was losing along the way. The way things were going, I

don't think our marriage would have survived another year or two."

She gave a tremulous smile. "So when you say
the loss is still too painful for me, I don't know how
to answer. I still grieve for Trent Hayward and the
part of me that loved him once always will...but I
grieve more for the loss of Maddie's father than for
my husband."

"Maddie's father, who died after an unsuccessful
meeting with *my* company."

"Aidan, don't go there. Your company's involve-
ment was incidental in the whole mess. He made
his choices all along the way, first to drink when he
knew he didn't have the head for it and then to get
behind the wheel of a car."

"Regardless, I'm so sorry. And then I basically
mowed you down on the street." He swore again, so
emphatically she had to smile a little.

"Also not your fault. We've established that was
an accident and I've suffered no lasting effect."

Except the loss of her heart, if she wasn't very,
very careful over the next few days, she added silently.

"From the very first, I wanted to tell you about
Trent and his last meeting with your company. It
seemed like an uncomfortable secret I didn't want
to keep but I didn't know how to bring it up."

"I'm glad you did. I can't believe you would come
to work at Snow Angel Cove at all. You must be sorry
you ever heard of me."

"How could I be?" she murmured.

He gazed at her, blue eyes glittering with emotions she couldn't name, and the moment seemed to stretch between them, as thick and heady as the chocolate he had melted for her.

This was dangerous territory, she knew. She had to go, before she made a mistake she would regret for a long time.

"And now I think I had better go to bed. I find confessions exhausting, don't you?"

He stood up as well. "Here's a confession for you, then. I haven't been able to stop thinking about that kiss the other night."

She stared at him, the empty mug heavy in her hand. Oh, yes. Dangerous territory.

"If we're being frank with each other," she whispered, "neither have I."

His gaze shifted to her mouth and she swallowed, already tasting him there. He made no move to kiss her, though, only continued to let the moment stretch out between them.

He was giving her control, letting her make the decision about whether there would be another kiss between them, she realized.

She tried to order herself to move away. The smart choice would be to take the mug into the kitchen, rinse it out and then escape to her bedroom.

She was tired of always making the smart choice. Why couldn't she dance close to the fire, for once in her life? Okay, maybe her toes might get burned, but at least she would be warm for a while.

When she was old and gray, she could see his face on a magazine somewhere and remember the time when he had wanted her, if only for a moment.

For all she knew, that kiss the other day had been a fluke. Didn't they owe it to each other to find out for sure?

With a sense of inevitability, she set the mug back down on the table with fingers that trembled and then, without giving herself an instant to talk herself out of the insanity of it, she stepped forward and lifted her mouth to his.

He let out a little groan, as if he hadn't been sure which course she would take, and wrapped his arms tightly around her.

His father's cocoa was delicious enough straight out of the cup. It was absolutely intoxicating when it flavored their kiss and turned it into a sensory experience of chocolate and heaven.

If the kiss the other night had been a shock of heat and fire, this one was slow and sensual, a soft, delicious exploration, learning each hollow, each curve. Completely devastating.

She was in deeper waters than she expected, with heavy, terrifying currents. Any moment now they would be closing over her head.

Desperate to return things to safer ground, she forced herself to pull away with a shaky breath.

"There." She forced a casual smile, though it made her teeth ache. "Now we've got that out of the way."

He gave her a long look out of those hot, gorgeous eyes that seemed to see entirely too much. "Have we?"

She forced herself to blunder on, though her skin felt hot, tight, itchy. "I told you, I haven't been able to get that kiss out of my mind. Every time I see or talk to you, the memory simmers just under the surface. You might be talking away about the house or about Haven Point or your family and the only thing I can think about is, wow, that man knows how to kiss."

He raised an eyebrow and she felt herself blush even more. "Thank you. I guess. Right back at you."

She wouldn't let herself find pleasure in that. Okay, maybe a little pleasure.

"Of course, we both agreed it was a mistake that shouldn't have happened. But as mistakes go, you're right, that particular one the other night was, um..." Incredible. Amazing. Off-the-charts sexy. "Noteworthy."

"Noteworthy," he said faintly. "And did you? Take notes, I mean?"

"I've been trying to forget it. It was a mistake, right?"

"Unwise, certainly."

"Bingo. I couldn't agree more. And now I'm going to have to spend the next week trying to forget this kiss, too. As if I didn't have enough to do, with your family coming in only a few days! Thanks for that."

The frustrating man actually seemed to find the situation amusing. "Well, then, I'd better try to make a lasting impression."

"Aidan," she began, but he moved forward with that inexorable focus of his and lowered his mouth to hers again.

This time the heat raged back, exploding between them with wild intensity, as if the earlier kiss had only been the warm-up act to the real thing. He held her close and she wrapped her arms around his back. She was vaguely aware of random sensations. The heat of him, the leashed strength of his surprising muscles, the wonderful, half-forgotten ache in all her girly places.

If he threw her back on the sofa and began ripping buttons and tangling zippers, she wouldn't have been able to protest.

She wrapped her arms around his neck, pulling him closer as her body turned liquid and soft. She wanted this man, so much she couldn't breathe around the hunger. She wanted to feel him around her, inside her.

As their mouths tangled, he groaned her name and the sound seemed to jolt her back to her senses.

They couldn't do this. As much as she wanted to make love to him right now, she sensed it would leave her shattered.

Somewhere deep inside, she at last uncovered a forlorn little shred of self-protectiveness. Though it was the hardest thing she had ever done, she managed to slide her mouth away from his.

"We have to stop. Please, Aidan."

He eased away, his breathing ragged and a slightly unfocused look in his eyes.

"Why?"

She scrambled for words, her thoughts as scattered as paper snowflakes on the wind. "I like you," she finally said. "I like you very much. And you're a fabulous kisser. As I believe we have quite firmly established. But I...I haven't even dated since Trent died. I can't just jump headfirst into the water with someone like you."

"Someone like me?"

She eased away another few inches and tried to tuck her hair out of her face with fingers that had a rather embarrassing tendency to tremble. "You're larger than life, Aidan. I've seen pictures of you with the kind of women you usually date—thin, gorgeous, perfectly made up. They're not frazzled mothers who drive an SUV with Cheerios under the seat and juice boxes in the cupholders. You're not interested in a relationship with me. The idea is completely laughable."

"Funny. I'm not laughing."

"Come on, Aidan. Be serious. You're the CEO of your own billion-dollar business and I'm a heartbeat away from being homeless."

"You've had a run of hard knocks. That's hardly your fault and certainly doesn't negate the possibility of a relationship between us. I don't think less of you for circumstances out of your control, El. You're one of the hardest-working women I've ever met. What you have done with Snow Angel Cove is amazing."

He wasn't listening and she couldn't seem to make her brain cells cooperate to come up with a cogent argument. "Thank you. But that's not the point."

"What is? This is the point, as I see it. I'm attracted to you. You're attracted to me. I like you very much and enjoy your company. I suspect you feel the same, though I could be wrong."

She shook her head. "You're not wrong."

"I already care about your daughter. As far as I can see, there aren't that many additional barriers that would keep us from pursuing this attraction."

On a logical plane, she would lose any argument she put forward. The reality settled over her with depressing force. "You forgot the most important one. Yes, I like being with you. Yes, I'm obviously attracted to you. You're the Geek God and I haven't been with a man in more than three years. I would have to be dead *not* to be attracted to you."

"You're saying it's only physical."

For some ridiculous reason, she thought he actually looked a little hurt by that.

"I'm saying that for the next week, you're my employer and that has to be the only relationship between us. I apologize for kissing you. It was completely inappropriate and won't happen again."

She didn't want their wonderful evening together

to end like this, with cold words and anger but, again, the words to make it right just wouldn't come.

"What about friendship? Any interest in that?"

Suddenly, for no reason she could have pinpointed, her throat felt tight and her eyes burned. "Of course. I told you I like you, Aidan. Far too much for my own comfort, if you want the truth. I just... I'm a realistic kind of girl. Life hasn't given me a lot of choice in that pragmatism. The way I see it, you're like a fairy-tale prince and I'm Cinderella without the godmother and the cool shoes."

And on that ridiculous, entirely too revealing statement, she moved toward the kitchen and her rooms. Before she left the great room, she turned back and found him standing by the fire, the glow silhouetting him. "Thank you again for a wonderful evening. I'm sorry I spoiled everything."

"You didn't spoil anything," he assured her, but she knew it was a lie.

She tried a shaky sort of smile and then hurried out of the room before she could make an even bigger fool of herself.

Once in the safety and privacy of her sitting room, she closed the door quietly behind her—no emotionally wrought slamming of doors here—then collapsed onto the sofa.

She felt completely wrung dry, as if she had just tried to swim the length of Lake Haven.

She couldn't believe what she had just said to him.

I like you, Aidan. Far too much for my own com-

*fort... The way I see it, you're like a fairy-tale prince
and I'm Cinderella without the godmother and the
cool shoes.*

The truth was deeper than that and far more serious. She was falling for him, just as she feared she
would. She was coming to care for his kindness,
his funny sense of humor, the rare vulnerabilities
he showed.

For her own self-preservation, she ought to pack
up her daughter and her things and drive away from
Snow Angel Cove and Lake Haven.

She could find a short-term lease somewhere in
Boise and start seriously looking for another job.

That would be the wisest choice.

She had made a commitment, however, and she
was a woman of her word. Aidan was counting on
her to see to his family's needs while they were here
and at this late date, he wouldn't be able to find
someone else.

Oh, Aidan and his family would survive if she
wasn't here. Between Sue and the cleaning crew that
would be coming in daily to help, she didn't doubt
the house party would run magnificently without her.

They would go on to have a wonderful holiday
without her. She, on the other hand, would know she
had made a commitment and then reneged on it. She
knew too well what being on the losing end of broken promises felt like.

Beyond that, Maddie had been through enough
tumult these past few weeks. She didn't need an-

other upheaval. Her daughter was happy here and was looking forward to spending the holidays at Snow Angel Cove. Her heart would be broken if Eliza packed her up again and hauled her to some impersonal hotel.

For her daughter's sake and for Aidan's, she would be a professional and do her job. No matter how difficult, she would keep her relationship with him professional, casual, friendly—and do her very best to protect her heart.

If she wasn't already too late.

CHAPTER EIGHTEEN

AIDAN SAT BY the fire for a long time after Eliza left,
trying to sift through the past few moments.

He felt like a different person than he had been
earlier in the evening—as if everything he was and
everything he wanted had just undergone a radical
shift.

After the doctors found his brain tumor, he remembered walking out of the office and into the
August sunshine, amazed to see people going about
their business, driving down the road, walking into
stores, eating in restaurants. How could life just
go on around him like normal when his world had
just been completely rocked on its axis and nothing
would ever be the same?

This evening spent with Eliza and Maddie felt
much the same, for reasons he didn't quite understand.

He had feelings for her. He wasn't sure how or
when they started, but he was coming to care deeply
for her courage and her strength, her sweetness and
warmth.

He didn't want to think about her and Maddie
leaving. But how could he convince her to stay when

she was throwing up barriers between them as fast as she could come up with them?

You're like a fairy-tale prince and I'm Cinderella without the godmother and the cool shoes.

He smiled a little at the silly analogy, though it bothered him that she saw the two of them through that filter.

He was no Prince Charming. His brain tumor had forced him to take a hard look at his life and he wasn't sure he liked what he saw. He was driven and focused, which could sometimes come across as cold and uncaring.

He might live in a nice house—a few of them, actually—and have a private jet at his disposal but that wasn't the heart of him. He would never argue that he liked the luxuries he could afford now. More than that, he liked that his family members were all comfortable financially because he had given them stock in his company early on.

If Pop didn't want to work another minute at the Center of Hope, he could have a more-than-comfortable retirement. Charlotte had been able to buy her candy store in Hope's Crossing and a nice house in a very expensive resort town real estate market. Dylan had bought his property in Snowflake Canyon. Jamie could leave the army right now if he wanted and never fly a helicopter again for the rest of his days.

All of Pop's grandkids could have their pick of

any university, thanks to the education trust funds
he had set up for each of them.

He liked the trappings of his amazing success but
beneath it all, he was a man who had come face-to-
face with his own mortality in recent months and had
come to realize it wasn't enough anymore.

He wanted a family.

He wanted someone to share his life with. He
wanted someone sweet and warm and generous, who
would light up when she saw him like Lucy did when
she saw Brendan, like Genevieve for Dylan or Charlotte for Spence.

He remembered talking to Dylan shortly after he
and Genevieve started seeing each other. Though he
had known he was risking a right hook, he had asked
his brother what he possibly saw in Gen, the spoiled
society belle who had finally managed to make his
wounded warrior brother smile again. They were
the most unlikely of couples but somehow they just
worked together.

Instead of reacting with his fists—or fist, in these
days, as his arm had been amputated—Dylan had
shrugged with that slightly besotted look he wore
most of the time these days.

"She calms the crazy," he had said simply, looking a little embarrassed to admit such a thing to his
brother.

Aidan hadn't known what the hell his brother
was talking about until right this moment. He was

not only drawn to Eliza on a physical level but on a deeply emotional one, as well.

When he spent time with her and Maddie, the usual frenzy of his thoughts—constantly racing from idea to idea and project to project—seemed to quiet to a low murmur, allowing him to simply *be*. It was a rare luxury, indeed, and one he suddenly craved with a fierceness that shocked him.

He sighed and sipped at what was left of his chocolate. It was cold now, congealed in the cup, and he quickly set it down again.

What was he going to do with her?

She *had* said one thing that rang with resonance. She worked for him. Yes, it had been a cobbled-together job offered more out of guilt and obligation than any real need, but she had proven herself indispensable.

He had a dilemma, then. He didn't want her to leave but he didn't want her to stay on as his housekeeper-slash-hostess, either.

Okay, solving problems was what he did best. He would set his considerable mind to it and figure out a way to convince her a relationship between them was not only possible but inevitable.

She might not have a fairy godmother, but she had him.

"SUE, YOU NEED to see a doctor."

Eliza frowned at Aidan's cook, who stood at the

big six-burner stove with her foot on a stool. She was pale and drawn, with lines of pain around her mouth.

"I'm fine. This is stupid. I'm just such a klutz."

"You told me you tripped. What exactly happened?"

"I wish I knew. It was just one of those weird things, you know? One minute I was walking along minding my own business, enjoying the night after the parade, the next I slipped off a curb and twisted my foot. I'm sure I was quite a sight, a dried-up old broad lying there in the gutter."

Sue tried to make a joke and smiled at Maddie, sitting at the work island doing one of her math worksheets, but as she twisted to reach for the egg carton on the countertop, she winced as if she had dropped a heavy cast iron Dutch oven on her foot.

She swallowed a moan and Eliza moved forward to grab the eggs for her and move them closer so she could reach. She *wanted* to haul the woman to the doctor herself. Worry was a hard knot in her stomach.

"Please, Sue. You need to sit down."

"Oh, don't fret about me. By tomorrow, I'll be in fighting form. You'll see."

"The only thing you're going to be fighting is me if you don't sit down and take some weight off that foot. I mean it. I can't believe Jim didn't take you into the E.R. for an X-ray last night."

"He wanted to, that old worrywart. I wouldn't go. Told him, I didn't need to waste our hard-earned money for a doctor to tell me it was only sprained. The only way I was going to that clinic was if he tossed me over his shoulder and dragged me there kicking and screaming. He knew it wasn't an idle threat—just like he knows darn well he can't lift me anymore, what with his bad back and all."

She hopped to the work island for the package of bacon she had left there. By the time she hopped the short distance back to the stove, she looked close to passing out.

"Good grief, you are one stubborn woman," Eliza exclaimed. "Sit down. I'm making breakfast. I can handle pancakes and bacon."

Sue looked as if she wanted to argue but didn't quite have the strength to do it. After a moment, she sighed and sank onto one of the stools around the work island. Tears of frustration and pain gathered.

"What am I going to do? Aidan's family is coming in two days."

Eliza snatched a tissue from the box on the counter and handed it to her, then grasped Sue's other hand in both of hers. "Please let me take you in for an X-ray. If it's a sprain, you can at least get some crutches so you're not hobbling around in pain with only that old cane you're using. Who knows? Maybe they can give you a brace or something, or one of those cool little knee walkers I've seen people use at the grocery store. You don't want to do more damage to it, possibly make things worse, right? If you can't even stand up, you won't be any use to Aidan while his family is here. You know that."

The older woman seemed to waver. "I hate hospitals."

Maddie slipped down from her chair and came over to Sue. This darling girl who had endured too many hospital visits placed a hand on the older woman's leg. "You shouldn't hate hospitals. The doctors and nurses only want to help you feel better."

"Is that right?" Sue gave a little chuckle at receiving words of advice from a five-year-old.

Maddie nodded. "Even when they have to hurt you, it's only so they can fix what's wrong with you, then you'll be all better."

Sue tugged at one of Maddie's braids "You're a pretty smart cookie, you know that?"

Maddie beamed at her and even though Sue looked tired and cranky and sore, she still smiled back.

"I don't have *time* for a sprained ankle," she said under her breath. "In forty-eight hours, twenty-plus people will be arriving here with empty stomachs."

"We'll make sure nobody goes hungry, Sue, I promise."

"You know what the worst thing just might be? Having to admit everybody else around here is right and I just might be wrong."

"We've all been there, right?"

Eliza smiled, thinking how very dear this woman and her husband had become in the time she had been at Snow Angel Cove. She wanted to be just like Sue some day, plucky and strong, opinionated and hardworking and efficient.

"Who knows? It might just be a sprain, just as you said, but you can't know for sure until you have it checked out. I'll just finish the breakfast and we can run over to the Lake Haven Hospital."

"Jim can take me. You've got plenty to do here."

Eliza started to tell Sue that everything else could wait but she heard the door of the mudroom open before she could, then Jim's and Aidan's voices.

"Speak of the devil," Sue said.

A moment later, the two men walked into the kitchen. Eliza's resident troop of butterflies started dancing around her insides again at seeing him for the first time since she had left his arms the night before.

"Morning," he murmured to all of them, but she was quite certain his gaze rested on her for much longer than was strictly necessary.

"Hi, Mr. Aidan," Maddie said cheerfully. "Sue needs to go to the hospital."

He blinked at Maddie's casual tone. "What?"

"It's nothing," the cook assured him. "I slid over an icy curb at the boat parade last night. I probably should go get a brace or something."

"I knew it!" Jim exclaimed. "I should have taken you there last night like I wanted to. Maybe if I had, it wouldn't have been so swollen that you couldn't even put your shoe on this morning."

"You're right and I was wrong. There. I said it. Happy now?"

She looked so miserable that Eliza couldn't help feeling sorry for her. Any trace of pity seemed completely inconsequential when Jim stepped forward and kissed the top of the woman's graying head.

"Now, how could I be happy when my darling girl is in pain?" the quiet cowboy said.

Oh. Eliza's butterflies stopped long enough to go as gooey as the rest of her. She glanced at Aidan and found him watching the older couple with a softness she didn't usually see there.

"Son, you mind if I take the Suburban?" Jim asked him. "She can stretch her leg out better in that."

"Not at all. I'll go pull it around for you."

He gaze Eliza a quick, unreadable look, then hurried back out to the mudroom and out the door.

"Can you go over to our place for my best black coat and my purse with the insurance information?" Sue patted Jim's arm, apparently resigned to her fate now and in action mode.

"You bet. Be back in a flash."

He practically galloped out the door.

"I think the darn thing might be broken," Sue admitted when it was just the two of them and Maddie in the kitchen again. "I've had sprains before and they never hurt like this one."

"I'm so sorry."

"What if it is? I'll ruin everything for Aidan and his family."

"You'll ruin nothing," Eliza insisted. "I told you, we'll figure it out. I can manage with a little help. You can sit right there at the work island with your cast up on a chair and tell me everything you need me to do."

"I wanted the holidays to be perfect for Aidan. It's important to him. Especially this year."

"Because of his brain tumor?" Eliza asked, after making sure Maddie had gone back to her work-sheets and was humming softly to herself, not paying any attention to them.

Sue looked surprised. "He actually let you in on the big dark secret? Wow. I'm shocked. You're one of only a lucky trusted few. He didn't even tell most of his household staff in California. He leased a house on the coast to keep it a secret and called me and Jim out of retirement to go help him there."

"Why the big secret? Do you know?"

Sue sighed and shifted her leg on the chair. Eliza caught a glimpse of her foot, swollen and discolored. It looked worse than a sprain to her.

"He said it was because of how it might affect the Caine Tech bottom line if news trickled out. Make shareholders question the direction of the company and who might take over if his brain tumor turned out to be fatal."

"What do you think?"

"I think he hates showing any sign of weakness. I don't know, that might be from having so many tough brothers or it might just be part of who he is, the same way he likes to believe he doesn't need anybody."

He was an independent, complicated tangle of a man and she was coming to care far too much about him.

Before she could answer, Jim came in.

"Is this the coat you wanted?" he asked.

"That will do."

He helped her slip her arms in just as Aidan came in from the other direction. It must have started snowing, as his ranch coat had little sprinkles of snow scattered over the shoulders.

"Your carriage awaits, madam."

"Thank you, darlin'."

She gingerly rose to her feet and started hopping to the door with the cane she had brought along. Aidan let her go only to the edge of the work island before he sighed and scooped her up in one smooth motion

"Put me down, you fool. You shouldn't be lifting anything, especially not someone my size."

"You weigh no more than Maddie over there and I carried her to bed last night."

Maddie giggled as the wiry cook flushed brighter than a poinsettia. "You're crazy. That's what you are. Loony as popcorn on a hot skillet. Put me down! Right now!"

"Stop wriggling around," he said with a laugh. "You're only making it harder."

She instantly subsided.

"What do you need me to do while you're gone?" Eliza asked.

"Finish fixing breakfast for his orneriness here," Sue said. "That should do it."

"You don't need to fix me anything," Aidan protested as he carried her out the door. Jim picked up Sue's purse and headed out after them. He paused in the doorway and turned back to Eliza.

"Whatever you said to convince her to see a doc, thanks a million," he said gruffly. "I owe you."

"Anything you think you might owe me has been paid in full many times over with the kindness you and Sue have shown to me and to Maddie," she said firmly. "Please call and let us know when you find out anything."

After they left, Eliza pressed a hand to her chest. How was she supposed to protect her heart against Aidan? Every time she turned around, she found more things to love.

She stood there for only a moment as she fought the bleak realization that leaving this place was going to hurt worse than anything she had experienced in a long time, then she rubbed her hands briskly down her thighs, threw on an apron and went to work.

Aidan came back inside a few moments later. He looked at her standing by the stove and frowned. "You really didn't have to make me breakfast. Toast and coffee would have been fine."

"Too late. It's already cooking. How do pancakes, bacon and eggs sound?"

"Delicious, if you want the truth."

He walked farther into the room and approached the stove, bringing in the delicious scent of snow and leather and him.

"What can I do to help?" he asked.

"Not a thing," she answered. "It's under control."

At least the breakfast was. Tension seemed to sizzle and pop between them like the bacon frying in the pan. She heartily wished she could go back and unkiss him. Okay, not a word, but it absolutely fit in this circumstance. She wanted to go back to those sweet moments they had shared on the drive home from the boat parade, when they had shared confidences and she had felt warm and safe.

Instead, all she could think about was being in his arms again.

"I can flip the bacon," he said.

"No need. It's just about there."

He looked as if he wanted to argue but finally crossed to the coffeemaker and poured a cup then carried it over to the island where Maddie had finished her math homework and had pulled out crayons and a paper.

"What are you drawing?"

"It's a feel-better card for Miz Sue."

"Wow. That's really good. She's going to love it. It's a horse, right?"

She nodded, her bottom lip firmly nestled between her teeth as she concentrated. It was a mannerism she had either inherited or picked up from

Eliza. "Yep. It's Cinnamon. See? There's the white patch on her face."

He peered closer. "Oh, sure. It's an exact likeness. Way to go, kiddo."

They shared a smile of perfect accord and something soft seemed to twist in Eliza's heart.

She quickly turned her attention back to crisping the bacon before setting it on paper towels to drain the grease. Breakfast, in her estimation, was the hardest meal of all to prepare because all the typical breakfast dishes only took a moment to cook and everything needed constant pouring, stirring or flipping.

She was nevertheless quite pleased with the results as she plated golden pancakes, fluffy eggs and perfectly cooked bacon then set it down in front of him.

"Thank you," he said, that unreadable look in his eyes again.

"You're welcome."

She fixed a plate for Maddie and one for herself. While she would have liked to escape to her little sitting room to eat somewhere she could put a safe distance between them, she couldn't come up with a good excuse to leave.

"Did you see Sue's ankle?" he asked when she finally sat across from him.

"Only a glimpse. It looked nasty. Swollen and horribly bruised. I must confess, I felt a bit like a hypocrite urging her to go to the doctor after my own recent history of being on the other side of the situation and not wanting to see a medical professional, either. To my untrained eye, it looked worse than a sprain."

"Yeah, I suspected as much or she never would have agreed to see a doctor. Well, that will make for an interesting house party."

"I told Sue I'll be her cook's assistant. She can sit there on a stool and tell me what to do. I might not be a culinary genius but I'm sure I can do an adequate job with a little supervision." She gestured to his plate with her fork. "I didn't poison you, did I?"

"It's delicious. All of it. But I didn't hire you to feed twenty people."

She swallowed a bite of pancakes, lush and delicious with the genuine gourmet maple syrup Sue stocked in the refrigerator. "I'm perfectly aware you invented a job for me to do, Aidan. We both know Sue could have handled everything on her own, with help from the girls she hired to take care of the laundry and housekeeping chores."

He opened his mouth but she didn't give him a chance to reply. "I'm not stupid. I know you hired me out of guilt because you felt bad for the little mishap we had that first day and you could see I was in a tough situation."

"All right. Maybe initially," he conceded. "But you have proved your worth a hundred times over. The house looks incredible—festive and warm and inviting. Everything is perfect, El, from the gourmet soap baskets to the little guidebooks you left in each of the bedrooms. I love her dearly but, let's face it. Sue could never have pulled off all those welcoming little touches on her own."

His praise made her glow. "I'm really happy you like it," she said.

"You've done the impossible here. You've created a home I am proud to welcome my family to for Christmas. But you have enough to do without adding kitchen duties, too."

"I can handle the meal prep. Don't worry."

"The minute Pop finds out something happened to Sue, he's going to be in here taking over. He has a thing about feeding people. And if Pop's in here, everybody else will follow. The issue isn't going to be finding enough help for the meal prep, it likely will be finding enough counter space for all the cooks who will be in here spoiling the broth."

She couldn't wait for his family to arrive and felt as if she already knew them all. Even before she actually met them, though, she already had the sneaking suspicion this would be one more thing about him she would miss when she left Snow Angel Cove.

CHAPTER NINETEEN

IN A RARE twist for him, Aidan couldn't seem to concentrate, no matter how he tried.

For the past thirty-six hours, he had been obsessed with a new project. He loved the completely natural buzz that sometimes bubbled through his veins when he knew he was on to something sure to be a hit—when he could sometimes spend twenty-plus hours straight at his computer, until his eyes blurred and his shoulders ached.

That same excitement hummed through him about the project he was currently developing, but at the moment he couldn't seem to focus on any of the three screens in front of him.

Little wonder, he supposed. The largest jet of the Caine Tech corporate fleet was wheels up at the moment, on its way here carrying his family, and was due to touch down in less than an hour.

After piddling around a little longer, he finally sighed, saved the encrypted file and shut down his network.

He wasn't precisely nervous. His family had visited him in California plenty of times—maybe not en masse like this, but he had hosted them in smaller groups without problem. Pop and Charlotte had flown out and spent a few days with him over his birthday weekend a few years ago. Dylan and Jamie had each crashed with him for a while between deployments.

Hosting everyone at Christmas added an entirely new dimension, especially at a new house. He wanted everything to be perfectly memorable, which turned out to be a hell of a lot of pressure. Who knew?

As he walked through the house, some of the stress eased. Everything would be great. How could it be otherwise? The house looked terrific, from the Christmas tree to the garlands to the glittery lights everywhere.

Jazz Christmas carols played softly on the excellent stereo system, something Eliza must have programmed since he had completely forgotten about it.

He meant what he said earlier. She had done wonders with Snow Angel Cove. It was cozy and warm, exactly as he wanted.

Now that Sue was temporarily sidelined, Eliza had been forced to step up in the kitchen, too. He found her there, standing at the work island before a huge stainless-steel bowl filled with a puffy mound of dough.

She wore a Christmas-patterned apron and was humming softly to the music. He watched her for a long moment, enjoying the graceful economy of her movements as she rolled bits of dough between her palms and transferred them to muffin cups, the way she nibbled on her bottom lip just as Maddie did, the little sprinkle of flour she left behind when she rubbed the back of her hand along her cheekbone.

He had been so consumed with the project, he had only seen her briefly over the past few days. Each time he did, he was surprised all over again by the way the world suddenly seemed a brighter, happier, *better* place when he was with her.

What would it be like to have her here all the time? Not here at Snow Angel Cove, specifically, but in his life, in his bed. In his heart.

He didn't think he made a sound as he watched her but eventually she must have sensed his presence. She looked up from the dough and her cheeks turned a little pink.

"Oh. Hi. I'm sorry. I didn't see you come in. How long have you been standing there?"

"Only a moment." He moved farther into the kitchen, wishing he had the right to wrap his arms around her from behind and tug her against him, to kiss the delicate skin at the nape of her neck, under her ponytail.

He pushed away the yearning. "You're on your own in here."

"I could tell Sue's cast was bothering her so I strongly encouraged her to put it up for a while, before everyone gets here. She's in my sitting room with Maddie. I believe they were about to watch a Christmas special."

"Sue is a little addicted to them."

"I suspect she may end up sleeping through this one." She smiled softly as she set another ball of dough in the muffin tin.

"You are truly a miracle worker if you could convince her to rest just before the chaos I call a family descends on Snow Angel Cove. How did you manage to pull that off?"

"I wouldn't have been successful if her foot wasn't killing her. Christmas is a terrible time to have a fracture and have to wear a cast."

Sue had ended up with what doctors called a Lisfranc fracture of the small bones in her foot from the twisting injury of falling off the curb. It hadn't required surgery but she was now hobbling around with a cast and a small knee walker to keep her weight off it as much as possible.

"Looks like she put you to work before she went to rest. What are you doing? Cloverleaf rolls?"

She gave him a sideways smile that made him hungry for more. "Careful, Aidan. Your culinary experience is showing. Sue might end up putting you to work."

"She knows I can hold my own if she needs my help."

"Actually, I think we have everything under control. Sue wanted me to make rolls to go with the turkey tenderloins we're making for the late lunch. She babysat me through her recipe to make sure I didn't overwork the dough but trusted me enough to make the balls for rolls on my own."

"They look great. Good job."

She made a face. "Thank you for not mentioning all the misshapen circles."

"I can't see any from where I'm standing."

"You must not be looking hard enough," she said.

He wanted to argue that he could see fine and everything within his view looked perfect but he was afraid that would sound cheesy.

"In my experience, we tend to see our own mistakes and weaknesses far more vividly than other people do," he said instead.

"Isn't that the truth?"

The lapsed into silence broken only by the soft music on the sound system, now playing a vibraphone version of "Winter Wonderland." Did she feel the tensile attraction tug and stretch between them or was it wholly one-sided? He wasn't sure but by the occasional sidelong glance she sent his way, he suspected the former.

"I know I haven't said it enough," he said after a moment, "but thank you again for stepping up to help Sue out with the meal prep. We really would have been sunk without you."

"I'm glad I was here."

"Again, let me just say that I'm terribly sorry I ran into you that day and I'm probably going to have nightmares about it forever, but somehow it turned into one of the best things that's happened to me in a long time."

"Oh." The word escaped her on a small breath of

sound and she gazed at him, green eyes wide, arrested. It took a great deal of wrestling for him to fight down the urge to lean across the work island and kiss her right there, over the bowl of cloverleaf roll dough.

"I mean it, Eliza. I'm very glad you and Maddie are here—and not only because you've been a lifesaver in the kitchen."

"I am, too," she said after a moment, and he knew it was a confession she didn't make easily.

"How long before your family arrives?" she asked, changing the subject quickly.

"Within the hour. Jim and I need to be leaving in a few minutes for the airport pickup."

"You have the list of room assignments, right?"

"Yeah. I looked it over this morning. It all should be fine."

"We talked about leaving most of the evening unstructured. We'll let people settle into their rooms before we put out the late lunch buffet style an hour or so after everyone arrives. Dinner tonight is pizza, which is already prepped, and then we have the sleigh ride on the agenda."

"Right. Okay."

He did a little mental reorganizing. He had entertained some vague idea of welcoming his family for a few hours and then going right back to his project but that wouldn't work. Jim would need his help handling the team of draft horses temporarily on loan for the sleigh ride.

"Do you have a route in mind?" she asked.

"Yes. We won't go far, just around the road that circles the ranch property and down by the cove."

"Oh, that sounds perfect. You'll have a lovely view of the stars and the moonlight down by the lake. Your family will love it."

"I hope so. You and Maddie will, too. She has been dying to ride in the sleigh ever since she spied it in the barn the other day."

Her mouth tightened. "We probably would enjoy it, if we were going with you."

"Of course you're going! You have to!"

"Is that an order?"

"If it has to be," he retorted. He hated when she threw the fact that she technically worked for him between them like razor-topped concertina wire.

"How can I go? I'll be busy cleaning up after twenty people and I don't feel comfortable sending my child along for someone in your family to babysit."

"First of all, the primary rule in my family is, if you don't work, you don't eat, as I've told you before. Everybody will help you clean the kitchen before we leave. Watch. Pop will insist on it. And second of all, you have to come. Fine, consider it an order, if that helps you sleep at night. We both know Maddie's heart would break if we left her home."

She was silent, brow furrowed as she concentrated on rolling the last bit of dough into a ball. "Can't you see how awkward this is for me? I'm a total stranger to your family. A total stranger who *works* for you! What are they going to think when I just start hanging around, going on sleigh rides and eating dinner with you?"

"They're going to think the more the merrier. And five minutes after they all show up, you will feel like one of the family. One of my pop's favorite Irish sayings is, there are no strangers, only friends you haven't met yet."

She huffed out her breath. "Do you always manage to get your own way?"

"Not even close," he murmured. How could she say that, when she came up with excuse after excuse to fight the feelings growing between them?

She gazed at him and her mouth trembled slightly, just enough that he knew he couldn't go another moment without kissing her. In this, yeah. He insisted on his own way.

As he lowered his mouth, she caught her breath and he saw her pupils dilate, then turned shocked when he only pressed his mouth to that dusting of flour on her cheek.

"You had a little something there," he said, his voice low.

"Oh."

Her lashes fluttered down and she leaned into him slightly, almost as if she didn't realize it. Just before he leaned in to kiss her—really kiss her this time—he heard the mudroom door slam and cowboy boots on the tile.

Jim.

He eased away and stepped back a pace just as the man strolled into the kitchen. Jim looked between the two of them with a slight frown, as if he sensed some of the sparkling tension in the room but wasn't sure of the origin.

"There you are, boss. We should probably get moving to pick up your family, since we'll each have to make a couple of trips to haul them all, plus their stuff, plus their dogs."

Right. His family. He needed to focus on his priorities here.

"You're absolutely right. Let's go."

Before he left the kitchen, he turned back and found Eliza pressing a hand to her cheek. She dropped her fingers quickly, eyes slightly defiant, then quickly turned back to the rolls as he headed out the door.

"No, really, I can do this," Eliza insisted, stacking another plate on the tray she was using to bus the dining room table. "I promise, I don't mind cleaning up by myself. Go on your sleigh ride while it's still clear, before the snow starts up again."

Dermot Caine, a sturdy, handsome charmer who had passed his striking blue eyes on to all his children, wagged a finger at her as he picked up silverware. "Nonsense, my dear. We aren't leaving you with this mess! With all of us pitching in, it won't take but a moment to have that fine kitchen sparkling once more. Then we can *all* go for a sleigh ride, hmm?"

Apparently Aidan had inherited more than his father's blue eyes. His stubbornness must be a family trait, too.

"It's not necessary," she tried again. It had become a point of honor to her but Dermot overrode her as easily as his son usually did.

"Dylan, Bren, Andrew. Snap to it, boys."

The men—far from boys and every bit as gorgeous as their brother—obeyed their father with alacrity and Eliza could do nothing but be swept along in the tide of Caines grabbing up plates and trays and bowls.

Spencer Gregory—*the* Smokin' Hot Spence Gregory, who turned out to be not only more gorgeous in person but amazingly nice, too—smiled as he picked up a bowl containing just a few corkscrew curls, all that was left from a massive pasta salad.

"That pizza was really great, Eliza," he said.

"Thanks."

"Fantastic," Brendan Caine, the biggest of the brothers concurred. "I do believe I could have eaten one pie all by myself."

"Sue did a great job, didn't she?" She refused to take undue credit when she had merely followed directions.

"Couldn't have done it without you, dear," Sue piped up from her spot at the kitchen table, where she was going over the menu for the next day.

"The boys and I will take care of these dishes," Dermot said before she could even reach for a dish-cloth. "Go on. You deserve to put your feet up and rest up a bit before our sleigh ride."

Argh. Wouldn't anybody listen to her? "I'm just going to wander through the house and see if I can round up any other dishes."

In her experience, cups and plates and bowls tended to be scattered far and wide as people car-ried snacks and drinks from room to room.

"Might as well, might as well. I need to put Dylan to work here with a dish towel."

"Sure. Why not make the guy with one arm do all the hard stuff?" Aidan's younger brother, the wounded army ranger, gave Eliza a teasing wink

"That one-arm thing sure comes in handy some-times. Didn't seem to stop you from kicking our butts at billiards earlier," Andrew, the attorney in the family, threw out.

They were bickering good naturedly as she headed out to canvas the other rooms.

In the great room, she saw Dylan's huge black-and-tan coonhound stretched out in front of the fire while a trio of much smaller dogs—a lean chihua-hua and a couple of tiny cute puffballs who had to be related—cuddled up to him.

The house had needed dogs, she thought with a smile. Old Argus in the barn didn't count.

His sisters were clustered in one of the sitting areas of the great room looking at a photo album one of them had brought along. Not wanting to intrude, she tried to give them a wide berth on her way up the stairs to the media and game rooms, but Charlotte spotted her.

"Eliza, that pizza was fantastic."

She pasted on a smile and headed toward the women. "Thanks, but Sue really did all the work. I'm an adequate prep cook but that's about it."

Lucy Drake, tall and lovely with long dark curls, gave her a smile. "I understand I need to pick your brain while I'm here. Aidan says you're the one who added all the wonderful little touches to our rooms like the water carafes by the bed, the basket of fuzzy socks, the little gift bags of fresh cookies."

"I would love to talk with you," she answered. "He says you have an amazing bed-and-breakfast in Hope's Crossing."

Lucy blinked. "Aidan called Iris House amazing? *Our* Aidan?"

"Yes. He had nothing but good to say about it. It sounds absolutely delightful."

"Okay." Charlotte leaned forward. "What is going *on* with him?"

Eliza studied the women warily. "With Aidan? What do you mean?"

The women exchanged glances. "This whole party!" Charlotte said. "Inviting us here."

"Most years we can count ourselves lucky if he flies in for a few hours on Christmas Day," Erin— the schoolteacher, she remembered, married to the attorney—made a face. "This year he was absolutely insistent that we all come and spend several days here at his new place. Do you know how tough it is to get us all together, with everybody's crazy schedules?"

She could only imagine. She had a feeling this was not a family that sat home waiting for life to happen to them.

"So what's the story with him?" Genevieve pressed.

Eliza shifted and tried to keep her features as impassive as she could manage. "I guess he has this lovely new house and was eager to show it off."

It sounded totally implausible, even to her, but she wasn't about to reveal the secret he had demanded she keep for him.

"That's another thing," Erin pressed. "Why this house? Why here? Why not buy in Hope's Crossing, where he could be closer to all of us?"

"I'm sure he had his reasons. You should ask him," she said, trying to edge away from the group.

"No, something is definitely up," Charlotte said. "This afternoon, he spent an hour playing billiards with the guys. An entire hour! Right after that, he was down here reading a Christmas story to your darling little girl and Faith and Carter."

"Why is that such a shock?" Eliza asked. Aidan had showed remarkable patience and kindness to Maddie from the moment they met.

"It just seems...out of character. Don't get me

wrong. I love my brother dearly. He's probably the smartest person I've ever met. He's loving and loyal and brilliant. But as long as I have known him, he has also been the most driven person I know."

"Personally, I find it odd that he invited us all here, spent a few hours with us and then disappeared the rest of the evening." Katherine Caine, Aidan's new stepmother, had a worried light in her eyes. "Is he ill?"

Oh, she had a horrible poker face. Nevertheless, Eliza tried her best. "I believe he has a project he's busy with right now."

"See, that's more like the Aidan we know and love," Lucy said. "It's the whole, *come stay at my new digs, I'll fly you out* thing that seems out of character to me. Something is definitely up."

Eliza picked up a couple of empty nut bowls from the table, careful not to meet anyone's gaze. "He loves his family very much. I think he just wanted a chance for everyone to be together."

That was as much as she was willing to say. Much to her relief, Maddie came galloping in with Carter and Faith close at her heels. As Aidan had predicted, the three of them had become immediate friends and Maddie appeared to be having a wonderful time with children close to her age.

"Mama, when is the sleigh ride? We want to go *now*."

"I don't know, honey. Soon, I'm sure."

"We're going to sit together and sing 'Rudolph the

Red-nosed Reindeer' and 'Jingle Bells' and 'Way in a Manger.'"

Aidan had been right about this, too. She couldn't have separated her child from the family activities. Maddie would have been devastated at being excluded. She was already having the time of her life and his family hadn't even been here half a day.

"Why don't you children go find your coats and hats and scarves so we don't have to look for them later?" Erin said in what was obviously her best schoolteacher voice. "I'll try to find out where things stand with the sleigh ride."

"And I need to take care of these," Eliza said, gesturing to the dishes in her hands. She hurried away from the women, grateful she had escaped what she feared would have soon become an interrogation.

His family had already been so kind to her. He had been right, they had absorbed her into their circle from the first moment, as if she had always been part of it.

She loved watching their interaction—the teasing of his brothers with each other, their careful respect for Dermot, the affectionate touches between husbands and wives. This was a family overflowing with love.

Half a day and she already felt as if the women could become good friends to her—if she could only keep from spilling secrets that weren't hers to share.

She delivered the dishes to the kitchen. The men had finished cleaning up—sort of. They had left a jumbled pile of soaked dish towels on the counter. She picked them up and carried them to the laundry room off the mudroom to add to the pile left over from the lunch cleanup. Hoping to save a little time later, she threw them in the washing machine and was adding laundry soap when she heard someone come in.

"Eliza. What are you doing in here?"

Her traitorous heart gave that silly little skip it did whenever Aidan was close. She looked up with a shrug. "We're already running low on dishcloths. I guess that's what happens when you have eight or nine people helping in the kitchen after every meal."

He laughed as he pulled on his coat, sending a ridiculous shiver down her spine.

Smokin' Hot Spence Gregory was great-looking, sure, and she could admit she still had a little bit of an embarrassing celebrity crush on him—but he had nothing on Aidan, with those lean chiseled features, vivid blue eyes behind his sexy geek glasses and that slow smile that made her feel like her nerves were stuck on some permanent agitate cycle.

"I warned you how it would be," he said. "Crazy and chaotic. The noise level from this house alone might be an avalanche danger for the surrounding mountains."

"They're wonderful," she said quietly. "If everything else you ever had was stripped away tomorrow, you would still be the most fortunate man I know. I am absolutely green with envy, Aidan. I wish they were mine."

His eyes softened. "El."

He stepped closer and she was mortified at the sudden burn of tears that sprang up out of nowhere. She had no way to protect herself when he called her that, like a sweet and private endearment.

She cleared her throat and pushed them away, "A word of warning. I was just cornered by the women of your family. They're quite formidable as a group, by the way."

"Tell me about it. They scare the hell out of me."

She smiled a little and busied herself by reaching into the dryer for a load of extra bath towels she had left there earlier. "Yes, well, they know something is up with you. You're acting very out of character, apparently, sending up red flags all over the place. Buying this house, inviting everyone here for the holidays, reading to the little ones. Everyone is very suspicious of your odd behavior."

"Did you tell them anything?"

She snapped a towel out between them, filling the air with her annoyance along with the sweet scent of laundry soap. "What do you think?"

He sighed. "I think it's probably not fair for me to ask so much of you."

Why did he have to make it so tough to stay annoyed with him? "It's not. You're a terribly cruel boss. I should complain to someone."

He laughed. "Take it up with Sue. She probably has a raft of complaints."

"Oh, yes. I'm sure. That you pay her too much and don't eat enough of her snickerdoodles."

He grinned down at her just as Dermot came in carrying a few more towels.

He stopped in the doorway and studied the pair of them. "Oh. Sorry to interrupt."

Eliza could feel herself flush. "You're not interrupting anything, Mr. Caine," she said swiftly. "We were just discussing the, um, fabric softener. Your son is very particular about what he wants, you know."

"Oh, yes. He always has been."

After a slight pause, he smiled. "If we don't go on a sleigh ride soon, I'm afraid there are some children out there who might start staging a revolt."

Aidan seemed to collect himself. "Jim should be bringing the sleigh around to the front right now. Eliza, grab your coat."

"Yes, my dear," his sweet father added in that irresistible Irish accent. "And don't forget your gloves, will you? It's a bit nippy out there."

Eliza headed for her coat on the hook, aware there would be no point arguing with either one of them.

CHAPTER TWENTY

HIS FAMILY APPARENTLY had disappeared.

Christmas Eve afternoon, Aidan emerged from his office to a house that seemed to echo with emptiness.

Where was everyone? The great room fireplace was on but the room appeared to be vacant.

How did twenty rambunctious people vanish into thin air?

He looked around, a little bleary-eyed from the three hours of sleep he'd had the night before and about the same the night before that.

After the perfect moonlit sleigh ride the night before, which his family had loved, he had escaped to his office to work until the early hours in the morning, had crashed on the sofa there for a few hours in an attempt to recharge, and then hadn't budged from his office chair since 4:00 a.m. trying to nail down the specifics of the project he was working on.

He was close. He could feel it. He wasn't sure he would be able to pull it off in time but if he failed, he would at least know he had brought his A game.

But he was completely exhausted, too. Apparently a man of thirty-seven couldn't run a marathon on a

few hours of sleep as if he were still in his twenties—
though still being trapped in recovery mode from
brain surgery might have something to do with his
fatigue.

"Looking for someone, are we?"

His father's brogue sounded from deep in one of
the wing chairs by the huge Christmas tree.

"Hey, Pop." He really *must* be tired if he hadn't
even noticed Dermot there.

He headed over as Dermot set his book down on
the table beside him. *A Christmas Carol,* he noted.
His father had reread Dickens every Christmas season Aidan could remember.

"Where is everyone?" he asked.

"Oh, here and there. If I'm not mistaken, your
brothers and the teen crowd took those snowmobiles
in the garage out for a test ride around the meadow
behind the house. Katherine and the girls went into
town for a little last-minute shopping. I believe the
little ones are up in the game room working on a
special surprise with the lovely Eliza. I keep hearing
random giggles floating down the stairs."

"Ah."

Just hearing her name made his heart give that
funny little helpless tug.

He pictured her as he had seen her last, on the
sleigh ride with his family, her cheeks pink from the
cold and her face lifted to the moonlight.

Despite all the arguments she had mustered
against going with them, he knew she and Maddie

had both enjoyed themselves when their turn to ride the sleigh had come around.

"And where have you been keeping yourself all day?" Dermot asked.

Yeah, he was just about the worst host in the world. He had lost a house full of twenty guests, hadn't he?

He sat down now on the sofa next to his father. "Working," he answered. The fire felt lovely. A few snowflakes fluttered down outside and beyond the trees, the lake was a vast, peaceful blue.

"It *is* Christmas. You remember that, don't you?"

"I know. I just have something I have to wrap up. It's taking more energy than I expected, that's all."

Dermot sniffed. "I won't tell you that you work too hard. We've had that argument more than a few times over the years, haven't we?"

"Yes." Aidan stretched out his legs, certain that if he sat here long enough he would fall asleep. "I still find the lecture quite ironic, coming from a man who has been known to spend every waking hour at his café."

"Only after your mother died," Dermot pointed out. "She insisted I keep to regular hours while you children were at home. I tried my best. I'm afraid the last few years I did spend more time than I should have at the Center of Hope, with all of you gone. The silence at home, you know. Sometimes it was more than I could bear."

The honest admission touched a chord deep inside

him. Yes. That was it. The fundamental shift in himself he had been trying to pinpoint. He had always been content with silence. He wasn't an introvert, as he loved his family and his few close friends like Ben Kilpatrick, but he had always been perfectly content on his own with a book or a computer.

Being the middle child in a large family and always feeling the odd one out had taught him to be independent and self-reliant, both good things.

He didn't want to be alone anymore. He wanted laughter and music and heady kisses.

He wanted Eliza.

"Everyone is having a wonderful time being together. What a gift you've given us, son."

He managed a smile. "I'm glad."

"Perhaps you should stop hiding out in your office so you can see for yourself."

"I only need a few more hours and then I'll be done. I'm sorry I interrupted your book. Go ahead and read, if you want—though don't you have it memorized by now?"

"Everyone should read Dickens once a year to remember the message in it. That we only find joy when we're giving of ourselves to others."

Dermot picked up the book again. Aidan sat on the sofa and closed his eyes, thinking this wasn't at all a bad way to spend Christmas Eve, drawing on his father's constant, steady strength while the snowflakes drifted down outside and the flames danced in the fireplace.

He might have fallen asleep just for a moment —
or perhaps longer, he didn't know—but the sound of
giggles woke him. He looked up and spotted Eliza
and the children coming down the stairs. She was
holding Faith's and Maddie's hands while Carter and
a couple of the little dogs scampered ahead of them.

For one glittery moment, their gazes met. Her
smile slid away and she gave him a solemn look then
hurried into the kitchen, pulled along by the children.

"She's a darling," Dermot said, looking over his
bifocals as the group disappeared down the hallway.

"Maddie? Yeah, she's a great kid."

"Maddie, yes. Her mother, as well. You could do
far worse," Dermot observed.

"I know, Pop. Believe me. I know."

"You care about her, don't you?"

He thought about passing off a trite answer but
didn't see much point. Dermot had always been entirely too perceptive. When they were kids, they
could never try to slip a fib past him without those
blue eyes picking out the truth.

Care was a mild word for this yearning, this thick
ache in his chest. He loved her. She was everything
he never realized he wanted.

"Yes," he finally answered. "I care about her. Very
much."

Just saying the words seemed to free something
clogged inside him, as if he had lifted a fallen tree
trunk out of a riverbed to let the water flow freely.

He loved her. He needed her in his life, rather

desperately. And Maddie, as well, with her generous smile and sweet courage. Now he only needed to convince Eliza that perhaps she might need him, too.

"Well, then," Dermot said, looking stunned and pleased at the same time. "Well, then."

"She doesn't want me. She told me as much. She thinks we come from different worlds. I'm not sure how to prove her wrong."

"You'll figure it out, son," his father said, with a perfect confidence he found humbling. "It's what you do, isn't it? Take a puzzle and work it through? But you might want to keep in mind that you can't win the girl when you're sitting at your computer."

He rose, reinvigorated to return to his project. In this case, he was hoping his father was wrong.

"Thanks for the advice. I'm going to put in a few more hours but, I promise, I'll see you at dinnertime."

"Just keep in mind what Charles Dickens said." He tapped the book in his lap. *"No space of regret can make amends for one life's opportunity misused."*

"I got it. Thanks, Pop. See you at dinner."

JUST BEFORE SIX on Christmas Eve, Eliza looked around the heavenly-smelling kitchen. "I think that's everything. What are we forgetting?"

Sue took in all the dishes and the warmers waiting to be carried into the dining room in a few moments. Though Eliza had helped out where she could in creating the feast—along with most members of the family at one point or another—Sue was quite firmly back in charge in her kitchen. Her foot wasn't hurting nearly as badly, she claimed. With the little knee walker, she could get around wherever she needed in the kitchen.

"That should be everything. The ham has been glazed, the potatoes are crispy and perfect, the rolls are baking. I think the only thing left to do is for you and I to freshen up for dinner."

Eliza shifted. "I still feel a little weird crashing their family dinner, don't you?"

"Not a bit. After all you've done to throw this whole house party together this last week and a half, you should be sitting at the head of the table. Everything has gone smoothly because of you."

That wasn't even *half* true but she didn't want to argue with Sue on Christmas Eve.

"Anyway, Aidan wants you there," the cook went on.

She thought of that fleeting, charged moment when she had been coming down the stairs with the children and had seen him in the great room talking to his father. The look in his gaze had left her feeling so jittery and off-balance, it was a wonder she hadn't stumbled over a step.

"Have you spoken with him today?" she asked.

"No," Sue admitted. "He's been making himself scarce. I think he's got some big project he's working on. He's been holed up in his office most of the day on those computers of his. I took him a sandwich earlier but I'm not sure he even touched it."

Eliza frowned. "He has gone to so much trouble to have his family here. You would think he would at least *try* to spend a little time with them."

She hated to see him become so obsessed with work that he missed out on this family holiday he had been planning since his surgery.

"Sometimes he gets like this. An idea comes to him and he can't rest until he figures out how to make it work. It's just one of his quirks. You learn to live with it."

She wouldn't be learning to live with it. She would be leaving Snow Angel Cove within the week and he would be taking his workaholic quirks back to California.

"It's Christmas Eve. He should let his brain rest for a few hours and enjoy the moment with his family."

"Maybe someone needs to go remind him of that. Someone whose opinion he cares about."

Sue gave her a meaningful look that made Eliza flush. It wasn't her place to offer opinions about anything—not that he would care what she thought.

"Good idea," she answered smartly. "Let me know what he says."

The other woman snorted. "You know I meant you, missy. At least go knock on his door and remind him dinner will be ready at seven sharp, whether he's there or not."

Eliza wanted to come up with some excuse to avoid the task—but how could she send Sue traipsing down the length of the house, maneuvering around kids and dogs, on her bad foot?

"Sure," she said, trying to give in as gracefully as possible. "I have to round up Maddie, anyway, in order to change for dinner."

Outside his office door, she paused for a moment and took a deep breath, willing down the silly butterflies that now seemed to be marching in time to *The Nutcracker* suite. Just as she reached a hand up to knock, the door opened from the other side and, abruptly, he was there.

He froze, looking confused and disoriented to find her outside his door.

"Oh. Hi."

She didn't know how to respond to that intense look in his eyes that made her feel young and giddy and very, very female.

"Sue just sent me to pry you out of your office. It's nearly time for dinner."

"Right. I set an alarm to remind myself. I was just heading that way."

He looked exhausted, she thought, his eyes blurry through those sexy glasses and his hair sticking up as if he had been running his hand through it.

She could clearly see his scar, raw, white and terrifying. Glimpsing this rare vulnerability affected her far more profoundly than it should. If he walked out to see his family now, everyone would see it. Questions would fly like sparks going up the chimney and his big, dark secret would be out.

Should she tell him, or should she let the truth come out? She still believed he was wrong to withhold that information from his family, especially after meeting them and seeing their love for him.

She sighed. She couldn't do it. She wouldn't be sneaky like that. "Before you go out there, you should probably take a minute to, um, do something with your hair."

"What's wrong with my hair?"

"Nothing, really. It's just...it's sticking up a bit and your scar is showing."

Telling herself it was no different from helping Maddie, she reached a hand up and pulled the locks gently back in place. He froze at her touch and then, for an almost imperceptible moment, she almost thought he leaned into her hand.

The air between them seemed to thicken, heavy with awareness, tension, all the unspoken emotions between them.

"Thank you," he murmured. In his blue eyes, she saw gratitude and clear awareness. He knew she was helping him cover up something she thought should already be out in the open.

She dropped her hand quickly to her side. "I hope you would do the same for me, if I had a brain surgery scar I was foolishly trying to keep from my family."

His laugh was low and rusty-sounding. "You know I would."

"Of course, here's another good way to keep secrets from them," she said pointedly. "Invite them all to spend the holidays at your lovely home but then just hide out the whole time in your office. They'll never suspect a thing."

He looked rueful. "I know. I'm sorry. It's been a crazy couple of days. I've got a last-minute project I'm trying to wrap up but I'm almost done."

"Well, we told everyone seven for dinner. It's close to that. Sue wanted me to let you know."

"Thanks."

She should walk away. Her time was not her own, after all. She still had to find Maddie and change her clothes and her daughter's, run a comb through her hair, maybe add a little lipstick, and then help Sue set out the dishes for the Christmas Eve feast. On a subconscious level, she knew all that. Still, she couldn't seem to make herself move away from him and the seductive warmth in those tired blue eyes.

"El. I need to—" he started to say but the doorbell rang before he could finish the thought.

"Probably a last-minute delivery," she said, grateful for the distraction. "Those poor drivers, having to be out on Christmas Eve. I'll grab one of the gift bags of cookies for him."

She picked one up off the console table in the hallway where she kept extras and pulled open the door.

It wasn't a delivery driver. It was a man in a uniform, looking handsome and friendly and delighted to be there.

"Jamie!" Aidan exclaimed. The happiness on his face as he spotted his brother just about took her breath away.

The other man just had time to give Eliza a flirtatious grin before Aidan grabbed him hard in a bear hug.

"You always have to make an entrance, don't you? Last I heard, you couldn't get leave."

The guy extricated himself and picked up his suitcase to come inside. "It was a last-minute thing. I didn't know until late last night, so I've spent all day catching stand-by flights."

"You should have called! I could have sent transportation for you."

Jamie—just younger than Aidan, she remembered—gave a cheeky grin. "Then it wouldn't have been a surprise, right?"

She could tell right away this one was a trouble-making charmer. Good thing her heart was no longer available.

"Your father is going to be over the moon," Eliza predicted with a smile.

Jamie turned to her and aimed all that mojo her direction. "Hello, there. I don't think we've met. I'm James. Younger brother to Geek Boy, here."

"I'm Eliza Hayward," she said with a polite smile. "Aidan's housekeeper. For the sake of the family, I'm glad you're here. But you have no idea how hard it's going to be to find a bed for you."

Jamie raised an eyebrow. "Do you know, I believe that's the first time any woman has ever said that to me before."

He was obviously a player, an uncomplicated flirt—at least on the surface. Because she caught just a glimpse of deeper layers beneath the light-heartedness— and because Aidan was so obviously thrilled to have his entire family intact and at his home—she decided to like the man.

"I'm not picky," he said. "I can sleep on an unused sofa or a couple of blankets on the floor. Even a pile of hay would work. Wouldn't be the first time somebody in a pinch had to make do with that on Christmas Eve."

"I think we can probably manage to keep you out of the stable," she said dryly.

He grinned and draped an arm over his brother's shoulder. They went in search of the rest of the family while Eliza hurried off to add another place setting and make arrangements for one more guest.

"This is great, Aidan. Really great."

The rare sentiment coming from Dylan as they looked at the packed table touched him. He loved seeing his youngest brother smile again after so many months when they weren't sure he would survive his injuries sustained in an ambush in Afghanistan.

His stomach growled. "Everything looks delicious, doesn't it?"

"Hope there's enough to go around now that Jamie rolled in. I would hate to have to fight you for the last piece of ham."

"You know you would lose, brother. I have no mercy and I fight dirty."

Dylan grinned. "You always did, which is one of the things we love about you."

The rest of his family had started to gather in small groups and take seats at the big dining table. Everyone looked so happy that his heart seemed to expand in his chest—just like the Grinch in the book he had read to the little ones the other day.

Down at the other end of the table, he saw Eliza sit down with Maddie sandwiched between her and Charlotte.

With all the in-laws and grandchildren, his family didn't fit all together anywhere else, even in Pop's big house in Hope's Crossing. Usually the children complained about having to be separated into another room. He had purposely had a huge table made from planed hickory logs so that he could have everyone together—though it was still tight, he had to admit. He might have to commission a second table to go next to it, at the rate the Caines were growing.

When everyone sat down, he turned to his father, whom he had seated at the head of the table out of respect. "Pop, do you want to say a few words before we eat?"

Silly question, he knew. Dermot was Irish. He always had something to say.

His father stood and smiled at his progeny. "Only this. What a year we have had."

He smiled at Katherine, elegant and graceful. She blushed and smiled back and Aidan couldn't help thinking how perfect they were. Their courtship had taken more than a decade but perhaps that only made it all the sweeter.

"Three weddings and another in the New Year. Our table is more crowded every year, just as it should be."

"Get your elbow out of my plate," Jamie teased to Charlotte, who made a face.

Dermot smiled at his squabbling children, then grew serious again. "Every family goes through struggle. Alas, nobody escapes pain in this world, like it or not. We are no different. We have suffered loss and sorrow, sometimes so great we didn't know how to get through it. But we are the stronger for our pain. It is our trials that bind us together. They remind us we must walk through the dark times so we can fully appreciate the light. The joy and love and miracles around us. I hope we never lose sight of how much we need each other, in good times and bad. *Slàinte*."

Everyone toasted each other. As he looked around the family at his brothers, at Charlotte, at their spouses and children and stepchildren, Aidan suddenly knew what he had to do. *I hope we never lose sight of how much we need each other, in good times and bad.* He had lost sight of that. Eliza was right. He had been selfishly confident he could handle anything life threw at him.

He had been so wrong.

He stood up quickly. "Before we eat, I...need to say something, as well."

Carter, the kid who was always hungry, made an impatient little sound but was quickly shushed by Lucy.

Everyone looked at him with expectant faces. His gaze traveled the table and finally stopped on Eliza, watching him with a curious expression on her lovely, calm features.

"Thank you all for coming. I know it's a little different having the holidays somewhere besides Hope's Crossing."

"Different but wonderful," Charlotte assured him.

"Right. Well, I just wanted to say how happy I am that you all took time out of your busy lives to come here at my request. Also...I owe you an apology. In retrospect, this might not be the appropriate moment for it when Carter there is ready to gnaw through the table but I don't know when I can get everybody together, sitting still. It will only take a second, I promise."

Eliza watched him with dawning awareness in her gaze.

He cleared his throat. "Something happened to me this year, something tough I thought I could handle alone. It's recently come to my attention that by keeping it to myself and not letting my family know when I was going through a rough patch, I was being selfish and maybe even thoughtless and insensitive."

"What is it, son?" Dermot asked. "What's happened?"

This was a mistake. He should have waited until after the holidays, maybe tomorrow evening after the burst of Christmas excitement had passed. He didn't want to ruin dinner. If he hadn't been so fatigued, he might have thought this through a little better and made a different choice. Or maybe he would have chickened out and not said anything at all.

Whatever, it was too late to back down.

He glanced at Eliza again. She gave him an encouraging smile and he felt almost light-headed from the approval there. A thought that had been playing through his mind for the past few days, random and scattered, seemed to coalesce into one clear realization. Loving someone—truly loving them—meant exposing your weaknesses to them, not only projecting your strengths.

With a sigh, he parted his hair to show the scar, his most glaring sign of weakness. "I had a brain tumor removed in September, the week after Pop and Katherine got married."

There was an almost audible collective indrawn breath and then the dining room erupted into a dozen different questions.

Everyone looked shocked, his father most of all,

and he was suddenly profoundly sorry for shutting them out.

"Don't worry, it was benign," he assured them quickly. "The surgery went well and they were able to remove the whole thing. I'm doing fine now, just some lingering fatigue and headaches once in a while and a little double vision if I'm at the computer too long."

"Aidan. Why didn't you say anything?" Charlotte exclaimed. "A brain tumor. I can't believe this! And you didn't want your family to help you?"

"I had what I thought were good reasons. The timing of the surgery, for one thing, just days after Pop's wedding while he was on his honeymoon. The distance between us, with the surgery in California and you all in Colorado. And," he admitted, "a good part of it was pride. I'm...not good at allowing myself to need other people. I'm learning, though. I invited you all here for the holidays, right?"

"Just goes to show that even smart guys can sometimes be idiot assholes," Dylan said gruffly.

He tore his gaze away from Eliza, who was smiling softly at him now, he saw, and maybe even wiping a tear or two away with her napkin.

"True enough. It was wrong of me to keep it from you. I'm sorry. I made a mistake. Contrary to what I would like to think, I do make them. This particular mistake won't happen again. We can talk about this later but for now, let's eat before all this delicious food is too cold to enjoy. Pop. Do you want to say grace or pick somebody?"

"It's your home, son. Seems to me you should do the honors, since you have more than most to be thankful for today."

Damn right. And he wasn't about to forget it.

With a nod, he reached for Charlotte's hand on one side and his niece Maggie's on the other and bowed his head.

CHAPTER TWENTY-ONE

ELIZA HAD NEVER slept well on Christmas Eve.

When she was a little girl, she had always been too excited. She hadn't necessarily wanted to catch Santa Claus in the act of hanging stockings or anything, she only wanted to stay up and capture every moment of the magic.

She would hide in her room with a flashlight under her covers, humming Christmas songs or reading one of her favorite Christmas stories or perhaps making one up in her head.

A quick check of her phone revealed it was past 3:00 a.m. This was becoming quite a habit during her stay at Snow Angel Cove.

Staying up all night on Christmas Eve might have worked when she was a little girl who could nap with her new toys tucked around her, after the rush and frenzy of opening presents was over. As a mother and as an employee, she didn't have that luxury. She was going to be exhausted in the morning.

She could sleep in a little, assuming Maddie did, but that was far from a certainty. Her only real job in the morning was to preheat the oven about nine o'clock and then add the breakfast casseroles she had helped Sue prepare the afternoon before.

Each of the siblings was to spend Christmas morning with his or her own family before they all came together for a casual, no-frills brunch.

She rolled over, trying for a more comfortable position. Her body was certainly tired after a long day and an even more hectic week preceding it, but her mind wouldn't seem to settle.

The evening had been wonderful. Her perfect image of a big, boisterous family Christmas. After Aidan's announcement, the family had been upset with him but they had all forgiven him for withholding the information, as she had fully expected.

After the delicious dinner, she had seen his sister-in-law Christine—a pediatrician in Denver—peppering him with questions while Charlotte and Dylan interjected a few of their own.

When the meal had been cleaned up, Dermot read the Christmas story from the New Testament in his lilting Irish brogue and then the children performed the short collection of songs they had prepared: "Jingle Bells," "Rudolph the Red-nosed Reindeer," Maddie's favorite, "Away in a Manger," as well as a medley of angel-themed Christmas songs in honor of the house's name—"Angels we have Heard on High" and "Hark the Herald Angels Sing."

It didn't escape her attention that Aidan had slipped out shortly after the children sang and didn't come back in again while the family was playing laughter-filled party games she had suggested or while they were all heading to bed.

Small doses of family worked best for him, apparently. She could understand that, she supposed.

She flipped her pillow and tried that side for a few minutes, then finally sighed and slipped from bed, surrendering to the inevitable. Sleep would continue to elude her until she managed to calm her mind. She would have some chamomile tea while she checked to make sure everything was ready for Christmas morning, then she would likely be able to drift off for a few hours.

Careful not to wake her daughter, she pulled on slippers and robe, then quietly made her way to the kitchen, where she plugged in the electric kettle and mentally went over the items on Sue's menu for the day as she waited for the kettle to heat.

When it was ready, she poured it over her chamomile then carried the steeping tea through the house, pausing for a moment in the great room by the huge tree that reflected a kaleidoscope of colors in the huge windows.

The younger children had insisted they keep the tree lights on all night so Santa could find his way. Even the teenagers had chimed in to agree with that one.

It was beautiful, she thought again. The whole house was the perfect holiday gathering place for an extended family, with a wide variety of entertainment options and warm, welcoming conversation spots as well as more private nooks for those who might prefer their own space.

Would the Caines come here again next year? Perhaps they would make it a tradition—or perhaps they would alternate between here and their homes in Hope's Crossing. Wherever they met, their Christmases would be filled with laughter and fun.

She felt a sharp ache in her chest at the thought and especially at the realization that she wouldn't be there to enjoy those future holiday gatherings.

This season spent at Snow Angel Cove would probably spoil her for all other Christmases.

She sipped at her tea, trying not to feel too depressed about it. She and Maddie had been fortunate enough to be welcomed into the Caine family circle for the holidays and it would be sour indeed for her to already bemoan that she couldn't have another with them.

She sat for a while alone in the great room with the gleaming Christmas tree. When she finally rose to go, she noticed a light on at the end of the hall.

Aidan's office.

Surely he wasn't still working in the early hours of Christmas morning?

Though she knew he wouldn't want to be disturbed, she couldn't seem to help herself from walking down the hall and knocking softly on the door. He didn't answer. Had he fallen asleep at his desk? she wondered. It wouldn't surprise her.

After a moment's hesitation, she pushed the door

open slightly, just enough to peek in, and then paused in the doorway.

He wasn't asleep. He was sitting with his back to her working on three different computers at once, his fingers flying over the keys. He had headphones on and was completely absorbed in his work.

She couldn't tell what he was doing—for all she knew, it might be Spider Solitaire. Whatever it was, she was utterly fascinated by his single-minded focus.

"There you are, you son of a bitch. That's it. That's it!" he suddenly said with a delighted laugh.

As she watched him work, one firm, unshakable conviction seemed to settle over her.

She was in love with him.

The realization rolled over her like a snowball building up bulk and speed as it rolled down a mountainside.

She was in love with Aidan Caine.

It seemed an odd moment for the epiphany, while she spied on him cursing at a computer, but there it was.

The feelings had been building, like that snowball, for days. She loved his stubbornness and his dedication, his love for his family, his gentleness with her daughter.

Her heart ached as she watched his fingers dance over the keyboard. Okay, she loved him. So what? This, right here, was exactly the reason she could never do anything about that love.

She didn't *want* a man who would be working with such single-minded focus at 4:00 a.m. on Christmas morning. She wanted a man who would be able to put her and her daughter first in his life.

He might go out and conquer the world all day long. She was fine with that—in fact, she loved that about him, too, his passion and his drive and his wild creativity. But she wanted to know she came first in his heart.

She had been married once to a man who had, in his efforts to give her and Maddie what he thought they needed, been unable or unwilling to provide what they needed most. His time, his heart.

She wouldn't put herself through that again.

Her chest ached and her eyes burned with tears as she slipped from the room.

She loved him and leaving would shatter her heart into a million tiny shards but she didn't have a choice. She had no place in his life, in his world.

Somehow she would stay until his family left. She had made a promise and she didn't take promises lightly. When the holidays were over, she would take Maddie and leave Snow Angel Cove and would throw herself into doing whatever it took to put back together the pieces of her life.

"This was my very best Christmas *ever*."

"Was it?" Eliza smiled and hugged her daughter. A grand total of six Christmases—three of them spent in the hospital—wasn't exactly a huge pool to choose from but Eliza still appreciated the exuberance.

"It has been wonderful, hasn't it?" She had decided she would discount the heartache that had settled in her chest like a nagging cough.

"Bob says it's his best Christmas ever, too."

"I'm so glad Bob is enjoying the holiday season," she said solemnly.

Maddie hopped around, apparently unable to contain her happiness in one spot. "Today after everybody opens their presents, we're going to go sledding and Carter and me and Faith are going to build a snowman and take Daisy and Max for a walk and maybe go visit Cinnamon."

"That sounds like a very full day and a wonderful Christmas."

Everyone had been so kind to them. Maddie would miss this place and this family so very much.

"Santa found me here, too, just like you said! I was afraid he wouldn't, since it's not even our house, but he knew just where we were."

"Santa is magic like that, sweetheart."

"I wonder if he found Carter and Faith, too."

"I don't doubt it for a minute," she answered with a tired smile.

As she should have expected, sleep had turned out to be impossible after she returned to bed. Heartache tended to have an insomnia-inducing effect, she had discovered, so she had still been lying awake when the first rosy fingers of dawn crept across the room to awaken Maddie.

"We should go see them. Carter and Faith."

"We'll find them in a bit. Let's try to build something out of the magnetic blocks first."

Her daughter was easily distracted. "Okay. Maybe the rocket ship."

"Perfect."

They were reading the directions to figure it out when Eliza heard a soft knock on the door. Perhaps Sue needed her help earlier than expected.

She rose from the little table in their room to open the door and was stunned to find Aidan standing there, his eyes bleary and his hair sticking up in every direction.

"Aidan. Hi. Merry Christmas."

"Merry Christmas."

An odd intensity seemed to seethe and froth around him. Through the lenses of his glasses, his eyes seemed to glitter with barely suppressed excitement.

"Sorry to interrupt your morning with Maddie. Should I come back?"

"No. We've opened everything. Santa must have a big backache this morning from carrying all of Maddie's gifts, right, sweetheart?"

Her daughter giggled and rushed to hug him. After a surprised moment, he hugged her back.

"Merry Christmas. Did Santa find where you live, too?" Maddie asked.

"Why, yes. Yes, he did. And he left a present for you under my tree. He must have made a mistake, since our names both have an *A* and a *D* in them."

He held several presents in his arms, two large gifts and a smaller one.

He handed the two bigger presents to Maddie.

"Are those for me?" she breathed.

"I believe they do have your name on it."

She took them, eyes wide. "Mama, can I open them? Right now?"

"Of course."

Aidan sat down on the sofa beside her, stirring the air with that luxurious, delicious scent of him. She tried to ignore it, ignore him, as together they watched Maddie handle the first clumsily wrapped package, trying to figure out what might be inside.

Had he wrapped it himself? Eliza wondered. She couldn't imagine him going to that kind of trouble but she suspected he had. Most of the presents he had ordered for his family had been wrapped by his assistant in California or had been delivered pre-wrapped.

It seemed significant, somehow, that he had taken the time himself to wrap this one for her daughter.

The first gift was a doll she remembered Maddie admiring at the town festival. Her daughter shrieked with glee and hugged him.

"Now the other one," he said.

"Is it another doll?" Maddie guessed. "Or maybe a game? Or a bunny?"

She continued to list about a dozen possibilities,

growing increasingly more ridiculous as she went, and Aidan finally tugged at her braid gently. "Open it and find out, silly."

"Okay."

She ripped the packaging with care and a moment later unearthed a beautiful leather-bound art set that Eliza would have been envious to own, filled with charcoals and watercolors and crayons, along with several pads of sketch paper.

"You're so good at art," Aidan explained. "Every artist needs good tools."

"I love it! I love, love, love it. Thanks. Thanks a *lot*." She gave him a wildly exuberant hug and Aidan laughed a little as he returned it.

"You are very welcome, sweetheart."

"Where's my present for him, Mama? Can I give it to him now?"

Eliza forced a smile, feeling foolish about their gifts after he had given Maddie such an obviously expensive art set. The two gifts were curiously symbiotic, she had to admit. "Sure. It's over behind the chair."

Maddie found her present and the one Eliza had made and brought them over to him.

"I get two? Wow. Thank you."

He opened the larger one first, Maddie's gift, and exclaimed with delight over the elaborate picture she had colored of Snow Angel Cove, with the lake in the background and little horses—of course—grazing in the meadow. Eliza had matted and framed it and thought it actually was quite good, for a drawing done by a girl who wasn't quite six.

"You did this? Seriously?"

Maddie nodded, clearly thrilled at his reaction. "It took me a whole half hour to do the barn."

"I love it! It's perfect. Do you know what? I'm going to take it back to California and hang it in my office, so I can always remember this Christmas with you."

Eliza's heart gave a little squeeze at the thought of him, years from now, looking at the picture and trying to remember the little girl who had once drawn it for him.

When he started to open the other one, she wished she could yank it away and tell him not to bother opening it but she couldn't figure out a graceful way so she sat mutely while he tore away the wrappings to uncover the scarf she had clumsily knitted to match the hat his sister had made him.

"You made this?"

"Yes. I'm worse than Charlotte, as you can see."

"No, I love it, especially because you made it. Thank you."

He gave her a genuinely thrilled smile. Suddenly, foolishly, she had to fight the urge to burst into tears.

How on earth was she going to leave this place? Leave him?

"Can I draw something *right now?*" Maddie asked. "Bob wants his picture with a wreath around his neck."

"I would love to see that picture," Aidan said.

"Okay." Doll in hand, she raced over to the small table in the corner, flipped open to a page in one of the sketchbooks and immediately went to work.

"That was very thoughtful of you," Eliza said. "The perfect gifts for her."

He was silent for a long moment and she watched his throat move as he swallowed. If she didn't know better, she would suspect he was nervous.

"I have one for you, as well. Two actually. Here. Open this one first."

It was wrapped just as the other one had been, with the addition of a lopsided bow. He held it out with a strange, expectant look on his face. Intensely aware of him watching her, she unwrapped the bow and then tore away the wrapping paper. It was a small white box, about the size of a cell phone.

When she opened it, she could only stare. It *was* a cell phone. *His* phone.

"You're...giving me your phone?"

He made a face. "Well, no. Sorry—I need that part back. Your present is *on* the phone."

He leaned over her and pushed a few buttons to unlock the device and then held out the screen to her. She didn't know what she was supposed to be looking at.

"We can change the name and the icon and everything. This is just a prototype. I've still got quite a bit of work to do but the bones are there and they're solid."

She looked at the screen and then back at him, feeling stupid. "I don't... I'm sorry. I don't understand."

He pointed at the phone. "This is your app. Trent's big idea. The productivity app he wanted to sell to Caine Tech."

She stared at him as a little trickle of nerves started at the base of her spine and worked up. Something was happening here, something so big she couldn't manage to wrap her mind around it. Trent's app?

"But...he never did anything. It never went beyond the initial concept and, maybe, I don't know, a few lines of code from his programmer friend."

"Cory Dykstra. I know. I've been in touch with him. He sent me everything he had, which wasn't much but was at least enough to get me started."

She felt as if she were swimming through some of Pop's hot cocoa, thick and sweet and totally impenetrable. She was completely exhausted and had awakened feeling so very sad, despite the wonder and the miracle of the holiday. Perhaps that explained why she couldn't seem to make her brain work well enough to figure out what on earth was going on here.

"It was actually a really great idea," Aidan went on, when she didn't respond. "Your late husband was right. Three years ago, I'm not sure we would have been able to pull it off with the limitations of existing technology at the time. I understand why my team didn't bite on the idea, but conditions right now are perfect. I think when this hits, it's going to hit big. After the holidays, I'll fast track my best development team on it to work out the bugs of what I've come up with so far, but I can see us taking it to market by summer and being at full throttle this time next year. Eventually I see this becoming one of those apps everybody has to own."

"Okay, stop!" she finally burst out. "What are you talking about? This isn't even a *thing,* Aidan. It was just a…a vague idea."

"It's a thing now. This is what I've been working on the last few days. It's raw, sure, but we can work with raw, right?"

She thought of him holed up in his office while his family was here, of the food he didn't eat and his hair standing up and the frenzied dance of his fingers on the keyboard.

"Why?"

He was starting to look perplexed, as if he couldn't quite figure out why she wasn't more excited about it. "What do you mean, why?"

"Why did you do all this?"

He shrugged, looking uncomfortable. "It's what I do."

He glanced at Maddie who wasn't paying them any attention. "After you told me about Trent, I was curious. I tracked down the minutes from the meeting Trent had with Caine Tech and the report my guys did about the idea. It intrigued me enough to search for Cory Dykstra to see if he had pursued it.

He had basically back-burnered what he had done, hadn't touched it in years, since Trent was the man with the vision behind the idea. He was happy to send me all he had and after that, it was just a matter of playing around with the idea and tweaking a few things here and there. Like I said, I could tell at once we were onto something."

He pulled an envelope from his pocket and handed it to her. "You're going to want to open this now."

She stared at him and then, with hands that shook, she opened the envelope. A single piece of paper slipped out onto her lap and she knew in an instant it was a check.

She stared down at it and the staggering number blurred in front of her eyes.

"What is this?"

"It's your initial payment from Caine Tech for rights to the idea. I know it's not much for now, mostly because we still have a lot of work to do to bring it to market. There will be an additional revenue stream down the line, I promise, with in-app purchases and possibly some subsidiary rights. You're going to want to get some good intellectual property attorneys on your side. I can put you in touch with some reputable ones. Cory will, of course, get a cut for his initial work."

He might as well have run her down with his car again. Somehow her lungs couldn't draw enough oxygen and she felt light-headed and shaky and stupid.

"And for the record, this isn't just me," he was

saying. "I vetted it past my inner circle at the company and everyone is really excited."

He reached for her hand and held it in both of his. "It's not a ball gown or those glass slippers I know you had your eye on. But it's freedom, El. You can do whatever you want now. You can buy that bed-and-breakfast you were talking about or put it away for Maddie's future medical bills or just chuck everything and move to Hawaii and surf for the rest of your life, if you want."

Aidan looked drawn and exhausted but brimming with excitement at being able to give her the gift of choice. She was stunned. Completely overwhelmed. No one, in all her life, had ever done such a thing for her and the magnitude of it awed and humbled her.

It wasn't the amount on the check that overwhelmed her—though that was certainly life-changing. No, she thought of standing outside his office in the night, watching his excitement and eagerness and energy. All of that had been for *her*, because he wanted her to feel like she had options. Possibilities. He had taken the bare bones of an idea and literally worked day and night on her behalf to turn it into a reality.

Oh, she loved this man.

He was brilliant and driven, yes, but also generous, kind, loving.

And he needed her, she suddenly realized. As much as he had craved having his family around him this Christmas after his brain tumor taught him what truly mattered, he needed her and Maddie to tug him away from the computer sometimes. To make him laugh, to watch sparkly boat parades, to help him *live*.

He needed her and he loved her, too.

She knew it with sharp, stunning clarity. She looked at the phone on her lap again. If he didn't care about her, he never would have gone to so much effort for her.

She would likely have to deal with these bursts of wild creativity sometimes, where he worked night and day on something that filled him with passion. She could accept that, as long as he, in turn, took time to pause and breathe and embrace the world around him with her and Maddie.

He squeezed her fingers. "Say something," he said, looking nervous all over again.

She couldn't seem to get any words out so she did the only thing she could manage.

She burst into tears.

OKAY, HE HADN'T expected that. As Eliza started to sob, Aidan switched instantly from wired, edgy, caffeine-fueled energy straight into panic mode.

"It's a good thing, El. I promise. A really good thing."

Instead of calming her, that only made her sob louder and he sat there like an idiot, not knowing what to do. In desperation he finally pulled her onto his lap, just as he would Maddie. "Don't cry, sweet-heart. Please don't cry. I'm sorry. Whatever I did, I'm sorry."

Why wouldn't she say anything? She only kept looking at the check and then at him and then sobbing all over again.

Maddie, drawn by the commotion, marched over with a frown. "Why is my mama crying?" she demanded. "It's Christmas. You're not supposed to cry at Christmas."

Aidan swallowed. "I'm not quite sure, to tell you the truth. Why don't you go get her a drink of water? That might help."

Maddie looked at her mother uncertainly then hurried out of their rooms to the kitchen

"What is it?" he asked Eliza, after her daughter disappeared. "Do you completely hate the idea? We haven't gone forward with anything, as of now. It's just a concept. I can stop the whole thing this minute."

"No. No. I love it. It's amazing. *You're* amazing."

Well, that was something. He tipped her chin up to search her gaze. "So why the tears?"

She looked at him out of green eyes that looked soft, dazed, overwhelmed. "You did this for me."

He shrugged, uncomfortable. "I *investigated* it for you, initially. But I followed through because I could see the potential right away. It's a good idea. It's going to make me a lot of money, El."

She gave a watery laugh. "Well, that's something. It's not the only reason, though, is it?"

The way she was looking at him made him feel as if he could race to the highest peak of the Redemption Mountains and back without breaking a sweat, even as tired as he was.

"Like I said, I wanted you to have options. I don't want you to ever again feel like you have to go to work for the next idiot who runs you down in the street."

"Oh, Aidan." She gave a soft, sweet sigh. "Is it any wonder I love you so very much?"

He almost toppled her from his lap onto the floor as shock and joy burst through him like exploding Christmas tree bulbs. *"What?"*

She laughed. "I love you. But then you're the genius. You must have already figured that out."

Love. A short time ago, just the word might have sent him running. Now he wanted to hold her close and have her whisper it in his ear, over and over.

"I hoped. I didn't know."

"Now you do. I love you. I woke up this morning, hating that my time here was ending and I was going to have to leave Snow Angel Cove and you."

A soft, seductive peace seemed to settle over him and he wanted to close his eyes and savor every moment of it. "You can't leave. As your boss, I'm ordering you to stay."

"Ha. Too bad. I quit. You're not the boss of me anymore, to quote your sister." She held up the check. "Rumor has it, I don't have to work a day in my life, if I don't want to."

"I suppose that's true."

He hesitated as the other idea that had been running through his mind since the night of the Lights on the Lake Festival pushed its way to the fore. "I do have another job for you, though, if you'll take it."

"What's that?"

"You've done wonders at turning Snow Angel Cove into a warm, welcoming home. How would you feel about doing the same thing to a town?"

Her eyes widened. "Haven Point?"

He nodded. "This town needs help, someone to pour life and joy and *hope* back into it like you've done for this house and for me. I can't imagine anyone better suited to the task. What do you think?"

"Oh. Yes! I would *love* that!" She gave a happy little laugh and he couldn't help himself, he kissed her. She wrapped her arms around his neck and kissed him eagerly. It was Christmas morning, he remembered, and right now he felt like a kid who had awakened to find every single thing he had ever dreamed of asking for and a whole hell of a lot he never even knew he wanted.

"For the record, I love you," he murmured. "And Maddie, too. You do know I'm never going to let you go now, right?"

Her smile was incandescent with joy. "I'm counting on it, Geek Boy."

He laughed and kissed her again. He wasn't sure how long they sat that way by the twinkly lights of her little Christmas tree, but sometime later, he heard a throat being cleared nearby.

He wrenched his mouth away and found Maddie in her little red nightgown standing in the doorway. She was holding a glass of water with one hand and his father's fingers in the other. Dermot beamed at him, looking pleased as pie.

"Can I come in now?" Maddie demanded. "Grandpop said I have to make sure you're done kissing."

Aidan grinned. "Oh, we are not done kissing, kiddo. Not by a long shot. I suppose we can stop for now, though."

Eliza hopped off his lap, fiery red, and accepted the water glass from her daughter and a hug from his father.

"Merry Christmas, my dear," Dermot said with his Irish brogue more pronounced than usual.

"And to you," she murmured.

As he watched them, Aidan thought of the gnarled, twisted journey he had traveled the past five months and how it had changed him. He hoped he never had to endure the uncertainty, the pain, the fear of anything like that again.

He thought of what his father had said, that a person had to survive the dark in order to fully appreciate the light—the joy and love and miracle of life.

Eliza was his light, his miracle, his joy.

His love.

* * * * *

Turn the page for a sneak peek at *Redemption Bay*,
the brilliant next book in RaeAnne Thayne's
Haven Point series.

CHAPTER ONE

THIS WAS HER favorite kind of Haven Point evening.

McKenzie Shaw locked the front door of her shop, Point Made Flowers and Gifts. The day had been long and hectic, filled with customers and orders, which was wonderful, but also plenty of unavoidable may oral business.

She was tired and wanted to stretch out on the terrace or her beloved swing, with her feet up and something cool at her elbow. The image beckoned but the sweetness of the view in front of her made her pause.

"Hold on," she said to Paprika, her cinnamon standard poodle. The dog gave her a long-suffering look but settled next to the bench in front of the store.

McKenzie sat and reached a hand down to pet Rika's curly hair. A few sailboats cut through the stunning blue waters of Lake Haven, silvery and bright in the fading light, with the rugged, snow-capped mountains as a backdrop.

She didn't stop nearly often enough to soak in the beautiful view or enjoy the June evening air, tart and clean from the mighty fir and pines growing in abundance around the lake.

A tourist couple walked past holding hands and

eating gelato cones from Carmela's, their hair back-lit into golden halos by the setting sun. From a short distance away, she could hear children laughing and shrieking as they played on the beach at the city park and the alluring scent of grilling steak somewhere close by made her stomach grumble.

She loved every season here on the lake but the magnificent Haven Point summers were her favorite—especially lazy summer evenings filled with long shadows and spectacular sunsets.

Kayaking on the lake, watching children swim out to the floating docks, seeing old-timers in ancient boats casting gossamer lines out across the water. It was all part of the magic of Haven Point's short summer season.

The town heavily depended on the influx of tourists during the summer, though it didn't come close to the crowds enjoyed by the larger city to the north, Shelter Springs—especially since the Haven Point Inn burned down just before Christmas and had yet to be rebuilt.

Shelter Springs had more available lodging, more restaurants, more shopping—as well as more problems with parking, traffic congestion and crime, she reminded herself.

"Evening, Mayor," Mike Bailey called, waving as he rumbled past the store in the gorgeous old blue '57 Chevy pickup he'd restored.

She waved back, then nodded to Luis Robles, locking up his insurance agency across the street.

A soft, warm feeling of contentment seeped through

her. This was her town. These were her people. She was part of it, just like the Redemption Mountains across the lake. She had fought to earn that sense of belonging since the day she showed up, a lost, grieving, bewildered girl.

She had worked hard to earn the respect of her friends and neighbors. The chance to serve as the mayor had never been something she sought but she had accepted the challenge willingly. It wasn't about power or influence—not that one could find much of either in a small town like Haven Point. She simply wanted to do anything she could to make a difference in her community. She wanted to think she was serving with honor and dignity, but she was fully aware there were plenty in town who might disagree.

Her stomach growled, louder this time. That steak smelled as if it was charred to perfection. Too bad she didn't know who was grilling it or she might just stop by to say hello. McKenzie was briefly tempted to stop in at Serrano's or even grab a gelato of her own at Carmela's—stracciatella, her particular favorite—but she decided she would be better off taking Rika home.

"Come on, girl. Let's go."

The dog jumped to her feet, all eager, lanky grace, and McKenzie gripped the leash and headed off.

She lived not quite a mile from her shop downtown and she and Rika both looked forward all day to this evening walk along the trail that circled the lake.

As she walked, she waved at people walking, biking, driving, even boating past when the shoreline came into view. It was quite a workout for her arm but she didn't mind. Each wave was another reminder that this was her town and she loved it.

"Let's grill some chicken when we get home," she said aloud to Rika, whose tongue lolled out with appropriate enthusiasm.

Talking to her dog again. Not a good sign but she decided it was too beautiful an evening to worry about her decided lack of any social life to speak of. Town council meetings absolutely didn't count.

Her warm mood lasted until a few houses from her own, when an older gentleman out clipping the tall hedge in front of his trim brick home whirled to face her, almost as if he had been lying in wait for her—probably *exactly* what he had been doing.

"I need a word with you, missy."

Her stomach dropped. Darwin Twitchell—the bane of her existence and the three previous mayors before her.

"Mr. Twitchell. How are you this lovely evening?"

"Terrible," he growled. He wore a perpetual frown, much like his English bulldog, Petunia, who adored him. Of the two, Petunia clearly had the more appealing personality.

"I'm sorry to hear that," she answered, trying to be polite.

"Oh, I doubt that. I really do."

She tried so hard to be nice to Darwin. It was almost a point of honor with her, but he was one of those perpetually unhappy people who twisted everything around and made it so difficult to be kind.

As both a natural-born and determined optimist,

she struggled every time she had dealings with the man—which was at least two or three times a week when he came to her with some kind of beef about the city.

A Korean War combat vet, Darwin had recently become a widower. In the months since, he had become even more sour, if possible. Though arthritis gnarled his fingers and he relied on a cane for balance and support, he still somehow managed to keep his yard and house exquisite, without a stray leaf or overgrown branch.

She considered it one of life's great mysteries that a man who seemed to be a festering pile of frustration could expend so much effort and energy into making his property into a restful oasis of blooms and trailing vines and sturdy, beautifully placed trees.

A mystery she would try to puzzle out another day, she told herself. She had a chicken breast to grill—after she dealt with whatever stick he had up his hindquarters today. Dealing with irate citizens was part of her description as mayor, like it or not.

"How can I make things better for you this evening?" she asked politely.

"How long have you had your name on the door at the mayor's office in city hall?" he demanded.

"Six months, Mr. Twitchell." Six difficult, stress-filled months. Why, again, had she ever thought this whole mayoral gig was a good idea? Oh, yes. Because she loved this town. Perhaps not every single inhabitant, though.

"Six months." Darwin scowled. Or maybe he was

beaming with happiness and glee. It was hard to tell, since all his facial expressions looked the same. "And how long have I been warning you about that bridge over the Hell's Fury?"

The expression was a scowl, then. Not really a surprise.

She forced a smile. "Just about every week for the past six months, Mr. Twitchell."

"I don't know why I waste my breath. You obviously don't care, since you haven't done a damn thing about it since you've been in office."

She tried not to let that sting, especially considering all the things she *had* accomplished in six short months. He was a lifelong resident of this town, one of her constituents, and she owed it to him to try to address his concern. As much as she wanted to hug his adorably grumpy-faced dog and walk away.

"The public works director is aware of the problem. We've talked to the state about it. It's on the list. We're waiting on a couple of grants and appropriations to come through. When that happens, it will be at the top of our list, I promise you."

"When will that be?"

"I'm afraid I can't tell you exactly. As I'm sure you're aware, it costs a great deal of money for that kind of project. Right now the city cupboard is a little bare for a major infrastructure repair."

"If this were Shelter Springs, we would have had a dozen new bridges by now. My nephew, the mayor, would never let things go this long."

She had heard the same argument plenty of times

over the past six months. According to Darwin, Mayor
Martin of Shelter Springs could walk the entire length
of Lake Haven without getting the cuffs of his tailored slacks damp.

"Now, Mr. Twitchell, we have our challenges, yes.
But the people of Shelter Springs have their own."

She would like at least one of their problems—
more tax revenue than they knew what to do with.

Instead, her downtown was dead and most of the
available property had been tied up for years by one
man.

Ben Kilpatrick.

Just the thought of him made her grind her back
teeth and grip Rika's leash a little more tightly.

"You'd better do something about that bridge or
there's going to be trouble, mark my words," Darwin grunted.

"I appreciate the advice, Mr. Twitchell," she lied.

"And another thing. Garbage collection. That darn
truck knocked over my can again for the third week
in a row! Does that fool driver even know how to op-
erate the thing?"

Apparently the mayor, by virtue of the office, was
responsible for every single thing that went on within
the city limits. Garbage collection was run by the
county, as Mr. Twitchell fully knew.

"It might have something to do with the slope at
the end of your driveway. It's a little tricky to set the
can down just so."

"I don't know why we ever had to switch over to
those stupid automated trucks. Who can even pull

those big cans out to the street, unless they're a super-hero or something? More trouble than it's worth, you ask me."

Who would ever be dim enough to ask Darwin Twitchell *anything*, unless he or she wanted to spend the rest of the day listening to his lengthy litany of complaints?

She drew in a deep breath, focusing on the scent of pine and lake instead of acrimony. Darwin was an object of pity. He had little to do but sit around and stew about everything wrong in his world, both globally and locally. The challenge of righting a tipped-over can probably represented all the things he could no longer do because of his age and physical limitations.

McKenzie forced a smile, trying her best to inject a little genuine compassion in it. "Next time the truck tips over your can when it's done taking your garbage, please leave it. I'll be happy to pick it up for you and roll it back to the house."

He harrumphed at that and she knew he would never consider leaving his can tipped over all day, waiting until she could get to it. He was so particular, he raked the gravel out on his parking strip if anybody so much as left a bike tire trail through it.

"Just find a damn garbage truck driver who knows what the Sam Hill he's doing. That's all I ask. Nobody cares anymore about doing a good job. They're all so busy on their computers, sending out nekked pictures of their whatsit."

She almost laughed aloud—why didn't anybody send *her* nekked pictures of their whatsit?—but she managed to contain it. "I'll talk to the county public works supervisor and ask him to remind the garbage collectors to be a little more careful."

"You do that. And take care of that bridge, too!"

He gripped his cane and made a sharp gesture to Petunia, who had the effrontery to be fraternizing with the enemy—or at least the enemy's cinnamon poodle—then shuffled back up his driveway with the dog trotting behind him.

She sighed and continued on her way. She wouldn't let one cranky old man ruin her enjoyment of this beautiful summer evening.

When she reached her lakeside house, however, she forgot all about Darwin and his perpetual complaints when she discovered a luxury SUV with California plates in the driveway of the house next to hers, with boat trailer and gleaming wooden boat attached.

Great.

Apparently someone had rented the Sloane house.

Normally she would be excited about new neighbors but in this case, she knew the tenants would only be temporary. Since moving to Shelter Springs, Carole Sloane-Hall had been renting out the house she received as a settlement in her divorce for a furnished vacation rental. Sometimes people stayed for a week or two, sometimes only a few days.

It was a lovely home, probably one of the most luxurious lakefront rentals within the city limits. Though not large, it had huge windows overlooking the lake, a wide flagstone terrace and a semiprivate boat dock—which, unfortunately, was shared between McKenzie's own property and Carole's rental house.

She wouldn't let it spoil her evening, she told herself. Usually the renters were very nice people, quiet and polite. She generally tried to act as friendly and welcoming as possible.

It wouldn't bother her at all except the two properties had virtually an open backyard because both needed access to the shared dock, with only some landscaping between the houses that ended several yards from the high water mark. Sometimes she found the lack of privacy a little disconcerting, with strangers temporarily living next door, but Carole assured her she planned to put the house on the market at the end of the summer. With everything else McKenzie had to worry about, she had relegated the vacation rental situation next door to a distant corner of her brain.

New neighbors or not, though, she still adored her own house. She had purchased it two years earlier and still felt a little rush of excitement when she unlocked the front door and walked over the threshold.

Over those two years, she had worked hard to make it her own, sprucing it up with new paint, taking down a few walls and adding one in a better spot. The biggest expense had been for the renovated master bath, which now contained a huge claw-foot tub, and the new kitchen with warm travertine countertops and the intricately tiled backsplash she had done herself.

This was hers and she loved every inch of it, almost more than she loved her little store downtown.

She walked through to the back door and let Rika off her leash. Though the yard was only fenced on one side, just as the Sloane house was fenced on the corresponding outer property edge, Rika was well trained and never left the yard.

Her cell phone rang as she was throwing together a quick lemon-tarragon marinade for the chicken.

Some days, she wanted to grab her kayak, paddle out to the middle of Lake Haven—where it was rumored to be so deep, the bottom had never been truly charted—and toss the stupid thing overboard.

This time when she saw the caller ID, she smiled, wiped her hands on a dish towel and quickly answered. "Hey, Devin."

"Hey, sis. I can't believe you're holding out on me! Come on. Doesn't your favorite sister get to be among the first to hear?"

She tucked the phone in her shoulder and returned to cutting the lemon for the marinade as she mentally reviewed her day for anything spill-worthy to her sister.

The store had been busy enough. She had busted the doddering and not-quite-right Mrs. Anglesey for trying to walk out of the store without paying for the pretty hand-beaded bracelet she tried on when she came into the store with her daughter.

But that sort of thing was a fairly regular occurrence whenever Beth and her mother came into the store and was handled easily enough, with flustered apologies from Beth and that baffled what-did-I-do-wrong? look from poor Mrs. Anglesey.

She didn't think Devin would be particularly interested in that or the great commission she earned by selling one of the beautiful carved horses an artist friend made in the wood shop behind his house to a tourist from Maine.

And then there was the pleasant encounter with Mr. Twitchell, but she doubted that was what her sister meant.

"Sorry. You lost me somewhere. I can't think of any news I have worth sharing."

"Seriously? You didn't think I would want to know that Ben Kilpatrick is back in town?"

The knife slipped from her hands and she narrowly avoided chopping the tip of her finger off. A greasy, angry ball formed in her stomach.

Ben Kilpatrick. The only person on earth she could honestly say she despised. She picked up the knife and stabbed it through the lemon, wishing it was his cold, black heart.

"You're joking," she said, though she couldn't imagine what her sister would find remotely funny about making up something so outlandish and horrible.

"True story," Devin assured her. "I heard it from Betty Orton while I was getting gas. Apparently he strolled into the grocery store a few hours ago, casual as a Sunday morning, and bought what looked to be at least a week's worth of groceries. She said he didn't look very happy to be back. He just frowned when she welcomed him back."

"It's a mistake. That's all. She mistook him for someone else."

"That's what I said, but Betty assured me she's known him all his life and taught him in Sunday school three years in a row and she's not likely to mistake him for someone else."

"I won't believe it until I see him," she said. "He hates Haven Point. That's fairly obvious, since he's done his best to drive our town into the ground."

"Not actively," Devin, who tended to see the good in just about everyone, was quick to point out.

"What's the difference? By completely ignoring the property he inherited after his father died, he accomplished the same thing as if he'd walked up and down Lake Street, setting a torch to the whole downtown."

She picked up the knife and started chopping the fresh tarragon with quick, angry movements. "You know how hard it's been the last five years since he inherited to keep tenants in the downtown businesses. Haven Point is dying because of one person. Ben Kilpatrick."

If she had only one goal for her next four years as mayor, she dreamed of revitalizing a town whose lifeblood was seeping away, business by business.

When she was a girl, downtown Haven Point had been bustling with activity, a magnet for everyone in town, with several gift and clothing boutiques for both men and women, restaurants and cafés, even a downtown movie theater.

She still ached when she thought of it, when she looked around at all the empty storefronts and the ramshackle buildings with peeling paint and broken shutters.

"It's his fault we've lost so many businesses and nothing has moved in to replace them. I mean, why go to all the trouble to open a business," she demanded, "if the landlord is going to be completely unresponsive and won't fix even the most basic problems?"

"You don't have to sell it to me, Kenz. I know. I went to your campaign rallies, remember?"

"Right. Sorry." It was definitely one of her hot buttons. She loved Haven Point and hated seeing its decline—much like old Mrs. Anglesey, who had once been an elegant, respected, contributing member of the community and now could barely get around even with her daughter's help and didn't remember whether she had paid for items in the store.

"It wasn't really his fault, anyway. He hired an incompetent crook of a property manager who was supposed to take care of things. It wasn't Ben's fault the man embezzled from him and didn't do the necessary upkeep to maintain the buildings."

"Oh, come on. Ben Kilpatrick is the chief operating officer for one of the most successful, fastest-growing companies in the world. You think he didn't know what was going on? If he had bothered to care, he would have paid more attention."

This was an argument she and Devin had had before. "At some point, you're going to have to let go," her sister said calmly. "Ben doesn't own any part of Haven Point now. He sold everything to Aidan Caine last year—which makes his presence in town even more puzzling. Why would he come back *now*, after all these years? It would seem to me, he has even *less* reason to show his face in town now."

McKenzie still wasn't buying the rumor that Ben had actually returned. He had been gone since he was seventeen years old. He didn't even come back for Joe Kilpatrick's funeral five years earlier—though she, for one, wasn't super surprised about that, since Joe had been a bastard to everyone in town and especially to his only surviving child.

"It doesn't make any sense. What possible reason would he have to come back now?"

"I don't know. Maybe he's here to make amends. Did you ever think of that?"

How could he ever make amends for what he had done to Haven Point—not to mention shattering all her girlish illusions?

Of course, she didn't mention that to Devin as she tossed the tarragon into the lemon juice while her sister continued speculating about Ben's motives for coming back to town.

Her sister probably had no idea about McKenzie's ridiculous crush on Ben, that when she was younger, she had foolishly considered him her ideal guy. Just thinking about it now made her cringe.

Yes, he had been gorgeous enough. Vivid blue eyes, long sooty eyelashes, the old clichéd chiseled jaw—not to mention that lock of sun-streaked brown hair that always seemed to be falling into his eyes, just begging for the right girl to push it back, as Belle did to the Prince after the Beast in her arms suddenly materialized into him.

Throw in that edge of pain she always sensed in him and his unending kindness and concern for his sickly younger sister and it was no wonder her thirteen-year-old self—best friends with that same sister—used to pine for him to notice her, despite the four-year difference in their ages.

It was so stupid, she didn't like admitting it, even to herself. All that had been an illusion, obviously. He might have been sweet and solicitous to Lily but that was his only redeeming quality. His actions these past five years had proved that, over and over.

Through the open kitchen window, she heard Rika start barking fiercely, probably at some poor hapless chipmunk or squirrel that dared venture into her territory.

"I'd better go," she said to Devin. "Rika's mad at something."

"Yeah, I've got to go, too. Looks like the Shelter Springs ambulance is on its way with a cardiac patient."

"Okay. Good luck. Go save a life."

Her sister was a dedicated, caring doctor at Lake Haven Hospital, as passionate about her patients as McKenzie was about their town.

"Let me know if you hear anything down at city hall about why Ben Kilpatrick has come back to our fair city after all these years."

"Sure. And then maybe you can tell me why you're so curious."

She could almost hear the shrug in Devin's voice. "Are you kidding me? It's not every day a gorgeous playboy billionaire comes to town."

And that was the crux of the matter. Somehow it seemed wholly unfair, a serious karmic calamity, that he had done so well for himself after he left town. If she had her way, he would be living in the proverbial van down by the river—or at least in one of his own dilapidated buildings.

Rika barked again and McKenzie hurried to the back door that led onto her terrace. She really hoped it wasn't a skunk. They weren't uncommon in the area, especially not this time of year. Her dog had encountered one the week before on their morning run on a favorite mountain trail and it had taken her three baths in the magic solution she found on the internet before she could allow Rika back into the house.

Her dog wasn't in the yard, she saw immediately. Now that she was outside, she realized the barking was more excited and playful than upset. All the more reason to hope she wasn't trying to make nice with some odoriferous little friend.

"Come," she called again. "Inside."

The dog bounded through a break in the bushes between the house next door, followed instantly by another dog—a beautiful German shepherd with classic markings.

She had been right. Rika *had* been making friends. She and the German shepherd looked tight as ticks, tails wagging as they raced exuberantly around the yard.

The dog must belong to the new renters of the

Sloane house. Carole would pitch a royal fit if she knew they had a dog over there. McKenzie knew it was strictly prohibited.

Now what was she supposed to do?

A man suddenly walked through the gap in landscaping. He had brown hair, but a sudden piercing ray of the setting sun obscured his features more than that.

She *really* didn't want a confrontation with the man, especially not on a Friday night when she had been so looking forward to a relaxing night at home. She supposed she could just call Carole or the property management company and let them deal with the situation.

That seemed a cop-out, since Carole had asked her to keep an eye on the place.

She forced a smile and approached the dog's owner. "Hi. Good evening. You must be renting the place from Carole. I'm McKenzie Shaw. I live next door. Rika, that dog you're playing catch with, is mine."

The man turned around and the pleasant evening around her seemed to go dark and still as she took in sun-streaked brown hair, steely blue eyes, chiseled jaw.

Her stomach dropped as if somebody had just picked her up and tossed her into the cold lake.

Ben Kilpatrick. Here. Staying in the house next door.

So much for her lovely evening at home.